PRAISE FOR JOAN MEDLICOTT
AND HER BELOVED NOVELS

"I have always enjoyed Joan Medlicott's books. The characters stay with you long after you finish."
　　—*New York Times* bestselling author Jude Deveraux

"As cozy as a cup of tea and a favorite cat. . . . Fans of Jan Karon and Ann Ross will enjoy these gentle novels."
　　—*Booklist*

"A must-read for women of all ages."
　　—*The Tampa Tribune*

"Genuinely inspiring."
　　—*Library Journal*

"Ms. Medlicott is attuned to the nuances of Southern life and draws her characters with affectionate understanding and an inspiring message of self-acceptance, courage, and survival."
　　—*The Dallas Morning News*

"A heartwarming adventure."
　　—*San Jose Mercury News*

The
THREE
MRS. PARKERS

JOAN
MEDLICOTT

POCKET BOOKS
New York   London   Toronto   Sydney

POCKET BOOKS,
a division of Simon & Schuster, Inc.
1230 Avenue of the Americas, New York, NY 10020

Library of Congress Cataloging-in-Publication Data
Medlicott, Joan A. (Joan Avna)
The three Mrs. Parkers / Joan Medlicott.—1st Pocket Books
trade pbk. ed.
p. cm.
1. Women—South Carolina—Fiction. 2. Conflict
of generations—Fiction. 3. Oconee County (S.C.)—Fiction.
4. South Carolina—Fiction. I. Title.
PS3563.E246T48 2005   813'.54—dc22   2004058642

ISBN: 0-7434-8796-6

First Pocket Books trade paperback edition March 2005

1   3   5   7   9   10   8   6   4   2

Manufactured in the United States of America

For information regarding special discounts for bulk purchases,
please contact Simon & Schuster Special Sales at 1-800-456-6798
or business@simonandschuster.com

To Edith and Alden Galloway, good neighbors and dear friends in Salem, South Carolina; to Abed and Gloria Yassen of the Steak House Cafeteria in Walhalla, South Carolina; and to my daughter, Polly, and my grandson, Christian, for sharing so much

ACKNOWLEDGMENT

It is my great pleasure to work with Micki Nuding, my wonderful, knowledgeable editor. She is wise and kind, intelligent and sensitive. All her suggestions and guidance have served to enhance my work, and I thank her from the bottom of my heart.

1

In the Beginning

Low-angling light shrouded the room in soft shadows. Soon the sun would set—not only on the world beyond her walls, but on the way of life Zoe Parker cherished. Standing at the sink in the large, rustic kitchen of her home on Amorey Lane, she lifted and lowered her shoulders in an effort to release the tightness. Her foot tapped an agitated rhythm on the scrubbed wood floor. Her hair, mingled shades of brown and silver, hung over her shoulder in a long braid, and she absentmindedly twirled the end between her fingers. *If I keep my eyes on the clock, maybe time will slow.*

The tall, silver-haired woman appeared calm, her face composed. Only the tremor in her hand as she clutched the handle of the Amtrak train's door betrayed the strain of the journey and her agitation.

The porter set her two brown suitcases on the wooden platform, then flexed his fingers, making the joints pop. "Mighty heavy, lady. Whatcha carryin' in there, stones?"

Winifred Parker stiffened. She now regretted refusing her daughter-in-law's offer to pick her up, telling Zoe she was perfectly capable of getting there by herself. But the ride from Goose Island to Portland, Maine, followed by the long train trip to Philadelphia, and then Amtrak's East-West Express to Westminster, South Carolina, had sapped her physically.

The porter stood immobile, waiting for a tip.

"Call me a taxi, young man."

"I ain't got no phone." He lifted his hands in a helpless gesture and shrugged. "Gotta get you inside for that, lady."

Extracting her change purse from her deep leather pocketbook, Winifred counted out a dollar in quarters. The porter scowled, pocketed the money, shook his head, turned on his heel and moved away, abandoning her with bags too heavy for her to handle. Already she regretted coming.

Zoe stared through the bow window over her sink into the darkening evening and thought about her parents. They had bought these forty-eight acres of woods and pasture outside Salem in Oconee County when land cost one hundred dollars an acre, and taxes on the entire property were two hundred sixty-seven dollars a year. Located in the Golden Corner, as locals called the westernmost tip of South Carolina, Salem could be driven through in the time it took to speak a seven-word sentence.

Her father had built the rambling ranch house of stone, wood, and glass on a rise overlooking the pasture with a view of the distant mountains of North Carolina. He laid the flagstone patio outside the living room, and installed the lights surrounding the patio and running along the steps leading down the hillside, across the narrow stone bridge spanning the stream, and through the pasture to the summerhouse adjoining the pond. Zoe loved that moment each evening when day and night fused and the lights came alive with a radiance and sense of celebration that thrilled her.

It was silly, frivolous, and perhaps inappropriate for a fifty-two-year-old woman, but it lightened Zoe's heart, on warm nights when the moon was full, to slip into a white cotton shift, descend the steps, and cross the bridge to the summerhouse. From there the lights gamboled on the surface of the pond, and Zoe would lie in the hammock, relax, and release her mind to conjure up Steven, his red hair burnished by moonbeams. As in her memories of their too-short marriage, he would extend his hand to her, and they would dance. These moments brought the realization that she was perhaps too much alone, even though she worked with a local theater group and was helping to write a grant proposal to fund the renovation of an old theater, a home for their amateur company. It was a change from her usual work for environmental causes, but she'd needed a change, and she enjoyed working with the artistic director and the company's manager.

The kitchen phone jolted Zoe from her reverie.

"Zoe, I am at your railroad station, which is hot and full of flies, an utterly dreadful place. Come pick me up. Hurry." Winifred's voice was crisp and curt.

"It'll take me three-quarters of an hour to get there," Zoe said. "Is there someplace you can get something to eat, or a place to rest?"

"I'll be fine. Just hurry." The phone clicked and went dead.

The streamers of fog settling on Salem's dark country roads vanished when Zoe reached the lights, restaurants, and gas stations that flanked the four-lane roadway to West-minster. A truck jackknifed across one lane of the highway slowed traffic to a crawl, and Zoe's already-tight stomach tightened further. She was going to be late. Winifred would probably be quite out of sorts by the time she got there.

Winifred slumped back on the uncomfortable wood bench outside the Westminster train station, raised her feet, and set them on one of the suitcases. It was over an hour since she had talked to Zoe, and she needed desperately to lie down. She clutched the edge of the bench and closed her eyes to stave off the dizziness. Good Lord, not now. With trembling hands, she rummaged in her purse and extracted a small flask of water and a bottle of tiny pills. She swiftly swallowed a pill, leveled her shoulders, and focused on a window of a building across the street. "I may be seventy-five years old, but I'm not done with life yet," she mut-tered. After all, her ancestors were long-lived folk: hardy men who had fished the harsh Atlantic off the coast of Maine and stoic women with few comforts in their lives.

But this journey had been interminable and exhausting. And although she hated to admit it, she had again been her own worst enemy. Her heavy twill slacks and long-sleeved silk blouse were totally inappropriate for the South Car-olina summer. Winifred shifted her jacket from her lap to the bench beside her. Her hand went to her throat, con-firming that her pearls—fine, delicate pearls appraised at ten thousand dollars, a fortieth wedding anniversary gift from her deceased husband, Theodore—were safe.

Zoe rounded the corner and the Westminster train station loomed ahead. Winifred Parker's fine-boned, aristocratic face was all angles and shadows, her blush and lipstick mauve in the harsh light. Her hair, which Zoe recalled always being impeccably coifed, lay flattened about her forehead and temples.

The old harridan's dressed for fall, not for eighty-eight degrees at night in July, Zoe thought. By refusing to fly and refusing to let Zoe meet her, Winifred had obviously endured a needless and exhausting ordeal.

Winifred glared at Zoe with indignant emerald green eyes. "Those horrid taxi drivers. One wanted to charge me a hundred dollars to take me to Salem. Another laughed when I told him my destination and drove away."

"It's a long drive." Zoe forced a smile. "And it's hard for someone unfamiliar with the area to find the place in the dark." She wrestled the heavy suitcases into the rear of her van, while Winifred stood frowning at her. As always, this woman had the power to make Zoe feel inadequate, as if she, not Winifred, had made a fool of herself.

Thick fog lay across long stretches of Highway 11, and Zoe held her speed to thirty-five. They hardly spoke except about the weather. Winifred perched on the edge of her seat, one hand on the dashboard, and declared unequivocally that of all the places she had ever lived, the weather was the most predictable and pleasant in Philadelphia. Then silence, self-conscious and thick as the fog, settled over them.

Miles later, Winifred asked, "How is Kathryn?" On the rare occasions over the years that she had had any contact with Zoe, Winifred had always called her granddaughter Kathryn instead of Katie.

"She's fine," Zoe replied, and crossed her fingers on the underside of the steering wheel. It wrenched her heart to see what was happening to her Katie. At thirty, her daughter's lovely red hair was already white, and each year, it seemed, lines burrowed more deeply across her forehead. She rarely smiled these days, and the Parker eyes, those stunning green eyes, were often joyless and dull.

"How is that child of Kathryn's, what is her name? Laura May?"

"Laurie Ann. She's older, bigger," Zoe said.

"What is the longevity of a severely brain-damaged child like that?"

"No one really knows," Zoe replied. "Some live to be twenty or more."

"Well! Your daughter has certainly wasted her life. In my day, that kind of a child would have been put in an institution. How old is she now?"

"Nine." Zoe tightened her grip on the wheel. "Hank wanted to institutionalize Laurie Ann, but Katie insisted on caring for her at home. They were divorced, you know that."

Winifred shook her head. "I'm not surprised. No man is going to stay with a wife who makes a child like that her whole life."

The cold, disdainful way Winifred said *child like that* infuriated Zoe. Her head throbbed, and her foot pressed down on the accelerator as if by driving faster, she could leave Winifred's unpleasantness behind.

In the long silence, the dark seemed darker and the drive longer. Zoe's mind drifted back to when she was still Zoe Amorey, age twenty-one, and wildly enthusiastic about being instrumental in saving a stand of old-growth trees from a developer's bulldozers. She and fellow students had tied themselves to the trees, taking turns around the clock, attracting the attention of the media and putting pressure on the environmental education department of the university to join with legislators on behalf of the trees. She was also about to receive her master's degree in education.

Steven Parker's fire-red hair, long and wild about his square, honest face, and those amazingly intense green eyes had startled her when she looked up from a game of checkers at an off-campus pub. He had stood to her right, his eyes warm and seductive. In that moment, Zoe had lost both the game and her heart.

Their attraction had been immediate and their romance fiery, and when she started down the aisle—two months pregnant, to her mother's chagrin and his mother's horror—Zoe had glided on air, the universe trembling in the palms of her hands.

After weeks of trying to prevent their marriage, Steven's parents had presented him an ultimatum: Zoe, or his law education and his place in his father's law firm. Steven chose Zoe, then enlisted in the air force and was stationed at Caswell Air Force Base in Fort Worth, Texas. There Kathryn was born with her father's hair and eyes, and Zoe embraced the role of wife and mother. Those had been the happiest years of her life. Then on a cloudless afternoon, as Zoe shaded her eyes from the glare of the setting sun, she saw Steven's plane become a speck on the horizon. The gusto, the intellect, the passion that was Steven Parker vanished on a routine training mission. And Zoe, after months of immobilizing depression, managed to pack their few belongings and returned with her two-year-old daughter to her parents' home in Greenville, South Carolina.

Zoe turned off the highway onto a dark, winding country road. Within minutes a hillside sign, "Alexander Cemetery," spectral in the fog, loomed on a rise to their left. Just beyond, Zoe turned the car onto yet another dark two-lane.

Moments later a white sign with deep-cut black letters, "Amorey Lane," sprang to life in the headlights.

"In order for 911 to respond to an emergency, they mandated that every road in the county have a name," Zoe said. "Most people named their roads after themselves, thus, Amorey Lane."

Winifred did not comment, but when the house came into view, she said, "My God, how can you tolerate living way out here?"

Zoe's stomach knotted. "I love it here." Already it was clear to her that their arrangement, negotiated by phone, would never work. Winifred Parker, imperious and willful, a woman of means, could never adjust to rural South Carolina, and Zoe dreaded losing her privacy. Her heart plummeted as she considered certain of her personal habits: a trail of shoes left here, there, and anywhere, the unwashed dishes piled in the sink all day, books and papers strewn haphazardly on tables, laundry lifted from the dryer and left unfolded. Every habit, every move she made, would be subject to the scrutiny of Winifred's censorious eyes.

Living with her mother-in-law, whom she had not seen or heard from in years, would be untenable. How could she have imagined otherwise? How could she share her home with a woman she disliked and who disliked her?

But so much was at stake. She'd lived through tough times before; she could again. She would swallow her pride, adjust, and adapt to her mother-in-law and the situation. After all, Winifred wouldn't be here very long.

"The house is very comfortable, and we have neighbors now. See those lights?" Zoe waved in the direction of the pasture and pond. In the distance, tiny lights played hide-and-seek among trees on the far hillside.

"Where?"

"Over there, on the hill across the river."

"What kind of people would move way out here?" The scorn in Winifred's voice was unmistakable.

"There are two retired couples and a family with children. Nice people."

Winifred ran trembling fingers along her strand of pearls. She had never trusted this unwanted daughter-in-law. In those first months after Steven died, she had expected every letter to contain a demand for money from his widow. None ever had. But for a very long time she had needed a scapegoat, someone it was safe to hate and to blame for the loss of her only child. She understood that now.

Winifred squinted into the darkness. The unending chatter of insects grated on her nerves. She dreaded the isolation, and worried about the distance from a hospital. Already she loathed the house on Amorey Lane. She loathed the whole area. *Damn life's capriciousness. Damn growing old.*

2

KATIE

Katie hunched over a pew in the rear of the hospital chapel.

"Why, God?" she demanded for the hundredth time. "Why?" Laurie Ann was dead. Katie relived the anguish of a day long ago in another hospital with her husband, Hank, whom she had loved and trusted, and with Laurie Ann only three days old.

Hank had stood at the foot of the hospital bed, one hand clenched about the cold metal railing, the other hand slicing the air with crisp gestures. Usually fastidious in his appearance, he wore his tie limp and loose about his neck. His suit was crumpled, and he needed a shave after a night spent in a chair. "We can't take her home. There are places for children like this."

Uncomprehending, Katie had stared at him. "Places?"

He leaned forward, his dark eyes determined. "Where they'll look after her."

Bands of fear fettered Katie's chest and she held the infant close. "She's ours, Hank. What you're proposing is unthinkable. We've got to take her home." Her eyes pleaded with him. "You won't have to do anything. I'll take care of her."

"She'll devour your time, Katie. We'll have no life. Don't you understand? She isn't normal. Nothing will be normal for us, for other children we might have, for our folks. Listen to me, Katie." Hank clenched his fist, raised it, then dropped his hand in an exasperated gesture. "Life sucks if you're taking care of a severely brain-damaged child."

Hank *couldn't* be saying these things. He was upset. He would feel differently tomorrow. "Can we talk about this tomorrow?" Katie wanted nothing more than to sleep and sleep.

He shook his head. "I can't do it. I'm just not noble enough to make this kind of sacrifice."

The whole bed trembled as he pushed himself away from the railing, and when it did not stop, Katie knew it was her body trembling.

"We've got to walk out of here without her and put this disaster behind us, or . . ." Hank looked away from Katie, then back again, and his eyes were determined. "Or you walk out with her alone."

Pain, wide and deep, assailed Katie, and for a moment she could not breathe. She looked down at the infant in her arms. "I'll have to walk out alone with her," she said. At that instant, their marriage ended.

Voices in the hospital hallway outside snapped Katie back to the small chapel, but the pain of that day, nine years ago, spilled into the present.

She slowly rose and walked up the aisle to the altar. The simple chapel was warmed by a large, round stained-glass window behind the altar, which was bare but for a green velvet cover that hung to the wood floor. Pleasant organ music filled the space but couldn't soothe Katie's anguish.

"I believed in you. I trusted you," she charged angrily. "You, my Father in heaven, my hope." Katie raised a fist. Her face crumpled into a mask of pain. "Laurie Ann's dead. My child is *dead*. How could you do this to me?" Raw and frightening, a howl of pain tore from her throat.

"Kathryn? Ms. Parker?" an Irish voice asked as the chapel door closed. "I'm Maudie O'Hara. I'm the nurse who tended your wee one, and I came to say how sorry I am. Is there anything I can do for you?" Tall, with rounded hips, full bosom, and auburn hair curling softly about her face, Maudie O'Hara leaned over the stricken woman. Tiny freckles danced across the nurse's nose, and empathetic violet eyes met Katie's. "Ms. Parker. 'Tis hard, I know."

Maudie's strong arms caught Katie as she crumbled. She helped her to a seat in a front pew, and Katie leaned into her and sobbed.

"I loved Laurie Ann so much. She was my whole life." She clutched her arms tight across her stomach. "I took care of her by myself—I pureed fresh food, fruit, vegetables, whatever she could digest. She couldn't feed herself, sit up, crawl, or talk. I'd take her outside strapped into her chair, and every single day I'd carry her to the bathroom and bathe her while she lay in a canvas sling. I'd talk to her." Katie clutched Maudie's hand and sought affirmation in Maudie's eyes. "Her eyes didn't focus. But I'm sure she knew what I was saying."

Maudie nodded sagely. "Wee ones understand more than most folks think they do, lass."

"Every morning, I'd meditate to stay calm and centered. I tried, God how I tried, to stay positive." Katie rocked back and forth against Maudie, and Maudie's soft body swayed with her. "Laurie Ann, my baby. What will I do now?" Tears dripped from her chin. Maudie handed her a handkerchief and Katie wiped her face.

"She'd been sleeping through the night since she was four, but then tonight . . ." Racking sobs came, and Maudie held and rocked her the way Zoe had soothed her long ago when she was a child and had bruised her leg or cut her finger. In the confines of the small chapel, it seemed to Katie that she and this comforting nurse were the only people on earth, and she wished never to reenter the world beyond.

"Earlier today, Laurie Ann had horrible seizures. Her back arched like a bridge, and she couldn't breathe. I could almost see her heart thudding in her chest. It was terrible. I tried everything I knew, but nothing worked. Why didn't the medics who came when I called nine-one-one save her or the doctors here? Why?" She looked at Maudie, the question huge in her eyes. Then her body went limp. "I've been so tired. I'm still so tired."

"And understandably so, love. 'Tis a lonely road, being a caretaker. People don't realize."

Katie sniffled and nodded.

"My Granny back in Ireland used to say, 'In all matters, God decides, we abide.' It's easier if we believe there's a purpose in it all."

"Is there?"

"I would rather believe there is."

Katie sighed. "Sometimes I feel there's no purpose in anything."

"Whatever one believes, 'tis easier if we believe in something." Maudie glanced at her watch. "Come now, lass, we best be going."

Katie dreaded setting foot on the floor where Laurie Ann had lived her last day. "Where are we going?"

"I need to get back to the floor. I'll be taking you to the

lounge near my station. You can rest a bit and call your family."

"There's only my mother, and she lives about an hour and a half away, in Salem."

"You can call her, or I'll call her for you. Why don't you come along with me."

Maudie put an arm about Katie as they walked down the hall and onto the elevator. Katie shivered as they exited on the pediatric floor, but Maudie kept a supportive grip on her arm and led her to the long, narrow lounge with tan leather furniture and tables strewn with magazines. Katie fished in her purse for pen and paper, then handed the nurse Zoe's number. "Please, will you call my mother?"

"Right away." She squeezed Katie's hand gently. "You rest now."

Exhausted, Katie removed her shoes and stretched out on the leather sofa. A moment later she fell into a deep sleep.

Zoe awakened to the harsh jangle of the phone on her bedside table.

"Mrs. Parker?" The voice was soft, with an Irish brogue. It confused Zoe.

"Yes, this is Zoe Parker."

"Nurse O'Hara here from St. Francis Hospital."

Zoe snapped awake. Sheet clutched tightly in her fist, knuckles pressed against her heart, she sat bolt upright in her bed. "What is it?"

"I'm calling for your daughter, Katie—"

"Oh God, oh my God, something's happened to Katie?"

"No. No. Katie's fine. 'Tis the wee lass, Laurie Ann. They admitted her last night, and I'm sorry to tell you that she's passed on."

"Laurie Ann's passed on. You mean she's dead? Where's Katie? I want to talk to my daughter, please."

"She's asleep in the lounge. The poor lass was exhausted. I'll go wake her and she'll phone you back." The phone went dead.

Slowly the door to Zoe's bedroom opened. Winifred Parker stuck her head into the room. "Is something wrong?"

"Yes. Katie had to take Laurie Ann to the hospital last night. The child didn't make it."

"It's just as well," Winifred muttered, then she disappeared from view.

Anger welled, but before she could reply, the phone rang. Zoe grabbed it. "Katie! Laurie Ann—I'm so sorry, darling."

As Katie spoke, Zoe slipped off her nightgown, grabbed her jeans from the floor near the chaise, and yanked them on. Shifting the portable phone from hand to hand, she shoved her arms into a blue-and-white-checkered blouse. Rummaging in a dresser drawer, she located two socks of the same color, then plopped on the end of the chaise, pulled them on, and slid her feet into scuffed brown loafers. "I'm on my way," Zoe told her daughter. "Meet you at the house. I love you."

Giving her tangled hair a quick brush, Zoe braided it, wound it about her head, and pinned it in place. She slapped water on her face and perfunctorily brushed her teeth, then headed for the kitchen.

Winifred set her half-empty glass of orange juice on the kitchen table. Her short silver hair, damp from a shower, was slicked back from her high forehead. She wore dark blue cotton slacks and a white, high-buttoned blouse on which rested the ubiquitous pearls; she held a dark blue jacket. "I am going with you. I am not staying here alone," she said, her hand fidgeting with the pearls.

Zoe downed a glass of juice. "Let's go, then."

3

WINIFRED REMEMBERS

Katie and Zoe sat alone in Katie's bedroom. Zoe had asked Winifred to make herself comfortable in the living room of Katie's small home. "I want Laurie Ann cremated and buried alongside Grandpa Zak and Grandma Ida," Katie told her mother. "I'll close up the house here and bring her urn to Salem by the end of the week. Can we have a memorial service for her at the graves?"

"Whatever you want, my love," Zoe replied.

Tears spilled from Katie's eyes and she hugged her mother. "Thanks, Mom, for everything, for all the years you stood by me and Laurie Ann."

When Zoe's parents had each died, their cremated remains had been placed in marble urns and buried on a small knoll near the pond on the land in Salem that they had both loved so deeply. Zoe had prepared the epitaphs for her parents' headstones, and the pink granite markers had been reverently placed above their respective graves. Today Katie would arrive with the remains of her daughter, and one day Zoe too, and perhaps Katie, would lie in this small family cemetery.

A redwood bench, a few feet back from the graves, was framed by a trellis upon which fragrant old-world roses bloomed in pink profusion all summer long. As Zoe sat there waiting for her daughter to arrive, she thought of how Katie had devoted herself to her own daughter. Nothing was too good or too much for Laurie Ann. Zoe was not sure she could have handled the lack of sleep, the endless lifting and bending and tending that Katie had done. Every week Katie had taken the child to a chiropractor, and a massage therapist came to the house every two weeks. Having had no life outside of Laurie Ann, no time for other interests all these years, Katie would find the adjustment extra hard.

Winifred's voice jolted Zoe from her musing. "So you intend to bury that child here?"

Looking down at Zoe from the other end of the bench, Winifred appeared as austere and unapproachable as she always had. Instinctively, Zoe pulled back. Ever since Steven had died, Zoe had sought to avoid confrontation and controversy with the woman. But the look of contempt on Winifred's face couldn't go unanswered. Zoe planted her feet solidly on the grass, turned, and concentrated on outstaring her mother-in-law.

"Winifred, that child's name was Laurie Ann. You negate her as if she were a nonperson. She *was* a person, and my daughter loved her. After the funeral, Katie's going to be staying here for a while. I'm not asking you to be warm or caring, but if you can't treat her kindly and respect her grief, I'll have to ask you to leave." Her fingers hurt from squeezing them together.

Winifred swayed a little. "Leave? But our arrangement—"

"I'll have to find a way *without* our arrangement. It'll be hard, but Katie's more important to me than any arrangement. Somehow I'll manage."

Winifred tilted her chin up. An ultimatum? From Zoe of all people? "Well, I will certainly make it my business to avoid her."

Zoe felt herself shaking with the effort it took to stand up to her mother-in-law, but a crow flew by as it might on any ordinary day, and the fragrance of old-fashioned roses filled the air. The world did not crumble about her. Emboldened, Zoe said, "That's not good enough. This isn't an armed truce. I won't have Katie walking on eggs in my home. It's her home too." Her eyes held a demand and a plea, and her voice softened. "Katie's all the family I have. And, well, we're all the family you have."

"I have other family. My cousin Emily."

"Then perhaps you'd find it pleasanter to be with your cousin." Zoe swallowed hard. "If you decide to leave, I'll take you to the train or to the airport right after the funeral." Trembling at her audacity, Zoe rose to her feet and walked away.

The sky was a cloudless indigo blue; the grass in the pasture was deep green and smooth as velvet. A small insect lighted on Winifred's hand. She flicked it away and sat down on the bench. No one had spoken to her as Zoe just had since she was a girl. No one had dared. Her throat knotted, and she fought back tears as she watched the younger woman hasten across the bridge and take the steps up to the house two at a time. The buzzing in her ears grew louder. Next would come swirling bands of dizziness to plunder her of vitality and hope.

Gripping the wooden slats of the bench, Winifred closed her eyes. She must fight off this marauder that threatened to bring her down. She breathed slowly and deeply. This time the world did not spin, and when she opened her eyes, they lighted on the pink granite stones.

IDA CANNON AMOREY, 1920–1987
Wise and kind, a woman who accepted others
and saw the best in them. She is missed.

ZACHARY FRANKLIN AMOREY 1918–1986
A man among men, a tower of strength.
His passing is a loss to many.

Ida had been only sixty-seven years old when she died. Much too young. Winifred had always scorned Ida's docility, her "live and let live" attitude, yet she remembered Ida as having the calmest face, the most serene eyes she had ever seen.

"I bet you weren't afraid to die," Winifred said, addressing the headstone. Was *she*? Yes, she was afraid—not so much of dying, but of how she would die. Wasn't that why she was here?

She thought of Zoe. Zoe possessed her mother's oval face and her clear, amber-tinged brown eyes, and she was as quiet as her mother had been. Never, before today, had she seen Zoe express anger. Winifred recalled a conversation with her cousin and confidante, Emily, the day after Steven had brought Zoe home to meet his parents.

"Nice girl? Pretty?" Emily asked over lunch.

"Pretty in an ordinary sort of way. Unsophisticated. A different class of people from us."

"What class is that?" Emily asked.

"Her father's only a bank teller. Steven's sowing his oats. When my son marries, it will be to someone of our own kind, not some rabble-rouser who tied herself to a tree." Winifred's carefully plucked and penciled eyebrows lifted.

Emily laughed. "Tied herself to a tree? Why?"

"To stop progress, development."

"That was gutsy of her," Emily replied.

"She's a stupid and misguided hippie."

"I guess you want Steven's wife to be someone from a rich, prominent family, preferably with a mother who boasts of membership in the DAR."

"Of course," Winifred said.

Emily snickered. "Still social climbing, eh, Winnie? I'm surprised you even talk to me. I'm a very ordinary, working-class relative."

No one else dared call her Winnie or remind her of her humble roots. Winifred's eyes grew stormy. In stony silence, they finished lunch. She and Emily had never again talked in any meaningful way, and in the last seven years they had not even seen one another. Lately she had found herself thinking about her cousin, missing her, and wondering where she was.

The day when Steven announced that he and Zoe were going to be married, they had talked in the sitting room, her favorite room in the stately Georgian house with its cool blue walls, gem-toned Persian rugs, overstuffed sofas, and mahogany tables polished so smartly you could see your face in their surfaces. On one wall, a china cabinet brimmed with crystal pieces of great beauty: vases, bowls, and pitchers Winifred had collected over time and planned to pass on to her eventual daughter-in-law.

The events of that day changed her feelings for that

room, and after Steven married Zoe, she never used the room for relaxation or personal pleasure. Winifred squeezed her eyes tight, recalling how she had wanted to scream in rage and frustration, but she had smiled and offered Steven a splendid Episcopal church wedding and a European honeymoon if they would wait a year. So much could happen in a year; she intended to make sure of that.

Then Steven delivered the blow that almost sent her tumbling to the floor. "We're going to have a baby."

"What in heaven's name did you just say?"

"Zoe's pregnant."

"Impossible."

"We love one another. Zoe's being pregnant has nothing to do with our getting married."

"Oh, my God. Steven, no. You're throwing away your life." If she could, she would have vaporized Zoe with a wave of her hand; the little vamp using her body to trap her son. Even now, thinking about it made Winifred's mouth and her entire body tighten. With smiling reserve, she had masked her anger at her son's wedding. Her husband, Theodore, had kept a secure grip on her arm, anchoring her body against the strong keel of his own when the young couple said, "I do," in a simple ceremony in a small, unassuming white church in Greenville, South Carolina.

Later, when she demanded that Steven come home to visit his parents without Zoe, he refused, and Winifred had raged to her husband. "It's that little hippie tramp. She's turned our son against us."

Steven and Zoe had a baby girl, and she and Theodore never saw their only son again. Winifred's eyes glistened with tears. How could she ever admit to anyone that she was a pretender to the blue-blooded lifestyle she had embraced?

She was not proud that she had banished the most important people, Steven and Emily, from her life.

The irony of it all was that now, due to odious circumstances, she was in Salem, South Carolina, a place she
hated, with the woman she resented and had for a long
time held responsible for the loss of her son.

4

IT'S OKAY TO CRY

Sleep was impossible. There was no surcease from the weight on Katie's heart, the crushing loneliness, or the uncontrollable tears. This afternoon they had buried Laurie Ann's ashes on the knoll alongside her great-grandparents. The short service had been conducted by a Unitarian minister, the father of one of Katie's students at the Faraday School, where for many years she had been responsible for the after-school kindergarten program.

"Laurie Ann was a soul come to earth to teach patience, love, and dedication," the minister said in his eulogy.

When the marble urn was placed into the earth and covered with soil, Katie sobbed. Now, at four in the morning, she sat in the comfortable living room, her favorite room in the house. Katie had always loved to sink into the overstuffed sofa, turn up the fire in the tall stone fireplace, and read, or listen to the music of Vivaldi, Beethoven, or Bach. But the room offered no solace now. Nothing did. Not her mother's understanding or kindness, not the cards and sympathetic phone calls from teachers and staff at her school.

Zoe stood in the doorway of the dark living room. "Katie, you in here?"

"I can't sleep, Mommy."

"Neither can I, darling. Shall I fix us some hot milk with honey or a cup of herbal tea?"

Katie shook her head and hiccuped. Tears trailed along both cheeks and pooled near her mouth.

"It's okay to cry. How can you not cry for Laurie Ann?"

Katie's eyes drowned in despair. "I killed Laurie Ann."

"Good heavens, you did no such thing." Zoe crossed the room and sat by Katie on the sofa. "What's this all about?"

"She was very sick with terrible seizures, and the doctor wanted me to bring her to the hospital. I refused until it was too late. Did I want her to die?" Bursting into tears, Katie buried her face in one of the large, soft pillows.

"Darling, Laurie Ann thrived with homeopathic remedies all those years. You loved your daughter. No one could have done more for a child or loved a child more than you did."

"Did I refuse to take her to the hospital because on some deep, unconscious level I hoped she'd die?"

Zoe took her daughter's face in both her hands and lifted it so that their eyes met. "Do you really think that, Katie?"

Slowly the anguish faded from Katie's face and eyes. She shook her head. "I feel uncertain about so many things." She fidgeted a bit, then asked, "How did you survive when my father died?"

The old ache squeezed Zoe's heart even after all these years. She sighed and took Katie's hands in hers. "I felt like you do now. Devastated. For a long time I lived in shadows, like being in a cave. You learn to take it one day at a time, and somehow you get through it. I had your grandparents."

"And I have you."

"Always." Zoe dabbed Katie's cheeks with a wad of Kleenex from her bathrobe pocket. "Your grandparents went through many hard times with me. I'm sure at times they worried that I might end my life."

"You thought about that? That's exactly how I feel."

"I know, darling, I know. When we lose someone we love, nothing makes sense. Life feels meaningless for a very long time." Her eyes held Katie's. "But we go on putting one foot ahead of the other. We get up in the morning, get dressed, brush our teeth and hair, go to work, and of course we hurt, and we cry. And then quite unexpectedly, one day we hear a robin sing, or we notice that the moon is full, or we have the urge to see some silly movie, and we've begun to heal." Zoe rose. "Come. Katie, I'll make some tea."

Katie pushed herself up. Zoe took her arm, and they made their way from the living room into the foyer, which was lit by a small nightlight. "Be careful," Zoe said, from habit. "The edge of that wall table is sharp."

"You've been reminding me of that since I was little."

"You're right. Sorry."

"Don't be sorry. It's familiar, comfortable. It's home."

As they sat side by side at the kitchen table waiting for the water to boil, Katie said, "So many people from my school came all the way out here for the funeral."

"You have many caring friends." Zoe pushed back her chair, walked over to the stove, and lifted the lid from the pot.

"You always peek, Mom. It never boils until you go away and forget about it." There was a hint of humor in Katie's voice.

Zoe smiled, glad that she had helped to lighten Katie's pain. It would return, of course, but for this brief moment the ache in her daughter's heart had eased a little.

5

❧

WINIFRED

While Katie and Zoe sat in the kitchen and talked, Winifred lay awake reading in the mahogany four-poster bed in the room Zoe called the Caribbean room. She found the lemon yellow walls cloying, and especially distasteful were those clichéd coral and turquoise tropical fish prints that hung between the windows.

Winifred tucked the white lace-trimmed sheet close about her, set the book on her lap, and closed her eyes. The years rolled away, and once again she lay in the cramped bed with her two younger sisters, Mary and Bethany, staring up at the cobwebs on the low ceiling of her childhood. Six of them had lived in four rooms: her grim-faced parents, her ancient grandfather with his gnarled hands, her two sisters, and herself.

Grandfather spent most days hunched in his chair by the fireplace, muttering rebukes to his daughter-in-law for producing no sons to carry on the lobster business he had passed on to his son, Jacob Oxnaur. Winifred, or Winnie as they called her then, had been even more repulsed by the old man than by the smell of fish that permeated the house and lingered in her clothes and hair. The way the old man looked at her when they were alone frightened her, long before she understood his insinuation.

The tiny, storm-battered house was one of six built on a promontory above a pebble-strewn cove, above a fierce ocean too frigid for swimming. Each day powerful tides sucked the steel gray water from the cove, exposing sandbars and boulders that extended out two hundred feet or more. Though often reprimanded and sometimes spanked by their mother for venturing there, Mary and Bethany were drawn to the cove the way the tide responds to the pull of the moon. One fall afternoon, with a northeaster predicted, her sisters walked out to the rocky point where sea and sandbars met and were swept away by the grasping, snarling ocean. Their bodies were never recovered.

Remembering it chilled Winifred, and she shivered. It had been a cold, foreboding day when her father planted the homemade crosses with her sisters' names alongside their grandmother's grave in the unkempt Goose Cove cemetery. It was her birthday. She was fourteen. No one remembered. Above the crosses, her grandfather shot suggestive glances at her. Winifred remembered feeling confused and ashamed of her budding breasts and hips. On that day, she determined to leave this impoverished and desolate place as soon as possible.

From then on, Winifred avoided being alone with her grandfather. The old man hardly left the house, but neither did her mother. Had her mother seen his greedy eyes following her daughter? They never spoke of it. At night Winifred kept her bedroom door bolted shut and a chair shoved under the doorknob. There were nights when she heard the shuffling of his feet back and forth in the hallway outside her room, and she would cover her head with a pillow.

During her last year in high school she had been encouraged by her teacher to enroll in a typing class, which led to her first job, in the office of a rapidly expanding trucking company in Portland. When the opportunity arose, she gladly transferred to Philadelphia, far from the inhospitable coast of Maine. Six months later, she resigned from the trucking firm for a position that advertised training as a legal secretary.

She had been beautiful then, people said, with her smooth, pale skin, long raven hair, and spectacular green eyes. And Winifred seemed instinctively to know the right blend of boldness and coyness needed to attract the attention of Theodore Samuel Parker Jr., the son and heir of the law firm. Against his family's wishes, their courtship progressed rapidly. Six months later they were married. Her snooty mother-in law, finally resigned to the situation, had remarked to a friend, "Wait and see. I'll make a silk purse out of this sow's ear." Like Professor Henry Higgins with Eliza Doolittle in *My Fair Lady*, she set about to transform her daughter-in-law.

Winifred had proved to be an apt pupil, watching, listening, and learning to hold her shoulders and head in a reserved yet gracious manner. Imitating her mother-in-law, she assumed an air of confidence. She mastered small things and large: how to set an elegant table; which fork and spoon to use with which dish; how to dress demurely but with style; how to employ, address, and dismiss servants. For a time she exceeded her mother-in-law in savoir faire when it came to organizing lavish and successful charity balls, and outdid her in strict observance of social protocol.

Once Steven started elementary school, Winifred did less socially and assumed the responsibility for her family's personal investments. Instinctively she understood money, and thrived in her own corner office on the third floor of the building owned by the law firm of Parker and Parker. What exciting and stimulating years they had been. In her blue business suit, shoulders erect, briefcase at her side, she would step off the elevator and stride purposefully down the hall. The secretaries and other staff members looked at her with respect and visible awe. In those heady days, Winifred felt like royalty as she greeted and nodded to everyone as she strode by them. Then, three years ago, Theodore died suddenly, and with no son taking over the business, protecting her interests, his cheating, lying partners took it all away from her.

"We're expanding. The workload dictates taking in new partners and creating a new board," said Tom Dockery, the senior partner and her husband's trusted friend, with false regret. All three of the partners came into her office two days later, their faces solemn, their voices embarrassed but unyielding. "Our bylaws limit the period of time anyone can serve as a board member."

"Why did this never come up before?" she asked.

"Ted insisted that the rules be bent for you."

In a moment she lost her office, her purpose, for by then, like most men, Winifred had filled her social needs at the office and at the firm's business and political functions.

When the book slipped from her lap and onto the floor, Winifred awoke and swiftly reached for it. Dizziness and nausea propelled her back onto her pillows, where she lay struggling to bring her body under control by breathing slowly and deeply, as her doctor had instructed. As the room stopped spinning, she saw that the bedside clock read six thirty a.m. She'd actually slept through the night.

After a long while, moving at the pace of a mud turtle, Winifred eased her legs over the edge of the bed. Holding first to the bedpost, then to the back of a chair, then to the end of the dresser, she slowly reached the bathroom and leaned heavily against the doorframe. Any sudden movement could send her sprawling. How stupid of her to leave her pills on the bathroom sink.

Dr. Robert Lavelle, her family doctor of many years, had said, "It's going to be hard for you, but you must slow down and keep stress to a minimum."

Easy for him to say.

She made it to the sink, turned on the water, and swallowed two of the tiny pills, then studied her reflection in the mirror. At sixty-five the skin on her face had still been smooth, but, now, at seventy-five, it no longer was. "How incredibly I've aged since Theodore's passing," she murmured as her fingertips traced the wrinkles that fanned across her cheeks. She turned her chin slowly from right to left. "Imagine, me, Winifred Parker, with a turkey neck." She hated aging. It brought more than creaking knees, more than slowing down and wrinkles. It brought illness, and fears of dying, and regrets. That was the worst—the regrets.

"Grandmother Parker," a soft voice called from the hallway outside her bedroom door. "Mom's making pancakes with fresh blueberries. Would you like to join us for breakfast?"

Do not skip meals, Dr. Lavelle had said. And despite the early hour, she was hungrier than usual. The country air, perhaps. "I'll be right there," Winifred replied.

Zoe had explained that Ida had furnished the house with a tongue-in-cheek, eclectic style. To Winifred's orderly mind, the house was an eccentric hodgepodge, every room jarred her senses. The decor of the kitchen was all country garage sale and flea market. White stars, eight inches point to point, were stenciled on the painted brown pine floor. Winifred felt uncomfortable stepping on them, as if by doing so she would mar them in some manner.

Unstained and never sanded, the kitchen walls were paneled with old barn siding. In one corner stood a mustard-colored distressed-pine hutch that was stenciled top and bottom with blue strawflowers. It housed an assortment of Early American artifacts: a cast-iron apple peeler, a dented tin milk jug, blue and white unmatched pieces of crockery, assorted red and white ceramic roosters.

On her first night here, when she had followed Zoe into the kitchen, Winifred's heart sank at the sight of the worn and scarred pine table and unmatched chairs. They reminded her of a smaller table and chairs, her family crammed about it, her grandfather's knee pressing against hers, his elbow poking into her side. She had always scrunched as far away from him as she could. It never seemed far enough.

As she sipped her coffee, Winifred thought that her granddaughter looked overly pale and much too young to be so drawn and haggard. A week of lying in the sunshine on a beach in Florida would do her good. She knew neither Zoe nor Katie had the money for a vacation. Well, they had best treat her with deference and respect before she would consider opening her purse strings.

"Did you sleep well?" Zoe asked.

"As well as I ever sleep," she lied. "Older folks lose their ability to sleep well, and when they do sleep, it's less than they used to. At least that's what my doctor tells me."

"I'm sorry," Zoe replied. "I thought maybe the country air would help."

Sitting up straight against the ladder-back chair, Winifred ate slowly and in silence.

Zoe attacked her pancakes.

Katie nibbled, then pushed hers away. "I'm not hungry." She rose and set her plate in the sink. Her shoulders slumped as she walked from the kitchen.

"She's quite upset," Winifred said.

Winifred had said little, smiled when appropriate, and stayed out of their way these last few days. Yet Zoe remained wary and vigilant. *Be careful*, her instinct warned. "Katie's been up all night. I found her crying this morning."

"Well," her mother-in-law said, "it's to be expected. When the purpose of your life is snatched away from you, it's astoundingly complicated and difficult."

I guess that's the closest she can get to sympathy. Zoe clamped her lips tight, moved to the sink, and began to fill the dishwasher.

"Can I be of assistance?"

Zoe shook her head.

Winifred was relieved. Asking had been a foolish pretense at cooperation; she feared her illness might overpower her if she bent to load the dishwasher.

6

THE SUMMERHOUSE

The morning stretched long and lazy. Reassured by the occasional sound of Zoe's and Kathryn's voices, which drifted to her through her slightly ajar bedroom door, Winifred rested, read, and sketched. Just before noon she heard a door close. The house grew quiet, too quiet. From her window she watched the other women walk arm in arm down the path and across the pasture to the summerhouse.

Time passed, and no one appeared to ask how she was or if she were hungry. "I might as well be living alone," Winifred muttered. Her heart sank as she thought how lonely her Philadelphia mansion had been without Theodore. Those last weeks in that house had been enough to drive her to suicide, but she had persevered, as she must now. She could fall back on injured pride and sit in her room and sulk, or . . . Winifred dressed in slacks and a long-sleeved blouse and fastened her pearls about her neck.

Then she left the house and followed the others down to the summerhouse.

The hexagonal gazebo they called the summerhouse was screened on two sides. The solid rear wall accommodated a two-burner gas stove, an under-counter refrigerator, hanging shelves for the unmatched pottery cups and plates, and a work shelf. The branches of an old oak shaded the summer-house, and potted ferns hung from the rafters, reminding Winifred of an old-fashioned porch. Along with a hammock, there were white wicker chairs with plum and white vinyl-covered cushions crinkled with wear. On a round wicker table, sandwiches were stacked high on a blue and white plat-ter. Alongside the platter stood a glass pitcher, its sides sweaty and glistening, three tall glasses, and an ice bucket.

Zoe lay in the hammock. Her moccasins, a *Health and Spirituality* magazine, and a magazine from the Sierra Club lay on the ground beside her. As Winifred approached, Zoe waved her hand toward the table. "Katie's made ham-and-cheese sandwiches and lemonade. I was about to come up to the house to ask you to join us for lunch."

She's trying to be polite, Winifred thought, feeling out of place. But then, where didn't she feel out of place these days? She settled into a chair, and for a time no one spoke.

Then Katie stood and shucked off her terry cloth robe. Long-legged and trim in a one-piece blue swimsuit, she walked swiftly to the end of the small wooden dock and moments later, every muscle taut, plunged into the water. Katie surfaced, dived, surfaced again, and sliced through the water with rapid strokes.

"Why do you call it a pond? It's more like a small lake," Winifred said.

Zoe's eyes followed her daughter. "It is, isn't it? My

mother used to call it Dad's folly. He kept encouraging the bulldozer operator to dig deeper and make it wider. I enjoy rowing. I row my dinghy on it sometimes, though it's not large enough to really get a good workout."

Winifred stood and held to a wooden post with both hands and searched the pond with anxious eyes. "What about snakes, water moccasins? Is it safe for Kathryn to be swimming there?"

"She learned to swim in that pond. We've never had any problems."

Kathryn had dived again but not surfaced, and anxiety tightened in Winifred's midsection. With a burst of spray Kathryn's head and shoulders emerged from the water, and the anxiety settled, only to stir again as her granddaughter turned and swam the length of the pond. Why such concern for this young woman? Her granddaughter, true, but until recently, a total stranger. "For goodness' sake, Zoe, call her in," Winifred said as if Kathryn were a child. At the surprised look on Zoe's face, she added, "She'll lollygag out there until her skin puckers."

"I imagine she finds it soothing." Zoe shifted in the hammock and it tipped precariously. "Katie used to take Laurie Ann into the pond every summer. I think it comforts her to swim."

Zoe's relaxed attitude annoyed Winifred. How could she, even for an instant, have imagined getting financially involved with Zoe? But here she was, and sooner or later they would have to talk about their hastily conceived arrangement and other serious matters. At that moment her granddaughter scrambled from the pond, wrapped the terry cloth robe about her, and joined them.

"I could eat a horse." Katie reached for a sandwich.

In the silence that followed as they ate, Katie picked up

her mother's strewn magazines and stacked them on the table. "Mom used to be very active in environmental issues. She helped clean up a river, stopped the plant upriver from dumping their crap into it," she told Winifred.

Zoe waved her hand dismissively. "That was a while ago. I haven't fought the good fight for several years now."

"Why is that, Mom?" Katie thumbed through the *Sierra* magazine. "You've always been involved in one cause or another. I remember you fighting with the city to have a stoplight installed in the block where my middle school crossing was."

"It infuriated me, so much traffic and no protection for you kids."

"Remember the time you led the struggle for recycling bins for glass, paper, plastics? I was fifteen when I carried a sign and picketed City Hall with you and your friends."

"Of course I remember. Too many cans and plastics end up in the public dump. But in the case of the river, I guess you could say there's a time for everything. I wrenched my ankle and tore ligaments getting to the river that last time and had to be carried out. But I've had the pleasure of seeing it running clear, brimming with fish again."

Katie set the magazine on the table. "You were laid up for weeks afterward. And you're probably right. There's a time for everything." Moving to the refrigerator, she swung the door open and hunkered down in front of it for a better view of its contents. "I don't feel much like lemonade. Let's see. Coke's all gone. Two bottles of ginger ale left, celery sticks, peanut butter."

Winifred realized that there was more to Zoe than she had thought, but her real interest was in her granddaughter, whom she watched with a mix of admiration and amusement.

"What?" Katie asked, standing and looking at Winifred.

"I was just thinking how well you swim, and how to the point and practical you are."

Katie flushed. "It's like that song from *Annie Get Your Gun:* I'm just doin' what comes naturally."

Zoe sat up, rolled out of the hammock, and slipped into her moccasins. "Let's get out of here before mosquitoes come and consume us for their dinner."

Katie collected the sandwich platter and the pitcher. "I'm ready to go up. How about you, Grandmother?"

Every joint of her body protesting, Winifred eased from her chair and looked about the summerhouse. "Yes. Let's go." While Zoe strode ahead, Katie adjusted her long stride to fit her grandmother's slower pace as they moved across the pasture. When they reached the patio at the top of the steps, Winifred paused to catch her breath. "Do you go swimming often?" She asked.

"I used to in the summer with Laurie Ann, on warm days. It was good for her. Now, suddenly, I can't seem to get enough of it."

"Water is therapeutic, or so I hear," Winifred said. "But remember, never swim on a full stomach. And never swim when you're alone."

Katie touched the older woman's shoulder. "Would you go down to the pond with me sometimes?"

"Why, yes, I would do that." An unanticipated flush of warmth filled Winifred's heart. "Just tell me when. I'll need a bit of time to dress and lace my shoes." She wore sturdy SAS shoes with laces and had brought four pairs with her—blue, black, tan, and maroon—and many extra pairs of laces. Theodore used to say her laces broke so often because she pulled them too tight. Too tight, like girdles in the old days when she was young. Where had those years gone: theater, dinner dances, elegant clothing? She and Theodore had been marvelous on a dance floor. It was perhaps the best thing they did together, other than having Steven.

"I'll give you plenty of time to get ready," Katie said.

Winifred liked this young woman. *Kathryn reminds me of myself. She faces life with courage. Even if I didn't approve of her choosing to raise that child and to lose her husband in the process, still, I have to admire her spunk.*

Thinking back, Winifred realized that what she had remembered about Zoe had been limited by her refusal to see the young woman as anyone other than the wrong person for Steven. Zoe's air of surety had put her off, and that whole tree thing was just appalling—or so she'd thought at the time. In fact, Zoe had been socially responsible, had stood her ground for a cause she believed in.

"Something's odd with the weather," Katie said, looking about them.

"Seems fine to me. The sky's clear."

"No," Katie said. "There's something in the air. I sense a change coming."

By evening a dense mist hovered above the pond. The air thickened and vaporous spirals whirled upward. An ominous silence replaced the chirruping of crickets. Worried, Zoe peered from her bedroom window. *The silence before a storm.* The evening news had reported that a tornado had torn through a town thirty miles away, leaving a path of twisted trees, shattered homes and lives. Of all life's natural disasters, tornadoes frightened Zoe the most. They gave little or no warning and roared in to divest you of all worldly goods, leaving you, if you were alive and unhurt, desolate on a pile of rubble.

At ten p.m. Zoe turned to the weather station on her bedroom television.

"Rogue storms have devastated the town of Lundsville, near Helen, in northeastern Georgia," the announcer declared. "The line of storms is moving due east."

So they'll miss Oconee County, Zoe thought, with relief, and she soon went to sleep.

7

SHARDS OF GLASS

Zoe was awakened by an enormous thud, as if some furious giant rampaging outside had flung huge boulders against her house. Glass shattered, the wind bellowed, and the house shuddered and surrendered to darkness. Zoe tumbled to the carpet and squeezed as much of her body as possible under her bed. She jammed the balls of her hands hard against her ears in an effort to blot out the howl of wind, and prayed for it to end. Finally the thunderous roar ceased as abruptly as it had begun.

In the frightening silence that followed, Zoe struggled to her feet. Reaching into the bedside table drawer, she pulled out a flashlight and stared in disbelief as her light scanned the room. Rain came through a shattered window onto the now-sodden carpet. Shards of glass defaced the bedspread, chairs, floor, and furniture. Blood dripped from a cut on the sole of her foot. From down the hall came Winifred's voice, "Zoe! Katie! Help me!"

Zoe grabbed a pillow, tore off the pillowcase, and wrapped it tightly about her instep. Then she limped from her room and down the dark hallway.

When Winifred had eased herself into bed that night, she thought, *Katie's right. There is something odd about this night, a smell or a stillness that doesn't seem right.* But then, she was accustomed to the sounds and smells of a city. From her nightstand, she picked up the detective novel *E Is for Evidence,* by Sue Grafton. She liked Grafton's books and knew her heroine, Kinsey Millhone, better than she knew Zoe or Katie.

At first the swells of sound and the trembling bed confused her, then the walls of the house shuddered. Windows imploded, sending bits of glass helter-skelter. The room plunged into darkness. The book flew off her lap, and it was all Winifred could do, clinging to the headboard of her bed, not to follow the book into a corner of the room. Something sharp struck her back, and she cried out. The silence, when it came, was as frightening as the roaring noise had been.

In the hallway, Zoe trained the flashlight straight ahead of herself and limped toward her daughter's room. Both Winifred's scream and Katie's silence terrified her, and she hastened past the older woman's room to Katie's. Curled in a ball, Katie slept, serenely, her arm hugging a pillow. She must have taken a sleeping pill. Relief brought tears to Zoe's eyes, and it took her a few moments to collect herself sufficiently to respond to the plaintive "Zoe! Zoe!" coming from Winifred's room.

The moment she saw Winifred, Zoe's heart softened. Disheveled and distraught, her mother-in-law lay on her side whimpering like a child. Pulling open a drawer in a small mahogany dresser near the doorway, Zoe found and switched on another flashlight. Immediately she saw the shattered glass and bits of trees and many leaves.

"There. It hurts, there." Winifred pointed behind her.

Below Winifred's left shoulder, blood stained her silk nightgown. Gently, Zoe slipped her arm about the older woman. Winifred's body shook uncontrollably.

"The storm's over now, Winifred," Zoe said softly. Her own foot throbbed, and blood seeped through the white pillowcase. She would need to tend to it soon.

"Over?" The older woman looked dazed.

"A tornado must have clipped us, but it's over now."

Winifred half raised her arm, then it fell back into her lap. "The windows."

"Mine blew apart too. That seems to be the major damage. Let's see how badly you're hurt."

Winifred pulled away. "I am fine now. See, my hand's stopped shaking." She extended a trembling hand toward Zoe.

"It's all right, Winifred. Turn on your side, if you can, so I can check your back."

Winifred complied. Being alone and ill was the nightmare that haunted her dreams. The fact that she had called out and someone had come was, she suddenly realized, reason enough to have come to Salem.

The nightgown was of high-quality silk and resisted tearing. Easing her hand beneath it, Zoe slid her fingers carefully along Winifred's back, and her mother-in-law winced.

"You lie here while I get my first-aid kit."

Bony fingers clutched her arm. "Don't leave me, Zoe."

"I'll be right back." Zoe handed Winifred a flashlight. "Don't try to get up until I sweep some of this glass. I'll get a broom and make a path to the bathroom for you."

Winifred could not have risen had she wanted to. "Kathryn?" she asked hesitantly.

"She's fine. I think she took a sleeping pill earlier and slept right through it. There are no broken windows on that side of the house."

Winifred's asking about Katie surprised Zoe. She limped toward her bathroom for her first-aid kit, taking out and setting up flashlights on tables on the way. Blackouts were not uncommon in the country, and there were flashlights and candles in every room.

Then she heard pounding on the front door and voices.

"Zoe! Zoe Parker." Someone had come to help them.

"I'm coming," she called, moving as fast as she could across the debris. But the solid oak front door was either stuck shut or twisted on its hinges, for it refused to budge. "I can't open the door."

"No problem, Zoe," a deep voice behind her said. "We just walked in one of them broken windows." Holding lanterns high, her neighbors stood before her.

Relief flooded Zoe and her entire body relaxed. "Bless you for coming. How did you know and get here so fast?"

"We were finishing up Bible study a piece up the road," Olive Holloway said. "Sounded like Lucifer, riding an old freight train. Someone said a twister'd hit up your road. We came a-running."

Ruben Holloway's wide shoulders were rounded from years of plowing and farming. Iron-gray hair curled about the edges of his baseball cap. His forehead was high, his face deeply furrowed. The middle finger of his left hand had been lost, to the second knuckle, in a tree-cutting accident. Olive was a strong, solid, well-rounded woman almost as tall as her husband. Her kind, open face wore an anxious look.

"My Lord, Zoe," she said, "we about died of worry for you."

"But what about your place?"

Ruben shrugged. "Don't know. It's in the hands of the Almighty. What's done is done; ain't a thing we can do 'bout it."

Zoe reached out a hand and touched his arm. "I hope everything's okay at your place with your animals." She stepped forward to embrace Olive. From down the hall came a plaintive call, "Zoe."

"My mother-in-law's got a cut on her back from flying glass. I was about to tend to it."

"I'll start right in sweeping this mess," Olive said.

"Where's Katie?" Ruben asked.

"Slept right through it. Lucky her room's on the hill side and not the pasture side."

"Well, bless her heart. She's had 'bout all she can handle, poor little thing," Olive said. "I'll just get me a broom and start in your bedroom."

The most damage had been done in Winifred's room. The settee was overturned, and a long shard of glass had pierced the upholstery, where cotton batting now oozed out.

Zoe washed and cleaned Winifred's cut, which was neither deep nor long, spread an antibiotic salve on it, and covered it with a bandage.

"Where's your robe?" she asked. "We need to get you up. The sheets need changing."

Winifred said, "On a hook behind the bathroom door."

But when Zoe tried to sit her up and tried to slip her arms into the silk robe, Winifred moaned and sank back onto the bed. "Oh, I'm dizzy," she said, lifting her hands to her head.

Zoe realized she couldn't do this alone. "Olive," she called, then explained to Winifred, "Friends came to help.

We'll get you settled on the couch in the den. There's no broken glass in there."

A moment later, her neighbor appeared in the doorway.

"Olive, this is my mother-in-law, Winifred Parker." Zoe turned to Winifred. "This is my good friend and neighbor, Olive Holloway." Then back to Olive. "My mother-in-law's a bit dizzy. Can you help me move her to the den?"

With the strong arms of a farmer's wife accustomed to hefting bales of hay, plowing pastures, and assisting in birthing calves, Olive helped Winifred to the den and onto the couch. "You're needing some tea to settle your stomach," Olive said.

Winifred shook her head. "Thank you, but no. I'll just rest. I'll be fine." She wished the woman would go away.

Her body trembling, Zoe spread a lightweight cotton blanket over her mother-in-law, lit a candle on the table nearby, and set a glass mantel over it for safety. On rubbery legs, Zoe made it as far as the doorway. Sweat beaded her forehead and trickled along her temples. She leaned against the doorframe. *If I could just lie down and not fall down.*

Once before, her body had betrayed her like this. It was that horrendous day in Texas when a tall, young officer stood at her door with the news that Steven would never be coming home. Shock coupled with fear had immobilized her then; it was immobilizing her now.

Zoe glanced over at the couch. Winifred's eyes were closed. From the hallway outside her bedroom came the swish of Olive's broom and the plink of glass into a trashcan.

Zoe slid down and sat with her back against the doorjamb, knees up, her head bent over her knees. It was frightening that in an instant life could plunge into chaos, or despair—while happiness seemed to arrive more slowly, with tentative steps, and could fly away like a startled bird.

Suddenly Zoe felt the strong hands of Olive on her shoulders, then under her arms, lifting her gently. Grateful for the help, she leaned heavily against her friend.

Olive led Zoe to the undamaged guest room and to the bed. She tended to the cut on Zoe's instep, then put a light shawl over Zoe. "Sip some of this here sugared tea, darling."

Zoe sipped.

Olive placed the cup alongside the bed, tiptoed to the door, and slipped out. Immediately Zoe buried her head in a pillow and gave in to great, heaving sobs.

Lying on the couch in the den, Winifred breathed slowly. She was relieved to be alone. Although her heart no longer pummeled in her chest, the nausea persisted. If she lay here quietly, she might be able to ward off a serious attack. Winifred look another long, slow breath. Closing her eyes, she breathed very slowly until she fell into a deep, sound sleep.

8

DILEMMAS

When Winifred awakened, the house was dark and very still. A great loneliness came over her, and nothing revived her bitter memories of her childhood more than loneliness. Work had been her salvation during many years of her marriage to Theodore. Active in humanitarian causes, she had addressed the issue of homeless and abused children and had convinced Theodore to establish a foundation to fund children's shelters. To raise awareness, Winifred had successfully traded on the Parker name for newspaper and radio advertisements.

And now it was all behind her and all she could do was lie here, feeling like a prisoner, and try to regain her energy and equilibrium. How would she do this when simply being in this house was stressful? Then she remembered Zoe responding to her call, ministering to her back, and for a moment she felt like an ingrate.

"Stress is your greatest enemy," Dr. Lavelle had warned.

Closing her eyes, Winifred imagined herself in her own lovely bedroom: all gold and cream, the high ceiling lending itself to the corona and drapes behind the beautiful carved mahogany headboard. This pleasant image faded before the memory of the building that had housed Theodore's law firm in Philadelphia. The name Parker and Parker no longer graced the front, which now read Dockery and Reynold. Her fury on seeing her husband's name replaced had known no bounds and had led to her first attack of this dreadful illness.

"Evicted," she muttered. "I was literally evicted by Theodore's partners, men I trusted." Her fists clenched. "Cunning bastards. They should rot in hell." Merely driving past the building had sent her blood pressure soaring.

"Don't go near that place," Dr. Lavelle had said.

But she had been drawn to the street, to the historic building, the way her sisters had been drawn to the cove.

Slowly and cautiously, Winifred eased up from the couch. Holding a flashlight in one hand, she leaned against walls with the other, steadying herself as she moved toward her bedroom. With a sigh of relief, she slipped into bed, and after a time bent over and opened the drawer of her bedside table, where she had secreted her sketchpad and pencils.

"How are you feeling?" Zoe's voice from the doorway startled Winifred, and she snapped the drawer shut.

"A trifle better, but I need to rest."

Zoe did not look the worse for wear. In cutoff jeans and an old T-shirt, with her hair braided and wound about her head, she looked thirty-five. Oddly, Winifred wondered why Zoe had never remarried.

"What are you doing?" Winifred asked as Zoe set down a bucket and began to sweep debris from a corner of the bedroom.

"I didn't know you were here. I thought I'd get the last

of the broken glass. We went over it earlier, but there are tiny pieces everywhere."

The sound of glass clattering into the bucket grated on Winifred's nerves. "Where's that woman who was here? Let her do it," she snapped.

"Olive did the hallways and my room. She and Ruben have gone to check on their home and their animals. They have pigs and cows. They were at church down the road when the tornado hit, and they came right over here."

"Well, get someone else in here to clean up this place."

"Katie and I can do it."

"Dammit." Giving off whiffs of irritation as powerful as perfume, Winifred beat the sides of the bed with clenched fists. "No. I won't have it. Call a cleaning service, or get someone to come in and do it. And for heaven's sake call a glazier to replace the glass, and this time get glass that can withstand hurricane-force wind."

"Tornadoes respect nothing—not steel beams, not triple-paned glass." Leaning on the broom, Zoe studied Winifred. "A glazier in Salem or Walhalla?"

"Certainly builders use glaziers. They must be available locally." Winifred lifted herself up on the bed; her voice brooked no argument. "Get out of here. Do as I say." Having expended all her energy, she collapsed back onto the pillows.

Zoe recoiled as if she had been slapped in the face and fled her mother-in-law's room. *I hate her. She's still as autocratic and mean-spirited as I remembered.* Back in the kitchen, she succumbed to tears. As soon as Winifred was on her feet again, she would ask her to leave, whatever the consequences.

The next morning, Olive sent over a cheerful young woman to help clean the house, and for the next few days Zoe avoided Winifred. But Katie, much to Zoe's annoyance, fetched and carried for her grandmother, brought her meals on a tray, sat and talked with her for hours.

"Do you think it's because of her age that Grandmother's taking a long time to recover?" Katie asked Zoe one afternoon, as they stood by the kitchen window and surveyed the torn and twisted tree limbs and smaller branches that littered the pasture.

Zoe tried unsuccessfully to keep the edge out of her voice. "Probably. I'm still shaking from that storm, and I wasn't hurt."

"Mom, what's going on? I know you've never liked her, but it's so raw, so obvious on both your parts. We haven't seen Grandmother in maybe thirty years and suddenly here she is. Why is she here?"

"She won't be much longer, so don't worry about it." Zoe strode from the house. Standing on the patio, she stared at the empty space where the storm had feasted on her beloved summerhouse and left bare bones in its place. Yet Winifred Parker tested her courage more than any storm.

Zoe walked down across the pasture. Luckily her parents' headstones and the bench were intact, covered only by a blanket of willow leaves. The trellis sprawled on the ground and tiny rosebuds peeked through its broken wood slats. Zoe sank to the earth near her parents' graves and rocked back and forth.

"Mom, Daddy," she whispered, "help me. How stupid of me to think that Winifred Parker would help me hold on to this property. She's as awful as she always was. After Steven died, she actually demanded that I give her his college ring." Zoe lifted angry eyes to the sky. "Damn you, Steven. Damn you for dying, for leaving Katie and me." She crumpled sideways, and her cheek touched the earth. Tiny bits of grass nudged her nose and tickled her cheek.

It was uncannily quiet. Zoe lifted her head. There, among the trees, stood Steven. It was not the first time she had seen him, but never this clearly or this close. "Oh, Steven." Zoe rose and staggered toward him. "Steven," she cried, but the image vanished, and she stepped back and sank down onto the bench. Her parents were dead and gone and could not help her, and neither could Steven, no matter what tricks her mind played on her.

Ironically, only Winifred could help. And there was no one to blame for her dilemma but Zoe herself and the foolish choices she had made, primarily inviting Alan Camaro into her life and home. But he had seemed so lonely, so vulnerable when she'd first met him. Her heart had gone out to him. What a huge mistake!

The bench was hard, as hard as the chair in the office of the vice president of the bank in Walhalla, where she had sat several months ago. Margaret Taft had always been kind. She had known and worked with Zoe's parents for years, and after their death continued to extend credit and more credit to Zoe. But that day Margaret Taft had asked Zoe to her office, had leaned forward across her desk, and had said in the kindest way, "Zoe, I'm afraid we can't give you any more credit on your land and house."

Uncomprehending, Zoe waited.

"Have you thought about selling some of your land, perhaps a piece on the other side of the hill, out of sight of your home?"

"I couldn't sell the land. My father wouldn't want that."

The vice president sat back. "Your father isn't here any longer, Zoe. Your loan is due next month. Taxes are overdue, and there's insurance. Can you pay these things?"

She couldn't.

"That area of the county is growing. Maybe there's some

kind of business you could operate—a lodge, perhaps? Or maybe a bed-and-breakfast. There are several fishing tournaments every year on Lake Jocassee. The lake's only fifteen minutes from you."

"I can't have strangers wandering about my land."

"Unless you have another source of income, or an investor . . ." Margaret Taft folded her arms across her chest. "I'd hate to see you lose the property. I wish you'd give some thought to what you might do with your land. It could be quite an asset, so close to Lakes Keowee and Jocassee. I understand your not wanting to sell it, but there must be something you would be willing to do."

Zoe's mind went blank. At that moment she wished she had a friend she trusted, someone who knew about loans and other money matters.

Mrs. Tate shuffled the folders before her and smiled. "You think about this," she said. "Get back to me next week."

It had been late April then. As Zoe drove home from Walhalla that day, she'd blamed everyone but herself. It was Alan's fault. The no-good, son-of-a . . . She had responded to his seeming vulnerability, his boyish good looks, and confused her need for emotional intimacy and companionship with sex; she had welcomed him into her heart and into her bed. By permitting him his way in everything, she had set herself up for the awful things that had happened. The initial delight in sharing her love and life with someone was overshadowed by the sadness and misery of later days.

She would never trust a man again. More than ever, she longed for a good woman friend her own age.

Zoe reached over and plucked a bud from the fallen rosebush and brought it to her nose. Even crushed, it bore the fragrance of a mature David Austin rose. She closed her eyes. It was August now, and time was running out.

Zoe had learned at an early age that being unobtrusive and pleasing to her parents, whose eyes lit up when they looked at each other, was her best route to inclusion and approval. Her dream had been a marriage that would replicate that of her parents, and the brief years with Steven had fulfilled that dream. Steven had smoothly handled the mundane matters of their lives. Afterward, it had been easy to return to her parents' home. They had taken care of the nitty-gritty of life, the finances especially, and her mother had always been there to comfort and encourage her.

Her father was wise, and she had trusted him. Over the years, when he attempted to interest her in the financial affairs of their family, she made excuses: too tired, too bored, too busy. He tried to explain that inflation would outpace her meager government pension and her salary as a teacher. "You don't have rent to pay or food to buy right now. You ought to be squirreling away your salary for a rainy day," he'd say.

She had ignored him and bought yet another pair of shoes or a dress for Katie. Truth was, had she not lived with her parents, she and Katie would have had neither home nor all the good things provided to them. She had intended to sit down with her father and go over everything sometime, but with teaching and weekends busy with one cause or another, sometime never came.

When her father retired from the bank, her parents sold the Greenville house, and moved to Salem. Zoe had moved with them to the house on Amorey Lane while Katie stayed in Greenville. Then Laurie Ann had been born, and both Katie's and the child's support systems had been anchored there.

Now, sitting in the sunshine, Zoe wondered how Katie had handled her money. How had she managed to support herself and Laurie Ann? There was some meager child support from Hank, just enough to pay for respite care so that Katie could work in that after-school program. And there had been some government money for a handicapped child. Katie had managed.

Zoe had screwed up her own financial affairs. What was she going to do now? How, without Winifred's money, would she be able to keep her house and land?

Zoe rose, brushed off the bits of dirt and leaves on her slacks, then strode to the edge of the pond. The water was murky, the banks marred by debris from the storm. After that talk with Margaret Taft last April, she had moped about, hankering for the past, while the days slipped into weeks, the weeks into months, and the date she must pay taxes and insurance and the loan grew closer. Then one day, lying in the hammock in her summerhouse, she had drifted to sleep and dreamed of Steven.

"Zoe, my love." Steven's voice had been barely a whisper. "Ask a relative for help." Zoe had jerked awake. A relative? What relative? She thought of Winifred Parker and immediately rejected the idea. Then a photograph slipped from the magazine on her lap, a picture of herself and Alan lying shoulder to shoulder on the grass, their shoes kicked off, an open picnic basket nearby. Anger, fear, and humiliation sent spasms through her stomach. Alan had plunged her into this crisis. With shaking hands, Zoe tore the picture into shreds, as she had done with all the others. *Damn Alan. If not for him* . . . It sickened her to finish the thought. Swallowing her pride, she had run up to the house, picked up the phone, gotten the number for Theodore Parker from the operator, and punched it in.

And so it had begun. Several tense and protracted conversations later, she and her mother-in-law had arrived at the arrangement that had brought Winifred to Salem. But now it seemed that had been a terrible mistake, and Zoe struggled with shame and a sense of helplessness, which increased with the estimates for replacing the windows and the sight of her smashed summerhouse.

As Zoe shilly-shallied about how and when to ask her mother-in-law to leave, it fell to Katie to select a glazier from the two suggested by Margaret Taft at the bank. After interviewing both glaziers, Katie consulted her mother, who waved her hand and walked away. Uncertain what to do, Katie turned to her grandmother.

"Just pick one. I'll take care of the bill," Winifred said.

Although her grandmother looked frail, when Katie introduced the glazier, Mr. Crowley, to her, Winifred's voice was that of a competent businesswoman, and her intense eyes examined the man as she questioned him about his credentials and demanded to know when he would begin and what guarantees he would provide.

Katie picked up where her grandmother left off, asking about the time frame and the density of the glass.

Winifred listened and approved of Kathryn's acuity, good sense, and direct manner. *Kathryn has potential. With Laurie Ann gone perhaps we can have a relationship. Salem would be more tolerable then.* And as Winifred studied her granddaughter's face, Kathryn's resemblance to Steven both pained and pleased her.

9

ILLNESS THAT BINDS

How long has it been since I really looked at myself, had a haircut, even shaved my legs? Katie slid her hand along the fine strands of fair hair on her legs. As a child she had believed in magic. As a teenager she had still believed that wishes would come true, and even with all the hardships of her life, Katie believed in possibilities. When her handsome husband, the man who had swept her off her feet, had betrayed her, she had held firm to her faith and believed things would work out for her.

For a long time after Hank left, Katie had buried her outrage. When her blood pressure soared and she started taking medication, her doctor warned her of a potential ulcer. Finally, driven by the news that Hank had remarried, Katie had sought counseling.

"This rage you feel toward your ex-husband shackles you to him," the therapist said.

"But he abandoned us. How could he do what he did to

me, to us? Why should he have good luck, and I have all the problems? I hate him."

"Your husband's a weak man. He couldn't handle the situation. Did you ever consider what life would have been like with him looking over your shoulder, probably criticizing you and drilling into you every day that you'd made the worst decision of your life?"

Over many painful sessions with the gently persistent therapist, Katie began to accept that she was better off without Hank. Slowly, she began to see the ways in which her hatred hurt her and to let go. But it was not easy, and for many months Katie fought against releasing her anger at Hank.

"These feelings you harbor have become habits. As long as you hold on to him, he'll have the power to frustrate and enrage you. You need to release him, to forgive him, to let him go."

"How do I do that?" Katie had asked, the tears rolling down her face.

"You begin by accepting the fact that you had, and have, no control over who he is, what he is, or what he does or does not do. You could not change his mind then, and you will never be able to change anything about him. He's moved on. You have not, and you need to."

On several occasions, Katie had stormed out of the woman's office. But the words haunted her, and eventually she gained detachment, that gift that freed her from Hank and from her bitterness. It had changed her life, and she would bless her therapist forever.

Katie propped a leg on the side of the bathtub and smoothed a foamy cream from ankle to knee and began to shave. Her blue T-shirt stretched like a second skin over her small, firm breasts. Years ago, when she was young, before

Laurie Ann's birth, people had complimented her on her deep green eyes and her copper-colored hair. But as time passed, her hair had turned gray, then white, and the compliments stopped. She rather missed them.

Sudden tears blurred her vision. Laurie Ann. It had been only ten days since they had buried her daughter, and the pain never stopped.

"Ouch." Katie stared down at where the razor had nicked her shin, then flung it away and sank to the hard, tile floor, sobbing.

When her tears subsided, she grabbed a hand towel and wiped the foam from her legs and the floor. Clasping the towel, Katie sat on the closed toilet seat and thought about Laurie Ann.

The minister had been right when he called Laurie Ann a teacher of patience and selflessness. Standing beside the freshly dug small grave, Katie had remembered a time, after a particularly bad seizure, when Laurie Ann's face had been tranquil, soft, and pure as God himself. In that moment Katie understood that she, Laurie Ann, and the whole universe were one, and she felt an ancient bond, extended back through time, that bound them together. It was love that flowed from Laurie Ann's heart and soul to her own, and gratitude, which made it easier to cope with the unremitting care required. Remembering that event comforted Katie, and she had not wept when the marble urn was placed into the grave.

Now she stood, threw the towel into the hamper, dashed water on her face, and returned to the business of shaving her legs. When she was done and the bathroom cleaned, she gazed at her reflection in the mirror. "Now, what am I to do with my life?"

*   *   *

At the kitchen sink, Zoe stared unseeingly toward the hillside. *I could simplify my life, raise chickens for their eggs and meat.* But the idea of killing anything caused her to gag. *I could buy a goat for milk, plant a garden, and stock the pond with fish.* What else could she do to cut expenses? Close off the bedroom wing to save heat. Use the den, with its gas fireplace, as her bedroom. Pick and can fruits, freeze vegetables, store home-grown potatoes in a root cellar. She would give up the car, if need be. Every penny of her small pension, everything she could earn selling jam, eggs, and organically grown tomatoes, would be stashed away to pay the taxes and insurance. *If* the bank could be prevailed upon to give her more time. She could not turn her life over to Winifred Parker; she would find a way to live alone again and be accountable to no one.

Maybe I could rent land, but only to like-minded people. A kind of community with rules against cutting trees or polluting streams. Just a handful of environmentally minded folks scattered about my forty-eight acres. I could select the locations, and I would hardly see them.

Zoe sighed and braced herself for her imminent confrontation with Winifred Parker. This morning, at breakfast, she would ask her to leave. When she was around Winifred, Zoe felt diminished and disdained, and it galled her that Katie spent so much time with her grandmother.

Good Lord. I'm jealous of that old woman, and I hate the feeling. She rehearsed what she would say, the firm tone she would use. "Winifred, before we go any further, surely you can see that our arrangement isn't going to work." Or would it be more decisive to say, "Winifred, I think it's best that you return to Philadelphia"? Or, "Winifred, I'm sure it's as plain to you as it is to me that your coming to Salem was a dreadful mistake."

"I'd like to talk to you, Winifred," Zoe said when the woman walked into the kitchen.

"Certainly." Winifred helped herself to a small glass of orange juice from a blue and white pottery carafe on the table. Pulling out a ladder-back chair, she sat stiffly, her hands folded on the handwoven place mat on the table in front of her. The juice remained untouched.

"Have your breakfast first," Zoe said.

"I only want juice," Winifred replied.

Zoe's mind went blank. Finally she managed, "This isn't going to work."

Winifred took a long, slow swallow of juice and set the glass down. "Juice is fine. I never indulge my appetite at breakfast."

"Not the juice. Our agreement. Don't you understand? Your being here."

"Ah," Winifred said, and drank again.

A hum exploded like a tornado in Winifred's head. The light in the kitchen seemed to dim, and the stars on the kitchen floor quivered, then rose to meet her. *I must get out of here and away from Zoe this minute.* Grasping the edge of the table, Winifred tried to stand. The ceiling, the walls, the countertop whirled. Sickening waves of nausea made it imperative she reach the sink immediately.

For an eerie moment, Zoe watched Winifred struggle to stand. With growing alarm, she saw Winifred turn white, saw sweat lather her face. Rushing to her mother-in-law, Zoe clasped her tightly about the waist and followed her pointing hand to the sink, where she stood helpless as the older woman retched. Finally, drained of strength and looking nearly lifeless, Winifred hung over the edge like a wet rag. "My bedroom," she murmured.

Winifred was tall and too heavy for Zoe to support. "Katie!" she called. "Winifred's had an attack of some kind. Hurry!"

Step by faltering step, Zoe and Katie helped Winifred to her room and into bed. In the soft, soothing voice of one schooled in comforting others, Katie said, "You're safe. You'll be fine in just a little while. Keep your eyes closed. Rest, dear, rest. I'm here." She wiped Winifred's face with a cool cloth and urged her to sip water. "Mom, you'd better call Doc Franklin."

It was not his habit to make house calls, but Doc Franklin had taken care of Zoe and her parents for many years and lived just a short distance away. The urgency in Zoe's usually calm voice alarmed him, and if her mother-in-law went to the emergency room at the hospital in Seneca, forty-five minutes away, they would undoubtedly call him, so it was easier to make a house call.

Time moved slowly while Zoe and Katie waited for Doc Franklin's arrival, and waited again after showing him to Winifred's room. When he finally joined them in the den, he lowered his large frame into one of the love seats. "This time she's had a bad attack," he said.

Zoe stared at his ruddy face, his high, balding forehead glistening with perspiration, and marveled that a man so big, with hands so large, could be so kind and gentle. But what was he saying? "Attack of what?"

"Ménière's disease."

"What's that?" Zoe's throat tightened.

"It's a middle ear problem. Chronic. Vertigo, nausea, vomiting, and profuse sweating accompany the attacks."

"Can she take medication for it?" Katie asked.

"Barbiturates like pentobarbital, but they'll knock her out. I don't have any patients with Ménière's disease who take their medication as prescribed."

"How often do attacks come?" Zoe asked.

"Could be months between episodes, or weeks. They last a few minutes, days, a week, or longer. It's got to do with a buildup of fluid in the middle ear. As a last resort, we can operate and selectively destroy the balance mechanism. Stress can bring on an attack. The tornado might have precipitated it." He leaned forward, reached into a bowl of M&Ms on the coffee table, selected six yellow ones, and popped them into his mouth.

"What can we do?" Katie asked.

"See that she maintains a low-salt diet. You should install safety bars on the wall near the bed so she's got something to hold on to if the dizziness hits her while she's getting up. Bars are absolutely essential in the bathroom and the hallway. She needs to go slow. No sudden movements, no bending or turning rapidly. I wouldn't let her unload the dishwasher, for example. And she should not drive. I gave her a tranquilizer, and here's more." He handed Zoe a small brown envelope, took a pad from his bag, and wrote a prescription. "One pill twice a day, for the next three days. She'll start feeling better tomorrow. Make her rest. Keep stress to a minimum."

Zoe's dreams of a life without Winifred crumbled. "The prognosis?"

Doc Franklin shook his head. "Well, there's no cure. She's a lucky woman to have you ladies to take care of her. So many older folks are alone these days. I've seen folks try to cope with this by themselves, crawling to the bathroom and lying there on the floor, or in their beds for days."

"How terrifying," Katie said.

Doc Franklin's hands grasped the arms of the love seat and he heaved to his feet. "Don't you worry now, Zoe, my dear. With good care, she'll be fine."

Oh, God, I'll go mad if Winifred stays here. Please don't let me be stuck with her for the rest of her life.

Winifred had told her on the phone, "I will have to come to see your place before I decide if I will lend you that money. And then if I decide to do it, I'll have to find a way to protect my investment." Protect her *life* was what Winifred had really meant.

His hand on the doorknob, Doc Franklin looked from Zoe to Katie. "If she can afford it, consider hiring a good home health care provider. Someone strong, who can help Mrs. Parker senior get around and drive her here and there." He plopped his hat on his head and regarded them with a mischievous grin. "Three Parker women, eh? Under one roof? Well, well." He chuckled as he stepped outside.

"I'll find someone," Katie told Zoe. "Do you mind giving up the extra bedroom?"

For a moment, Zoe resented Katie's taking charge, but that quickly gave way to relief. Bless Katie's willingness to assume responsibility.

"Of course not," Zoe said. She didn't use the fourth bedroom.

When Katie slipped her arm about her shoulder, the gesture comforted Zoe. Outside, some leaves, caught in an eddy of wind, swirled and danced on the patio. How much our lives are like those leaves, Zoe mused. Sometimes tossed about, sometimes wedged firmly in place, sometimes nudged along and not by our own volition.

Katie's voice drew her back. "Now I understand why you let her come, Mom. You're not really angry with her anymore. You're absolutely wonderful." She hugged her mother.

Zoe was silent, unable to tell Katie the truth, or how deeply she resented the woman's intrusion. For years, Laurie Ann had consumed Katie's time. Now, when Zoe and she could finally do things together, Katie was assuming responsibility for her grandmother's care.

The old witch doesn't deserve this kind of attention or care from us. I'm furious at her, even though I hate feeling so unforgiving.

10

❧

THE ARRIVAL OF
MAUDIE O'HARA

A week later, Zoe opened the front door and looked up into the violet eyes of the tall redhead she recognized from Katie's description as Maudie O'Hara.

Maudie extended her hand. "You must be Zoe. Pleased I am to meet you." Her hand was warm and soft, and her intelligent eyes searched Zoe's face.

"Welcome." Zoe withdrew her hand. "Katie's gone to the grocery. Winifred's asleep."

With energy and optimism, as if she were mistress of the situation, Maudie stepped into the house. "If you'll show me my room, I'll be setting down my things."

"Would you like some tea or coffee?"

"If Mrs. Parker senior's sleeping, I'd thank you for a spot of tea." She smiled, and Zoe found that she liked this tall woman. Suddenly things seemed not so dreary.

Maudie followed her across the black-and-white-tiled foyer and into the bedroom hallway.

"Katie's and Winifred's rooms are on the end. You'll have to share a bathroom with Katie. I hope that's all right."

"Of course it is."

Deep crown molding added warmth to the bedroom walls, painted a fresh spring green. Peppermint-striped wallpaper on one wall provided an interesting background for the simple wrought-iron four-poster bed. Yards of lace fabric were looped over the slender iron frame to create a delicate canopy. White lace curtains fluttered in the breeze. Scattered on the pine floor were handwoven rugs of various sizes and colors, while a standing lamp with a fringed shade provided a good reading light behind an inviting high-back rocker with mauve cushions.

"'Tis a wee bit of heaven," Maudie exclaimed. "A bit grand, I'd say."

"Cozy, not grand. My mother was a frustrated decorator. Every room in this house has a theme. I guess you could call this one American Country." She pointed to the bed. "Handmade quilt. Decorating isn't my forte, so I've left it all as it was."

The room commanded a pleasing view of the grassy hillside and woods. In winter, when the trees were bare, an occasional foraging deer was visible, and now and then a red fox dashed by. This had been Zoe's room, the room she had shared with Alan. When he left, she had moved into her parents' larger room and made it her own by adding a bookcase, artwork that pleased her, and a solid, square bedside table with a surface large enough to accommodate magazines, books, a pad, a pottery jar in which she kept pens and pencils, and a tall brass lamp.

"My room's across the hall. It was my parents' room.

The decor is French." She shrugged and smiled. "Tufted satin headboard, full-length gilt mirror, French provincial chaise, armoire, you know."

Maudie nodded. "I admire your mother's being so free-thinking and confident."

"Outwardly she was quiet, almost shy, but she was strong, with a mind of her own." Original, Zoe might have said, and a bit eccentric, judging by the way Ida had furnished the house: the formal black-and-white-tiled foyer with a crystal chandelier, the informal living room all wood and stone, a ragtag country kitchen, and strikingly dissimilar bedrooms. Yet to Zoe, it seemed a desecration to change anything.

"Pleased I'd be to see all the rooms."

Zoe hesitated. "Mine's a mess, with books and magazines everywhere. And the bed's unmade." She threw open a closet, disclosing six feet of hanging space with white plastic hangers and sturdy shelves for storage. "I hope you'll have enough room for your things."

"Aye, that I will."

"I'll put a kettle on for tea. The kitchen's just down the hall past the den." Zoe closed Maudie's door and stood for a moment in the quiet hallway, surprised at how much better she felt.

11

THE CARPENTER

Dimly aware that something special or wonderful had been with her in a dream, Zoe awoke with a smile on her lips. The smell of honeysuckle wafted through her open window, and from the distance came the sound of hammering. Hastening from bed, she pulled on jeans and a T-shirt, then slipped her feet into moccasins. Every inch of this property was familiar to her: where rhododendron shrubs grew the tallest, where poplars and oaks and maples clumped thickest, where sunlight seduced wildflowers, where poisonous jimsonweed with its bell-shaped blue flowers grew, and the vine-covered cave that had once sheltered her and saved her life. There was no place where anyone should be hammering. The sound seemed to be coming from down by the pond.

Yesterday she had asked Maudie O'Hara to join her for a walk down to the pond.

"I wish I could," Maudie said. "But I'm scheduled to take

Mrs. Parker senior to the Greenville Mall. It's a diversion for her. She's led such an active life, as you know."

What Zoe knew about Winifred Parker could nestle in the eye of a spider.

Maudie seemed to need to justify their going. "Shopping at the mall or just walking about keeps her busy. Please do ask me again. I'd love to take a stroll about your property."

The hammering, which had stopped for a few moments, resumed. Zoe grabbed a cinnamon bun from a box on the kitchen counter, then hastened down the steps and across the pasture. A squarely built man of about thirty, his thick hair a light brown, stood hammering a wooden brace between two posts in what had been the summerhouse. Stepping from the support column, he turned to her, his eyes dark under thick brows.

"May I ask what you're doing?" she said. "This is my property."

His smile transformed his bearded face from intense to quite handsome, though his front teeth overlapped slightly.

"Then you must be Zoe Parker. Katie hired me to rebuild this place—a summerhouse, she called it." His arm swept the area. "Screen on four sides, solid on two. Said it was a surprise for her mother."

"For me?"

"If you're her mother. But sure as roosters crow, you're too young to be that."

The worn leather tool belt hung low about his waist, exposing a line of skin between T-shirt and jeans. The skin was white in contrast to the tan of his face and arms.

"Since you're here, could we take a minute and go over the plans I've roughed out, to be sure it's what you want?" He picked up a roll of draftsman's drawings and started toward her.

She didn't trust any strange man, and involuntarily she stepped back until the firm earth no longer met her feet. She slipped in the mud, lost her balance, and then the chill water of the pond closed about her. She came up blinking, coughing, her hair billowing out before it snagged on something. When she tried to jerk loose and could not, Zoe screamed. She felt ridiculous. How many times had she been swimming in this pond?

Zoe heard the splash as the carpenter plunged into the pond. "It's okay," he said as he drew close. "We've just got to untangle your hair from this branch. Relax, and I'll have us both outta here in a jiffy."

Leave me alone! "If you'll just stop trying to help me, I can do it myself." She grabbed her hair, yanked hard and freed it, leaving long strands behind. Zoe swam to the bank and slipped and slid up the muddy side, losing both moccasins in the process. She was halfway to the house before she looked back. The carpenter had climbed out of the pond, bringing her moccasins with him.

"Mom, you're all wet. What happened?" Katie asked when she met Zoe on the patio.

"I was talking to your carpenter and stepped back. I lost my footing, and ended up in the pond."

"The carpenter? Oh, you mean Jon. Jonathan Bickford." Katie's eyes brightened when she spoke his name.

"I guess that's who it was." Zoe wrung the ends of her shirt and drops of water splattered on the patio. "I've got to go in and change."

Katie followed her inside. "Do you like him, Mom?"

"We met briefly and not under the most propitious circumstances. He dived in after me. What did he think, that I couldn't swim?"

"He was probably trying to help you, Mom. What would you have him do, stand there and watch you?"

Now they were in Zoe's room, and she began to tear off her wet clothes. "Excuse me a minute, Katie. I'm going to have a quick shower."

Katie waited. Once the shower had been turned off, she stood at the door and told Zoe, "I heard of Jon from your insurance man in Walhalla. He recommended Jon highly."

"Who's paying for all this?" Zoe bent forward to wrap the towel about her hair.

A moment of silence, then, "Grandmother. She wants to do it."

Zoe opened the door. Swathed in a bath towel, she stood there looking at her daughter. "Really? Interesting."

"Are you being sarcastic, Mom?"

"No, I'm not. It's just that I'm not accustomed to generosity from Steven's family. I don't know quite what to say. Right now, I need to clear my head. I'm going to take a long walk in the woods."

"I'll see you later, then." Katie turned and walked from the room.

12

⁓❧⁓

HERO TREES AND DREAMS

The forty-eight acres Zoe inherited from her parents consisted of fifteen cleared and thirty-three wooded acres. The land undulated, rising to heights that afforded great views of distant mountains and falling into valleys and gullies bordered by deep banks of rhododendrons. Little River—a meandering, mild, and shallow river except in springtime, when torrents transformed it into a monster that gobbled its own banks and sometimes flooded the bottomland—bounded the property on three sides. Rutted tracks, remnants of an ancient logging road, skirted sections of the river. In other places, high, rugged slopes thwarted easy access from the land above.

Zoe started up the hillside. Looking back, she saw Katie join the carpenter. Both of them waved to her and she waved back, then moved swiftly toward the tree line. Two long strides and the woods closed about her. With each step into the green, leafy world, Zoe felt lighter-hearted. She had a sense of belonging to this land, as if it had been in her family for generations and generations. In fact, she had been thirteen when her parents first bought the land and brought her here, and Zoe never forgot the awe she had felt, staring up at the huge pines and oaks rooted in earth, reaching to heaven.

Familiar with every dip and rise, Zoe stepped over rotting logs, avoided the thorny clumps of blackberries that thrived in sunny clearings, circumnavigated tangled shrubs, prickly vines, and newly downed limbs.

Finally she stood in a circle of tall pines. Years earlier, she and her father had come upon this circle of eight small, slender trees.

"Let's name these trees after characters in Greek mythology," he said, and he named them Priam and Paris, Achilles and Hector, Agamemnon and Castor, Ulysses and Menelaus. Then he told her the story of the Trojan War, how Paris, the son of King Priam of Troy, fell in love with the beautiful Helen, wife of King Menelaus of Greece, and fled with her to his home in Troy, and how the warrior king, Agamemnon, led a fleet against Troy.

"For ten years, the conflict waged with no victor. Then the Greeks sailed away from Troy, leaving behind a huge wooden horse. The Trojans threw wide the gates of Troy and brought it inside. That night a trapdoor in the belly of the horse opened, and Greek soldiers poured out. They ravaged Troy. In fact," he told her, "the saying 'Beware of Greeks bearing gifts' comes from the tale of the Trojan horse."

"Was Helen given back to her husband?" Zoe remembered asking.

"She was."

"Did she want to go back to him? Did she love Paris?"

"You can read all about it in Homer." That Christmas he

had given her a copy of both the *Iliad* and the *Odyssey*, which she still treasured.

Season after season, the hero pines grew taller and taller until their branches closed the space above, and what little sunshine penetrated the glade below cast a mysterious green glow.

At the end of his last illness, Zachary Amorey insisted on coming with Zoe and her mother to fill a bushel basket with fallen pine cones for making Christmas decorations. They had sat on the earth and picnicked with cheese, bread, and wine, and her dad read to them from his favorite poem, Wordworth's *Intimations of Immortality.*

> Our birth is but a sleep and a forgetting;
> The soul that rises with us, our life's star,
> Hath had elsewhere its setting,
> And cometh from afar;
> Not in entire forgetfulness,
> And not in utter nakedness,
> But trailing clouds of glory do we come,
> From God, who is our home . . .

Three days later, Zachary Amorey died peacefully in his sleep.

"What a wonderful way for him to go," someone wrote in a sympathy card.

"What a horrid thing to say," Zoe's mother had sobbed. "We had no preparation, no time to say good-bye." *Did one ever have enough time?* Zoe wondered.

Zoe settled on the ground below Agamemnon and waited for the customary sense of a loving presence to fill her. "Here I am, Steven. Mom. Dad." She hugged her drawn-up knees and spoke aloud. "Katie's going to rent out her house in

Greenville. There's no better place to heal than here." Zoe sighed. "But now there's Winifred Parker and a nurse, a nice woman, to look after her. Did you have some sixth sense that one day I'd need all those bedrooms, Dad?" Her voice grew plaintive. "I'm thrilled to have Katie here, of course, but I'm never alone anymore. The house is rarely quiet. Someone's always in the kitchen." She tipped her head as if listening, then said, "Winifred's seriously ill. She didn't tell me before she came here. I'm angry about that."

A shaft of sunshine slipped between the pine needles high above and lit Zoe's hand. She peered at it quizzically, as if seeing for the first time the brown spots sprinkled there. She touched one of the oval-shaped spots, and thought that this was the finger she had used to dial Winifred's number after her dream of Steven.

Would she have called Winifred if that picture of herself and Alan had not fallen from the magazine? In her dream, Steven had not actually suggested that she contact his mother, just a relative. But who else was there but Winifred?

With her finger, Zoe traced a ridge of rough, scratchy pine bark. "I had to call her," she whispered to the tree trunk. "To save my land and you, my precious trees."

Her father had always said, "Make decisions slowly. Remember, every action generates a reaction." But she'd had no choice in this case. *Make the best of it,* she told herself, even though she resented having to listen to Vivaldi and Beethoven with earphones just to please Winifred, who didn't care for classical music. "But what bothers me most," she said aloud, "is that I haven't found the right moment to talk to Winifred about our arrangement. Why is this so hard for me to do?"

Don't dwell on all that. Prefer peace. Things will unfold for you.
Had someone said that? Had she imagined it?

Prefer peace!

There was truth in those words, for the more she fretted about Winifred, the angrier she became, and the greater her unhappiness grew. "So what shall I do?"

Zoe stretched out on the ground with her arms behind her head, eyes closed, and ignored the rumbling in her stomach that reminded her it was almost lunchtime. She dozed for a time and dreamed of a mist, a forest, and a bearded gnome wearing a rusty red belted tunic and a fern green hood. He smiled down at her.

"Welcome, Zoe. I've been waiting for you." His voice rippled upward as notes on a scale.

"Why?" Zoe asked.

He winked at her.

"You live here?" she asked.

"I do." His laugh came, shimmering waves of sound.

"What do you want?" she asked.

"Reverse the question. What do *you* want?"

"Money and my mother-in-law gone." Thinking of Katie, she added, "Winifred is intrusive and takes over everything and everyone."

"Well." The gnome tapped his bearded chin. "Be careful or your anger will chase away what you *do* want." Then he vanished.

Zoe awoke with a start. Such an odd dream. Angry? Yes, she was angry, and justifiably so. She slowly retraced her steps through the woods, down the hillside, and past the pond.

The carpenter was not there, but his work was apparent in the new posts and the framework for the walls. *Good! Let Winifred pay to rebuild the summerhouse.* She owed them plenty for all the years she had abandoned them.

13

HANDS IN FRIENDSHIP

Zoe opened the front door and followed the sound of schoolgirl giggles to the den. Standing in the doorway of the sun-filled room, she stared at the off-kilter tableau.

Katie sat cross-legged on the Oriental rug, her back against the love seat on which her grandmother sat. Winifred's shoes were off and her stocking feet were outstretched on the small sofa. The sleeves of Winifred's silk blouse were rolled to the elbows, the buttons open at the neck. The pearls, symbols of pride and arrogance to Zoe, were missing.

Maudie strode in from the kitchen with a tray piled high with sandwiches and placed them on an end table. "Ah, Zoe," she said. "What a time we've had of it today. A tire on that new car of Mrs. Parker's punctured, and you wouldn't believe who knew how to change it."

Katie looked up at Winifred and patted her grandmother's leg. "Granny did."

When had Winifred become Granny? When had this trio become so comfortable with one another that Winifred would kick off her shoes, and they could behave as if they had been close for a lifetime? The sense of having been betrayed swept over Zoe.

Zoe had eschewed telling Katie about the details of her horrendous relationship with her father's family. Katie knew that when she was two years old, with Steven gone, she had been diagnosed with deadly meningitis. The doctors at the military hospital had argued before finally agreeing to give her a new experimental sulfa drug that had saved her life. Zoe had never shared the bitter truth about the helplessness and anger she had felt when she had turned to Winifred Parker for help and been rejected yet again. Winifred's refusal to help remained unforgivable.

"Please, please," Zoe had begged. "Just do this one thing for us. Please, fly us home to my parents by ambulance plane. I'm devastated over Steven and worn out. I can't cope alone any longer."

"What kind of parents do you have?" Winifred asked coldly. "Let them drive to Texas and get you."

But Ida had been nursing her husband during his slow recovery following gallbladder surgery, and Winifred had slammed the phone down before Zoe could explain. Yet Zoe had decided early on to avoid vilifying her husband's family, perhaps in some silly hope that eventually they would reach out to their only grandchild. Until Katie was four, Zoe had sent them pictures. How could they resist the little girl who, with her curly red hair and green eyes, looked so like Steven? But Theodore and Winifred Parker had never responded.

Zoe now struggled to quiet the hurricane of emotions roiling inside her. Shielding Katie from the truth had backfired, and now Winifred was appropriating her home and her daughter.

Prefer peace.

There they were again—the words she had heard in the woods. The hairs on her arms stood erect.

"What's wrong, Mom?" Katie's eyes followed her mother's quick look about the room.

"Nothing," Zoe replied.

"Mom, you look bewildered, and your face is all red. Come, sit." She patted the love seat across from Winifred. "Maudie made us sandwiches."

But Katie did not rise to welcome her, and it was Maudie who took Zoe's arm and propelled her to the love seat. "Off your feet," she said. Against Zoe's protests, she untied the laces and removed Zoe's walking shoes, then slowly rotated her thumbs along the sole of one foot.

Zoe would have liked nothing better than to lie back and relax, but not in front of Winifred, for those sensations of pleasure brought with them a loss of control, a sense of vulnerability. Zoe pulled her feet away from Maudie's hands. "Thank you."

"Had a fine time in the woods, did you? Seen the little people?" Maudie asked, sitting back on her haunches.

Zoe stared at her. Was the gnome in her dream one of Maudie's little people?

"You know," Maudie said, "leprechauns."

"Ah," Zoe said. "No."

Maudie laughed. "Well, maybe 'tis only we Irish who can see them." She rose. "I'll be getting us drinks."

Maudie seemed to take the light with her, and silence settled over them until Katie asked, "What kept you so long in the woods, Mom?"

Zoe took a deep breath. "I fell asleep in the glade."

"I've never understood how you can lie down on the hard ground and actually fall asleep," Katie said.

Was her daughter belittling her? Zoe had planned to tell Katie about the gnome and her dream but decided not to do so. At that moment, Maudie returned with a pitcher of tea and glasses and began to pass the drinks and sandwiches. Her presence had a leavening effect.

Zoe turned to Winifred. "Did you find what you wanted at the mall?"

With Zoe's arrival, Winifred began to feel uncomfortable. Her daughter-in-law loathed her, but the emotion was no longer mutual. Her dislike of her son's wife had long since spent itself in bitter diatribes written to Zoe at three in the morning, torn to smithereens at seven, and washed away in rivers of tears shed for Steven. It had been so easy to condemn Zoe and to blame her for Steven's death. At some point, that had changed.

But it was clear that Zoe had not forgiven, much less forgotten. And hearing Zoe's voice that day on the phone after all those years, she had instantly reacted negatively. Her voice had hardened, and her words grew clipped even as her heart pounded in her chest.

She was old and ill. She wanted an end to the anger and recriminations. She needed these women now, especially her granddaughter, whom she was beginning to care for deeply.

"We never got to the mall," Winifred said. "Maudie was the one who actually changed the tire, and as we were closer to Pickens than to Salem, we drove there and had lunch at a drugstore counter while the damaged tire was being repaired."

"I don't know anything about tires or changing them," Maudie said. "But Mrs. Parker senior does, and she told me how to do it, step by step."

"How did you know about changing tires, Granny?" Katie asked.

Winifred smiled. She knew how to do many things, things learned in childhood when survival often depended on being able to implement what one had seen or been told. How many times had her hands turned blue with cold while changing tires on her father's ancient truck? After all these years, she could still conjure up his harsh voice and his words. "Get on out there and change that tire. Don't dawdle. Get a move on." It was that or the back of his hard, callused hand.

"We found a quaint little antique shop in Pickens," Winifred said, ignoring Katie's question. "All those empty stores in Walhalla. It's a pity no one's opened an antique shop on Main Street. It would do very well, I imagine."

"Why do you think so?" Zoe asked, more out of politeness than interest.

"Katie tells me that people from Florida and Georgia pass through Walhalla on their way up to the summer mountain resorts. Many of them stop for lunch at the Steak House Cafeteria, she says. If there were a shop in Walhalla, they might shop for items for their mountain homes, or to take back as gifts."

Zoe shrugged and busied herself positioning a pillow behind her back. "Not for me. Selling jam's the closest I've come to business."

"I didn't know you sold your jam, Mom."

"It is delicious," Maudie said. "Especially the blackberry."

"Jam? You make jam?" Winifred asked. "I'd like to have some."

"I'll get some for you." Maudie rose and went to the kitchen, then returned with a jar of jam, slices of whole wheat bread, and a knife.

Winifred slathered the bread with butter and jam, then took a bite. "This has a lovely full-bodied flavor."

"Mom makes great jam," Katie said. "I used to take jars of it home to Greenville at the end of the summer and give them as Christmas gifts to my colleagues at my school. They loved it."

"With a designer label, this jam would sell anywhere," Winifred said.

Zoe said, "Olive taught me how to make jam. I sold it at the tailgate market in Walhalla, but I'm no businesswoman."

Winifred slid her feet to the floor and sat up straight, then rolled her sleeves down. "No. I don't imagine that you are a businesswoman. I believe that Kathryn has a fine mind for business, but I wager you can spot antiques a mile away."

"I have no interest in ferreting out antiques."

In the silence that followed, Winifred sighed. She felt old. Tired. Ill. She could take Maudie O'Hara and return to Philadelphia. She didn't need Zoe or Kathryn. Or *did* she need Kathryn? Daily, she grew fonder of her granddaughter. And truth be told, as she listened to the interactions between mother and daughter, plus snatches of conversation between Zoe and someone on the phone regarding a grant Zoe was writing, she was realizing how much she had misjudged Zoe.

The problem now was that she didn't know what to say to her daughter-in-law about the past, or anything else. How could she bridge this gap between them? Not everyone wanted to make it to the top; not everyone was assertive, as she had been. Zoe had her own strengths and interests, important interests concerning the environment, especially in today's greedy world. So, she hadn't managed her money well. Winifred knew that she, herself, didn't handle people well.

Suddenly, without thinking, she set down her cup, leaned forward, and held out her hands to Zoe.

*   *   *

Katie's heart skipped a beat as she watched the exchange between her mother and grandmother. Zoe's suspicious eyes were also curious, and in Winifred's flushed face Katie saw caution and calculation, withholding and longing. For years her grandmother had seemed not to care one whit about her, but things had changed. Katie recognized affection in the way her grandmother's eyes now softened when she looked at her, and in the caring tone in her voice when she spoke to her.

Katie had discovered that she and her grandmother had more in common than she had with her mother, which surprised her. Zoe had been her rock and comfort all of her life, someone to admire and look up to, and Katie loved her. Yet the differences between mother and daughter were real. Zoe tended to procrastinate over major issues, but once decided, she let nothing stop her in pursuit of her goal. Katie and Winifred, on the other hand, acted immediately, without much deliberation. They were organizers, planners who saw the broad picture. Both ways were valid.

The intensity of her mother's dislike of Winifred struck Katie as irrational. Why would her mother invite Winifred to live with them if she disliked her so much? Zoe had implied financial problems but never elucidated the extent of them. Over the years, she had poured out her heart to Zoe, but what did she know about her mother's life these last few years? Where did the money come from to maintain this house and land? Had Grandpa Zak and Grandma Ida left Zoe a financial inheritance as well as the property? The undercurrent of anxiety surrounding her mother was palpable. Something serious was afoot, and there were too many unanswered questions. Katie determined to get to the bottom of them.

On top of all this, like a carrot on a stick, Winifred's idea for an antique shop intrigued Katie. Would her mother be the fly in that ointment? Would she have to choose between her mother and grandmother? Dear God, she hoped not. And now her grandmother had done the most extraordinary thing. She had smiled, set down her cup, leaned forward, and extended her hands to Zoe.

Katie held her breath. The air in the room seemed electric.

Explosive emotions and strange mood shifts came unannounced these days, and they left Zoe trembling. Rummage for antiques through someone's musty basement or stifling attic? Finagle a priceless family treasure from some old lady? What did Winifred know about her? Nothing! Nothing at all.

Zoe rose and, without a glance at any of them, walked from the room.

14

❧

REVELATIONS

Katie kissed her grandmother on the cheek, then followed her mother to her bedroom. Shoving aside a magazine, she sat on the edge of Zoe's bed. Books, newspapers, and magazines seemed to be everywhere. A dresser drawer had been left open, and Zoe's shirt was haphazardly flung across the back of a chair. Suppressing her instinct for orderliness, Katie forced herself to sit and wait for Zoe to explain her behavior in the den. But Zoe remained silent.

Depleted by nine years of being the sole caretaker of Laurie Ann, as well as a reluctant after-school teacher, Katie was both adrift and depressed. But with one simple statement made earlier by her grandmother, things had changed in her mind. "I believe that Kathryn has a fine mind for business," Winifred had said, and those words replayed in Katie's brain and filled her with pride. No one, not even her mother, had ever credited her competence in stretching her meager income to provide the home and care needed for Laurie Ann.

No one at school had ever credited her with the orderliness with which her after-school kids played and interacted. Some after-school classrooms were chaos. Not hers.

All her life, Katie had unquestioningly followed her mother's lead and disliked her father's family. After all, they had abandoned her and her mother. But why this had been so was never clear to Katie. Surely Winifred and her husband had loved their only son, and by extension ought to love their only grandchild.

It pained Katie to think that Winifred might leave and return to Philadelphia, but why would she stay here in the face of Zoe's hostility? She had Maudie to go with her. No! *She* would go with Granny herself. Maudie liked it here and could do private duty nursing or work at the hospital in Seneca. Maybe Mom would rent her a room. Katie would feel better knowing that her mother was not alone again. The more she considered this scenario, the more feasible it appeared, especially as Zoe and Maudie seemed to like each other.

Katie studied her mother's melancholy face. Whatever passions and anguish lurked behind Zoe's kind eyes and loving manner were a mystery to Katie. In the last few years their daily telephone calls had been confined to practical matters such as work or Laurie Ann. They never spoke of dreams, hopes, longings, fears that haunted them in the night. It was as if personal matters of greater depth were forbidden topics.

Only once, years ago, had there been a brief moment of intimacy when her mother spoke with excitement about a man she had met named Alan. The tone of her mother's voice, the quickened breathing, indicated that she liked the man very much. But what had come of it? Where was he now? What had happened between them? When Katie had asked about him, Zoe stood abruptly and walked away, just as she had today from Winifred's outstretched hands.

Well, this time she would not allow Zoe to sabotage the moment. This time they *would* talk about the past, and she would sit here for as long as that took.

"Mom," Katie said.

Zoe jumped as if startled.

Katie rose from the edge of her mother's bed, went to the chaise, and waved her hand up and down in front of Zoe's face. "Where are you, Mom? Talk to me."

"Don't do that, Katie." Zoe brushed Katie's hand away. "I'm trying to think."

Katie selected a *Fine Gardening* magazine from the pile on the carpet. "Then I'll lie on your bed, read this magazine, and wait. I'm not leaving until we talk."

"About what?"

"About what just happened, for starters."

"Nothing happened."

"Something certainly did happen. Granny offered you her hands in friendship. Why did you walk away? And I want to know more, much more. Like about your life before I was born, and why we never saw or heard from Granny or my grandfather in all those years."

Anger flared in Zoe's eyes. "So you suddenly want to know everything that happened over thirty years ago? Well, let me tell you, young lady. Before you were born, and your father died, that woman hated me. After Steven's death, she . . . I wasn't good enough to marry her son." She lifted her quivering chin. "Winifred Parker let me know that in every way possible."

"In what way? What happened, Mom?"

Zoe's shoulders slumped. "So much, Katie. It's hard to retell it all."

"That was a long time ago. Granny's living with you, with us, now. Surely you two came to an understanding?"

"No. Not an understanding—a possible financial arrangement for me, and obviously a home for her, where she could be taken care of by me. The money issue's not even settled, though."

"The money issue?"

"I asked her to help me financially, though I felt like Faust selling my soul to the devil." Zoe's slender frame trembled.

Katie resisted the impulse to hold and comfort her mother. "Okay, start with her illness. You knew about that, right?"

"No. She didn't bother to tell me that."

"She didn't? But I thought . . ."

Zoe's brows furrowed. "Well, don't think or assume anything."

Katie quelled her growing irritation. *Don't push*, her instincts warned. "Then tell me. Start anywhere."

Zoe folded her legs under her on the chaise. "All right. When you were two and nearly died, Winifred Parker refused to help us. Steven was dead, and you were very sick. She turned her back on us. I was a wreck by the time we made it home to South Carolina and my parents."

"Why wouldn't she help? What kind of help did you ask her for?"

A dam broke inside of Zoe. "You know that I was pregnant with you when Steven and I married. Winifred hated me, called me terrible names—bitch and tramp! But she had never spoken a kind word to me even before she knew that I was pregnant."

"Mom, I didn't mean to upset you."

"She ignored your birthdays and Christmas. She lorded it over my parents on the rare occasions they met." Zoe leaned forward, her knuckles white from grasping the arms of the chaise. "You want the truth? The Parkers issued my Steven an ultimatum—his law education and a future with the family firm, or us—you and me." Zoe lowered her face into her palms for a moment. "Before we were married, Mr. Parker asked me to come to his office. When I arrived, he silently sat behind his huge desk and wrote a check to me for fifty thousand dollars. Winifred stood behind him, gloating. She snatched that check and poked it in my face. Do you know what she said?"

Katie shook her head.

"Winifred said, 'Whether it's Steven's child or it isn't, and I seriously doubt it's my son's child, this should cover its birth and more. Afterward, I suggest you give the child up for adoption.' I was humiliated and so furious I couldn't speak. I tore the check into pieces and threw it on his desk."

Katie drew a deep breath. "I'm stunned. That must have been horrific for you. But Mom—it's so long ago. Someone must start somewhere to put an end to all the anger and blame." She paused, then whispered, "Why didn't you tell me any of this years ago?"

Zoe slumped. "Oh, Katie, I wanted to protect you. I sent them pictures of you for years, hoping that when they saw how much you resembled your father, they'd want to get to know you, that they would fall in love with you and help you."

"But they didn't."

Zoe wrapped her arms about her shoulders as if to hold herself together. "I've never said this aloud, but for years I considered your grandmother responsible for your father's death. Steven had always dreamed of being a lawyer. When his parents disowned him, the air force offered law school and he signed up."

"Law school? But wasn't he a pilot?"

"Yes, because your father liked flying. Law school would come after his term of duty was over, compliments of the air force."

"He died on a training mission, didn't he?"

"Yes. He trained other pilots. I'd watch his plane take off and return so many times, it never occurred to me that he'd never come back. Katie, I loved him so very much." Her shoulders shook. "If his parents hadn't refused him the funds for law school, hadn't cut him out of their lives, he would never have enlisted in the air force."

"My gosh." Katie kneeled by the chaise and held her mother. "I'm so sorry."

Zoe's quivering body leaned into her daughter's. "It's all right, darling. We survived Theodore and Winifred Parker then, and we'll survive her now."

But Katie was worn out with surviving. More than anything, she craved harmony and a peaceful place in which to grieve and time to heal. She longed to be mothered and supported, the way Zoe had nurtured her when she was young—kissed her bruised knee or elbow, made fudge when she was sad, played games with her to distract her from scratching her face when she had the measles, and when she became a teenager, assured her that her pimples would go away. *We grow up*, Katie thought, *and we grow more and more alone.*

"I want us all to forgive the past and begin to take care of one another. The three of us only have each other," Katie said. "There's been too much pain, too much aloneness."

"I don't know how to forgive the past, Katie."

Katie sat down on the chaise. "What do you know about Grandmother's life?"

"Nothing."

"Did you know she came from a dirt-poor fishing village on the coast of Maine?"

Zoe lifted her eyebrows. "The snooty Mrs. Parker, a fisherman's daughter? That's ridiculous."

"Her sisters drowned when they were little girls. Her grandfather was what we'd call a dirty old man. She got away from him and her family as soon as she finished high school. When she fell in love with her boss, and his mother couldn't stop the marriage, she molded her daughter-in-law into a version of refinement where snobbery, arrogance, materialism, and appearances were top priority. Winifred's mother-in-law hired an elocution teacher and she made Grandmother walk for an hour each day with a book on her head so she'd learn to stand and move correctly."

Zoe stared at her daughter. "And I'm supposed to feel what, now that you've told me this?"

"Oh, Mom." Katie lifted her hands in exasperation. "I just want you to try to forgive her. I'm so tired of feeling unloved by half my family. We're so alone, you, me, and Grandmother. What I pray for is that you two find some way to meet halfway. I'm not asking you to love her, just relax with her. Try not to be so wary of her, not to hold on to anger and resentment any longer."

Zoe wondered, *How can I do that? How can I quell the sense of outrage I feel when Winifred steps into the kitchen in the morning, or when I hear her roaming about the house at night?* Was there a handbook that taught forgiveness? She simply did not know how to begin.

Zoe stroked Katie's cheek. "Let me think about all this. I'm very tired now, darling."

"Think about it, Mom. It would mean the world to me, especially with Laurie Ann gone." Tears glistened in Katie's eyes as she kissed Zoe. "I need a family. We all need a family."

15

ZOE CONFESSES

Maudie O'Hara had found herself desperately homesick in America, yet returning to Ireland was never a consideration. After leaving home and becoming a nurse, she had found her Irish family oppressive and narrow-minded. Surely there were families who laughed together, whose fathers were not drunks, where hope and optimism reigned. When Katie had called and offered her the opportunity to live and work with her family, Maudie didn't hesitate a second. She found Greenville noisy, the traffic horrific. Her work in pediatrics often left her in tears. Children dying seemed so unnatural. She had fallen in love with Salem and the pastoral countryside. The Golden Corner of South Carolina reminded her of Ireland with its lush greenness and open landscapes, and she liked the Parker women, all of them.

But it was clear that they were as dysfunctional as her own family, only in different ways. From the start, Maudie wondered at the dissonance between Zoe and Winifred, the speculative mistrust and hesitancy in their voices. They sparred more than talked.

Aye, the old woman acts indifferent and hard-hearted like my old granny did, but a bit of attention can melt that iceberg of a heart. So Maudie had set about to do just that. And she was making progress, but what would happen now that Zoe had so hurtfully rejected her mother-in-law's overture of friendship?

So caught up were they in their tug of war that neither had looked at Katie to see her reaction.

Tossing and turning, Maudie could not sleep. *I'll go to the kitchen and get some hot milk,* she thought. But as she passed Zoe's door, the light beneath it drew her attention.

The soft knock on the door startled Zoe out of a half sleep. It was two in the morning. Her heart thudded. "Katie, is that you? What's wrong? Come in."

"It's not Katie. I saw your light and thought maybe you couldn't sleep." Maudie stood in the doorway clasping her yellow terry cloth robe tight about her waist.

Zoe sat up. Her unbraided hair hung in long strands about her face. "I must have fallen asleep with the light on. Can't you sleep?" She tucked a long twist of hair behind an ear.

"May I come in?" Maudie asked.

Zoe hesitated, but it would be hard to fall back to sleep anyway. "Sure, come on in."

"Would you like a bit of a massage for your shoulders and neck to relax you again? 'Tis guilty I feel, waking you up."

Zoe's spirits lifted. It had been a long, long time since she'd had a massage. "Sounds nice." She swung her legs over the side of the bed and her feet felt for her slippers.

"Sit right over there in that chair." Maudie nodded toward the straight chair in front of the vanity. "I'll be a moment getting the lotion."

Maudie disappeared, then reappeared, and positioned herself behind Zoe. "Now just relax." Maudie rubbed her hands together to warm the lotion before applying it to Zoe's skin. "In the hospital, I'd give my wee patients a bit of a rub when they were feeling better." She was silent for a time while she worked, then she said, "I saw how upset you were with Mrs. Parker senior tonight."

Zoe stiffened.

"Sorry to bring that up. Just relax."

Zoe closed her eyes. She liked Maudie and would miss her very much if Winifred left and took the nurse back to Philadelphia with her. Zoe had never had many close women friends: her roommate at college, but they'd lost touch years ago; and another air force wife, whom she'd lost touch with also. The bond between Zoe and her mother had strengthened over time, and having a close female friend had seemed irrelevant. The Holloways loved her, but they were more surrogate parents than friends. Zoe had badly needed a friend before, during, and especially after Alan, and she needed one now.

As Maudie's hands worked the kinks out of Zoe's shoulders, her concerns faded. "Thank you, Maudie. Do you have family in America?"

"No. I left a fine sister at home," Maudie said. "We used to give each other shoulder rubs."

"Do you miss your home?"

"Only my sister, Emma, and she's married now with children and lives in Wales. In the village where I grew up, too many of the men were out of work. My brothers and my father drank. The women had babies. When I think back to it, I see gloom, both in the weather and the attitude of the folks."

"I'm an only child," Zoe said. "Katie's an only child."

"Katie's a brave one, taking care of her daughter like she did."

"Yes, she is. I love and admire her. Unfortunately, Mrs. Parker and I never liked one another, not from the day we met. I hadn't seen her in over thirty years until she came here a few weeks ago."

The silence between them felt safe and comfortable. After a time Maudie asked, "Will Mrs. Parker senior be going back, then?"

"Maybe. Katie's pressing me to mend fences. It's not easy, when there's so much hurt and anger. I don't know how to put an end to it."

In the mirror, Zoe watched Maudie behind her listen attentively as she ended the massage.

"It's sorry I am, for whatever passed between you and Mrs. Parker senior."

"They were difficult times, Maudie." Zoe rose. "Thank you for the neck and shoulder rub; it felt great. I'll sleep like a baby now. Get some sleep yourself."

When Zoe next looked at the clock on her night table, it was five a.m., and when she looked again, it was ten a.m. The house was quiet. Zoe stretched in long, lazy movements and thought of the quiet, nonjudgmental way Maudie had listened. If she were to tell Maudie about Alan, would Maudie think less of her?

She turned on the water in the shower and stepped under stabs of cold water that pricked her breasts and belly. Years ago, in their first apartment in Texas, she and Steven had lived for a week with a broken hot water heater. They had showered together, clinging to one another as streams of cold water pounded them. Afterward, lovemaking had warmed them. Zoe turned her back to the cold water. Remembering Steven no longer tore her heart in two. She was grateful to have known and loved him, grateful for the daughter they had produced.

Wrapped in a big white towel, Zoe dropped onto her chaise and flipped on CNN to watch the news for a while. It was eleven when she finally ambled into the kitchen, where she was surprised to find Katie sitting at the table with the want ad pages of the *Seneca Journal* and the *Clemson Messenger* opened before her.

"Morning, Mom," Katie said brightly, looking up and offering her cheek for a kiss. "Maudie took Grandmother to Walhalla. She said you had your light on late and to let you sleep."

"I fell asleep with the light on. Maudie saw it and came in. We talked. She gave me a neck and shoulder rub, which really helped me get back to sleep." When it popped from the toaster, Zoe buttered her bread and spread jam on it. "What are you doing?"

"Seeing what kind of job I might get in the area. I'd like to stay with you this winter." She smiled. "If you can tolerate having me around."

"Depends on how you cook," Zoe teased, tousling her daughter's thick, white hair. *Color this hair of yours, Katie,* she wanted to say. People went white almost overnight from fright, she'd heard, and surely excessive stress caused white hair too. Zoe removed the orange juice from the refrigerator and poured herself a glass. Katie resumed her search of the ads until Zoe rose, placed her dirty dishes in the sink, and said, "Let's sit in the living room, Katie. I'd like to talk to you."

Through the high, arched windows, soft light flooded the room. A book Katie had been reading the day before sat on a table, its bright yellow bookmark indicating the page she would return to. On the mantel beside Ida's silver candlesticks were photos of Zoe's parents in dark mahogany frames, and on the chairs sat needlework pillows that Ida had worked on during many a winter evening. Her father's pipe stand retained a whiff of his tobacco, faint but evocative to Zoe of his tenderness and love. Zoe took comfort from the familiar things.

"Long ago I determined not to burden you with my problems," she began, "but now I want to explain how I got into this pickle and why your grandmother is here."

Katie curled her legs under her and rested an arm on the back of the couch.

"Several years ago, I found I didn't have enough money to pay twenty-two hundred dollars in property taxes and insurance. I borrowed from the Blue Ridge Bank in Walhalla. Then the roof leaked and had to be replaced, so I borrowed again, and other repairs were needed over time. The next year I took another loan to pay the taxes and insurance on the property, and the next, and next, until the bank wouldn't give me any more money. I don't have the money I need to pay this year's taxes and insurance on the house and land. Last year I didn't pay the taxes or the insurance either. I didn't even pay the interest on the loan. This spring the bank served me a notice of foreclosure."

"My goodness, Mom. How much do you owe the bank?"
Zoe sighed. "Thirty-nine thousand dollars. I have no insurance on the house, as you may have realized when the windows were smashed."

Katie had wondered why her grandmother had asked no questions and merely handed Mr. Crowley a check. "Granny knows all this, doesn't she?"

Zoe averted her eyes. "Your grandparents left this place clean and clear with no mortgage, and I've borrowed to cut the meadow, to dredge the pond, to clear the river of beaver dams. Beetles killed some of the pines, and they had to be removed. A high wind tore the screen in the summerhouse, and I had to replace that. It never ends. Look at this house: the wood on the outside needs staining; the inside needs painting." She put her hands to her head. "I thought I could live on my pension from the government, but inflation's eaten that up. And last year I needed four new tires for my car."

"You've been living on the edge."

Zoe nodded. "I'm in a financial morass." It was easier to take the blame rather than reveal to her daughter the truth about the money. "Sometimes, at night, I start to panic. I tell myself that I'll think about it tomorrow, like Scarlett O'Hara when she couldn't cope."

"Is there anything that can be done to generate cash?" Katie asked.

"The bank had lots of suggestions: sell land, turn this place into a fishing camp, rent land for mobile homes. I couldn't do any of those things. I've simply felt immobilized."

"I can understand that," Katie said. "Where does Grandmother fit into all of this?"

"I was at a loss what to do. There was no place else to turn, so I phoned her. I expected her to yell no and hang up, but she said maybe she would give me a loan so I could pay back the bank. The caveat was that she would come here to see what she was being asked to invest in. I was desperate, so I agreed. I thought, she'll come, look, give me the loan, and take the first train back to Philadelphia. I didn't know she had been ill or that she intended to stay."

"It must have been a dreadful shock when Doc told us."

"Yes. So to make matters worse, I feel tricked and trapped." Then she turned her mind from Winifred and back to her other problems. "My dad used to try to get me to sit with him and learn about investing, the stock market, bonds—ways to make money grow. I simply wasn't interested. Living with them all those years made me complaisant, and I spent all of my income on extras for you. Nike sneakers, summer camp, tennis lessons."

"They paid my college tuition, medical insurance, and much more, didn't they?"

"Yes. They did."

"Well." There was no judgment in Katie's voice, only curiosity. "Did Granny give you the money?"

"Not yet. She hasn't said a word about it. Neither have I, and time's running out."

Katie sat back. "What are you waiting for? Why don't you bring it up?"

"Every day I intend to, and something happens. For example, yesterday I had a call from Bill Hicks at the theater group. He wants some changes made to the grant proposal we've been working on, so I went into town, and it took longer than I had anticipated. And frankly, it feels like begging. I dread it. I'm afraid she'll look down her nose at me, make me feel insignificant and even more incompetent than I already feel."

"So, Granny came here knowing how sick she was. She needed someone, a home, and her pride stopped her from asking for help." Katie looked pensive. "Seems to me you're on equal footing. She needs you, and you need her."

"Winifred doesn't need me. With her money, she could take Maudie back home with her or hire other nurses to care for her."

"If that was what she wanted, she'd have done that, Mom. Trust me in this. Talk to her as soon as possible. You won't feel put down." Katie's eyes grew sober. "When's the bank's deadline?"

"September twelfth," Zoe replied.

"That's only a week away. We need to get this taken care of."

Katie had said *we*. That little word sank deep into Zoe's heart, and she felt less alone and scared.

"But there needs to be a reconciliation between you two," Katie continued. "I believe that Grandmother wants to bury the proverbial hatchet. The question is, can you do it, and do it before it's too late?" She squeezed her mother's hand. "Give her a second chance. If you'd hurt someone, wouldn't you want a second chance?"

"What makes you so sure she won't pack up and return to Philadelphia?"

"Return to what?"

Zoe said, "She talks about a cousin, Emily."

"She doesn't even know where Emily lives. They haven't spoken or seen one another in years."

"How do you know so much about her?"

"I ask her things, and Grandmother talks to me about her life. That's how I know she wants to make things right with you."

For a moment Zoe resisted. "We don't need her. We could sell the land and walk away from here. You and I could live in your house in Greenville and both of us teach."

"Sell our home and the woods you love so much? You don't really want that, do you, Mom?"

Slowly Zoe shook her head; tears spilled from her eyes.

"Then let's be practical. Let's say we all stay," Katie said. "Talk to Grandmother. I'm sure she doesn't expect you to open your arms and heart to her overnight, but make a start—for my sake and yours. We must pay off the bank, renew the insurance, and pay the back taxes. After that, we could both teach to buy some time while we figure out how to make this land pay its way."

Zoe snorted. "Or we could open an antique shop."

"At her age and being ill, you don't really think Grandmother was serious, do you?"

"Yes. I think she's serious. There was that glint in her eye."

Zoe wondered how she would ever overcome her irritation with the way Winifred clinked her spoon against the glass when she stirred iced tea, or her annoyance when her mother-in-law insisted that every dish be placed in the dishwasher the moment it was used. Yet if she overcame her annoyance, if she smiled instead of scowled, if she took Winifred's hand—if and when it was ever extended again—and if she complied with everything her daughter wished, maybe the money crunch would end. The interminable pressure, the headaches that sent her to her bed, would be over.

Katie's next question unnerved her. "So, Mom, since we're being honest, tell me who Alan was, and why you never talk about him anymore."

Zoe's mouth turned as dry as parchment. "Not today, Katie. I'll tell you soon, I promise. We'll take the boat out on Lake Jocassee tomorrow, just the two of us, and I'll tell you then."

16

INDECISION

That night, Zoe lay in bed unable to sleep. The air outside was heavy with humidity, and her mind felt as thick and burdened as the night itself. Tomorrow she would take the rowboat out on Lake Jocassee and, in the quiet calm of the lake, confess all to her daughter.

These past few years, since Alan left, good decision making had eluded her, and often she felt as if she were sliding down a chute with no brakes, nothing to slow her descent. What would Steven, so cool and clearheaded, say if he were here?

"Never make important decisions when you're caught up in anger or fear or the urge for instant gratification, not even desire." He was right, of course.

Zoe sat up and switched on a light on her bedside table. In the far corner of the room, her father's desk, as solid as he had been, reminded her of how bereft of sound council she was. "We all have a tragic flaw," her mother used to say.

"Mine is impatience. My mother's was indecision, like Hamlet."

"What's mine?" Zoe had asked.

"You never quite let go of things," her mother said.

It was true. She resisted letting go of old furniture, old clothing, even worn-down shoes. How was she going to let go of the past and make peace with her old nemesis?

"I can't do this," Zoe muttered. "I can't. But oh, God help me, I must."

Prefer peace.

Let the anger go, the voice in her head said. *Forgive! It's time.*

But how could she erase in a few days the rejection and pain of all these years? Katie credited the old woman with virtues Zoe doubted that Winifred possessed. Her hands knotted into fists. "What should I do and how?"

Why, she asked herself, if she hated Winifred so much, had she felt no rancor toward her the night of the tornado, only pity and a desire to help her?

Zoe had expected the lash of the older woman's tongue, but instead, after the storm, Winifred had seen to the replacement of the windows and hired a woman friend of Olive's to set the house in order. Winifred had also hired Jon to rebuild the summerhouse, her summerhouse. Zoe appreciated that.

Looking back, she realized that money had always framed their relationship: the bribe Winifred had offered Zoe, money denied for plane tickets for herself and Katie after Steven died, and now, Zoe's desperate need for money. "Tell me, Steven," she whispered. "How do I do this for Katie, for our daughter?"

The reply floated into her mind. "Act kindly. Act as if you have forgiven."

When daylight ushered in a sky streaked with gold and mauve, Zoe went into the bathroom and splashed water on her face. The mirror reflected a lower lip that quivered and eyes that brimmed with tears. "I'll try, Steven. For you, and for Katie. I'll remind myself of her recent kindness and act as if I too want this reconciliation."

17

THINGS SAID AND UNSAID

The glorious September morning cooled Oconee
County, cooled the house on Amorey Lane, and cooled the
hearts of its occupants. Today Zoe and Katie would trans-
port Zoe's faded fiberglass dinghy to Lake Jocassee, and she
would tell her daughter the truth about her life these last
few years.

The lakes of Oconee County bore melodious Indian
names: Keowee, Place of the Mulberry, and Jocassee, Place
of the Lost One. For Zoe, Lake Keowee evoked the mascu-
line principle in nature. A mecca for developers, the land
surrounding it thrust into the lake, creating bays, coves,
and inlets. Lake Jocassee, fed by waterfalls cascading from
the high cliffs of the North Carolina mountains into recep-
tive feminine depths, was four hundred feet deep. Its cre-
ation had buried in its depths a town and Jocassee Valley.
Dedicated to recreation, its shores were intruded upon only
by Park Service facilities: boat ramps, picnic areas, and a

Lilliputian beach. Zoe came to Jocassee to row and sail, to fish and drift, and to dream.

She and Katie hauled the lightweight dinghy from its storage place behind the house and secured it to the top of her van. When they turned onto Highway 11, Katie commented on a parcel of land that was piled with pyramids of crushed building stone, and she noted a small, weatherworn house in the process of being renovated. A child's swing and a bicycle marked a return to habitation.

"A young couple from New Jersey bought it," Zoe explained. "There are lots of new people from up north around here now, retirees, or younger folks hoping to live off the land."

Far from any city, Oconee County nurtured a quiet and stable way of life. Winters were temperate with minimum snowfall. The rich soil yielded abundant fruits, vegetables, and grains. Near Walhalla, the town of Senaca was expanding, with a good bookstore, the Booksmith, and new chain stores and motels. Forty minutes away, Clemson University dominated Clemson, and another half-hour drive brought you to Anderson with its mall shopping and a sense of bustle and growth.

They began the descent to Lake Jocassee via a series of sharp curves. At the main boat ramp stood grandfathers in overalls, middle-aged women with middle-aged spread in jeans, and teenagers in skimpy shorts, all waiting for husbands, sons, or boyfriends to launch speedboats, cabin cruisers, pontoon boats, or skiffs. Quick as lizards, children, their faces rosy with excitement, darted indiscriminately among family members and strangers as they played tag.

"There are so many people here," Katie said. "I'd looked forward to being alone with you, Mom."

"I forgot it was Labor Day weekend. Don't worry. Once we're out on the lake, we'll be private."

The only regular exercise Zoe embraced was walking in her beloved woods and rowing. Rowing loosened the tightness in her back and shoulders, and Zoe enjoyed the sense of power and control she derived from it. She needed this now if she were to stay calm and speak honestly to her daughter.

Above the lake, awash in light and bathed by air so transparent that every fold and ridge seemed touchable, the mountains loomed. The women launched the rowboat, and then Zoe pulled hard on the oars. The pale green water near the shoreline slipped away, replaced by deepening shades of blue until the boat rounded a curve and entered the shade of trees overhanging a deep and silent cove. There the water became a murkier green.

Zoe lifted the dripping oars and set them inside the boat, then cast a small anchor overboard. "Nice here, isn't it? It's one of my favorite spots."

"It's wonderful, Mom." Katie leaned forward from her perch in the bow. "And I especially like having you all to myself."

"I've missed you too. It's good to be just the two of us."

Katie's eyes clouded. "I miss Laurie Ann. I wake up in the morning expecting to hear her cry, but it's just quiet. Too quiet. It's worse in the afternoon. I walk around feeling empty, lonely, useless."

"It'll take time."

"It hurts so much, Mom. How much time?"

"I can't tell you that, but it will be easier after a while. Meantime, I'm glad to have you here with me."

Katie looked up, raised her arms to the dome of trees above them, and heaved a deep breath. "It's good to be home. I could never have gone on alone in that house. I'm lucky—not everyone has a place of refuge, or caring people they can turn to when life gets to be too much."

For a time they were quiet, and when Katie finally spoke, she came directly to the point. "Tell me about this Alan person, Mom."

Zoe's hand slid along one of the damp oars. "It's hard. It makes me sick to think of him, much less talk about him. It's not something I'm proud of." She was silent a moment. "Actually, I'm ashamed to tell you." She brought her palms to her cheeks, hot to her touch.

"Ashamed? I can't imagine you doing anything you'd be ashamed of."

"There's a first time for everything, I guess." Leaning over, Zoe dipped her fingers into the cool water, then dampened her cheeks and forehead. When she spoke, her voice was low and hoarse. "He was stunningly handsome, like Omar Sharif, the movie star. Maybe I was flattered that someone as good-looking as Alan wanted me, or maybe it was loneliness or a midlife crisis. I don't know. But what I did, Katie, was degrade myself, my values, my self-respect."

"What do you mean, degrade yourself?"

"At first, he seemed so needy. I wanted to help him, to comfort him and make him happy." She shrugged. "People should watch others' behavior and what they say, to see who another person really is, but who pays attention to warning signs when you're in love?"

"Warning signs? Like what?"

"His quick temper, his self-centeredness, his impatience with me, the way he spoke of his mother with contempt. I ignored all those things. I wanted to ignore them. Run like the devil from any man who has no respect for his mother, Katie."

Zoe looked her daughter squarely in the eye. "I met Alan in the market, of all places, in the fruit section. He asked me how to tell if a melon was ripe. We chatted a bit.

He was new in town, he said, and seeking a quiet life. I could understand that. We went to the Steak House Cafeteria in Walhalla for lunch, and we talked some more. He was pleasant. He invited me out, and we had dinner a few times in Seneca." She hesitated a moment. "Next thing, he moved in with me."

"Just like that, he moved in with you?" Katie asked.

Zoe looked away. "I probably invited him. I can't remember now. Maybe we never discussed it, and it just happened. It felt right at the time. At first it was fine. We were consumed with one another, or at least I was." Zoe blushed. "It had been a long time for me. After a few weeks, I realized that Alan never wanted to go anywhere—not for dinner in Seneca, or even lunch in Walhalla. He rarely left the property. We shopped for food together some of the time, but mainly he just sat in the house or by the pond, and sometimes he walked in the woods with me."

"Didn't he have a job?"

"He said he was a consultant for light industrial plants in the area, that he was a specialist in diversity training, but he never went anywhere or made any phone calls, and no one called him. At first I was flattered. I assumed he preferred being alone with me. I didn't want things to change, so I never asked questions. I chose to ignore his obvious irresponsibility, and I never asked about his work or the lack of it."

Katie asked softly, "Being in love blinds you, doesn't it, Mom?"

"Yes, it does." Zoe's voice was low and strained. "For a few weeks, I felt beautiful. He had a way, when he wanted to, of making me feel special. But then, one day, Olive and Ruben Holloway came over to visit. Alan was rude to them, and when they left, he cursed them and raved on and on that they had come to spy on him. He flew into a rage, stormed off to his car, and left. He was gone for days. I was frantic. When he came back, he wouldn't say where he'd been. Instead, he accused me of having people check him out and yelled that I preferred spending time with them rather than with him. I explained that Olive and Ruben were old friends, like family to me, and that they had probably come over because I hadn't called them in a while, and they wanted to make sure I was all right. They'd had no clue that he was there."

"That must have been scary. Did he understand and calm down?"

"No, he didn't, not at all."

A yellow leaf of a poplar tree drifted down and landed on Katie's hair. Zoe picked it off and cradled it in her hand. Then she gently set it adrift in the lake, pulled the anchor from the sandy bottom, and slipped the oars back into the water with a plop. She settled into the smooth rhythm of rowing, and soon they were skimming along close to the shore. Zoe plunged the oars deep, and pulled into another cove with a steep shoreline. Lanky trees yearning for sunshine leaned outward, providing shade. On the boulders near the shore, green moss swished and swayed with the water.

"So, Mom," Katie asked, "what happened with Alan? You had an affair. What's to be ashamed of? So far, I see a woman who's head over heels in love and having the time of her life, and a guy who's possessive, self-centered, and probably unreliable."

"And egomaniacal, devious, and a con man," Zoe said. "And mean. Incredibly mean. Nothing in my life prepared me for what he would dish out."

It wasn't long before Alan had started playing games,

punishing her by withholding sex and disappearing for days without any explanation. She had been frantic with worry, then fearful that she had bored him and that when he vanished, he'd never return. When he did come back, sure of himself and cocky, she'd give him anything, let him *do* anything. It was all so sordid, Zoe felt nauseated just thinking about it. Trailing her hand in the water, she avoided her daughter's probing eyes. "He wasn't a nice man. You couldn't depend on him, not in any way."

"I'm sorry, Mom. What made you want him back? Was it sex?"

"Yes. The sex was good at first." It had been fantastic in ways she had never imagined. Zoe fixed her eyes on the green moss clinging tenaciously to the rocks. The hypnotic effect of their swaying motion calmed her, even as she remembered a day when she went to the mall in Anderson for a crotchless teddy that Alan had insisted she buy. She had worn dark glasses and a large floppy hat to hide her face. Then came her sputtering request for the black teddy, and the saleswoman who tried to foist a red and then a blue teddy off on her. No, she had insisted, she must have black. Alan would be furious and cruel if she returned with anything else.

"Black turns me on, baby," he had said earlier that day.

They had had yet another fight that had escalated into his striking her, nearly knocking her to the floor. Alan relished fighting; the adrenaline surges empowered him and made him feel alive. When he grew calm, after he apologized again and again, their lovemaking bore a frenzied intensity. Alan brought chaos into her placid world. How could she tell this to Katie? She had loved him, forgiven him time and time again, and wanted him desperately. And she had hated him and, by extension, hated herself.

How could she tell such things to her daughter? Yet she owed her some explanation, and she needed, finally, to purge her own soul by telling at least a part of it. Gripping the sides of the boat, Zoe said, "He didn't like my clothes. He criticized everything I said, did, wore." Her voice grew bitter. "He made me feel as if I were a nothing."

Tell Katie about the physical abuse. Tell your daughter he struck you more than once and that you feared for your life.

One day she'd returned home from the market and seen a yellow sports car in her parking place. Sensing that it was a woman's car, Zoe slipped off her shoes and moved silently as a cat down the hallway. After a moment's hesitation, she grasped the knob and swung the bedroom door open. She watched Alan's naked body rise and fall above a woman's long, tan limbs. Blond hair fanned out on Zoe's pillow.

Zoe had turned and run. Grabbing her shoes in the kitchen, she had raced across the pasture and around the pond. Terrified of how he would punish her for what he would call interrupting him, she had scrambled up the hillside. Out of breath, in fear for her life, she had squeezed into the shallow, hidden cave and huddled in a tight ball against the rear wall. Time stopped. Then she heard him trampling in the brush and heard his voice calling.

"Zoe. Come on back home, baby. That stupid blonde doesn't mean a damned thing to me, you know that, baby."

Zoe hardly dared breathe.

The sound of branches breaking and of leaves crackling grew closer.

"I know you're here somewhere." More tromping. Closer. "Wherever you're hiding, come out, you hear me?" His rage, barely under the surface and disguised with difficulty, spilled out. "Damn bushes."

He's probably stumbled into the blackberry patch not two dozen feet away.

"Come on out, baby." A few seconds later. "You damn well better get yourself out here, and fast."

The thud of a heavy stick against the bushes grew closer. Surely he would hear her heart thumping. Surely he would hear her ragged breathing.

The wall of the cave against which she cowered was rough and cold, but she hardly felt it. Only a layer of vines and brambles separated them. If Alan found her, he would use his fists or the heavy stick to injure her, maybe even kill her. Or he would beat her, cripple her, and leave her in the woods with no way to call for help.

His cursing grew louder and more menacing. "Zoe, where the hell are you? I'll beat the hell out of you when I find you!" Then his voice softened. "Just kidding, baby. I'll let you off easy." More cursing. His boots hit the earth hard as he moved past the mouth of the cave, then stopped. *He had found her.*

In that instant Zoe knew that she would fight him, and that she would die. She hardly breathed. The seconds became years. Then his boots pivoted and moved away. Soon his voice grew hoarse, his curses faint. Zoe shook with terror, and silent tears coursed down her face.

After an interminable time, Zoe heard the blast of his motorcycle start up and the engine roar as he revved it hard before burning rubber on the paved road. When the sound faded, Zoe finally succumbed to sobs that racked her body. For an eternity she sat in the cave huddled over her knees, immobile and aching.

The Holloways found her there, crouched like an animal, shivering, near delirium and unsure if they were friend or foe. Olive said, "It's me and Ruben, honey. When we couldn't find you at home, and we saw what he did to the house, we come looking for you up here. I was praying mightily to find you. Praise God. You come on out now, honey. We're gonna take you home."

She shook her head. "No, not home. No."

"Our home, Zoe. We're gonna take you to our place, where you'll be nice and safe," Olive said. "He's gone. That terrible man is gone. I prayed on it, and he's gone."

Ruben lay on his belly on the ground and urged her out. "Just ease on out here, Zoe girl. I'm gonna carry you down the hill."

Weeping, she crawled out and into his arms.

"Easy with her now," Olive said. "She might be hurt."

"Don't you worry none, Olive. Zoe's gonna be just fine."

Ruben lifted her gently and carried her down the hill to their ancient Chrysler. Olive drove. They asked no questions as they brought her to their farmhouse, where Olive put her to bed in their upstairs bedroom. For the next three days, Zoe burned with fever. They fed her soup by the spoonful, and Olive replaced damp cloths on her forehead and rubbed her down with alcohol. Zoe would remember shapes, muffled sounds, and moments of fear quickly overridden by a sense of comfort and safety. On the fourth day, Zoe opened her eyes to dappled sunshine. Even before she could talk, her mind flashed back to the blond. Who *was* she? Jealousy, regret, and rage mingled with shame and fear in Zoe's heart.

How could she tell all this to her daughter now?

"Mom? You're crying. I'm so sorry." Katie's voice brought Zoe back to the present.

She wiped her eyes. "Alan brought another woman home one time. I found them. I ran and hid in my cave. The Holloways found me. I'd once shown Olive where it was when we were picking blackberries for jam." Though it was so hard to say, she managed, "Alan was physically abusive, Katie."

"He *hit* you?" Katie leaned forward with a quick jerk, setting the boat rocking. "Oh, Mom, how terrible. Why didn't you kick him out after the first time?" A vein throbbed at her temple. "I can't bear the thought of some horrid man striking you. The bastard, the damned bastard."

Unconsciously, Zoe's hand found her cheek. "Alan Camaro wasn't a man you could say 'get out' to and have him go."

"You could have left, gone to the Holloways, the police."

"I know that now, Katie. But I found out the hard way that a woman in that situation believes she loves the man, and that he loves her and truly regrets his behavior. That's what he says, and he lavishes her with apologies and gifts afterward, and she wants very much to believe he's sincere. I clung to the hope that he'd keep his word, that he'd change. Then one day I woke up to the fact that he was just plain mean, and by then I felt trapped, and I was terrified of him. And believe me, Alan was someone to be afraid of."

"I wish I'd known. I'd have driven down here and kicked him out for you. We could have done it together."

Zoe shook her head. "I couldn't let you become involved in such a thing. One time we had a minor disagreement down at the summerhouse. He went berserk, screamed that I was a stupid idiot, kicked over chairs, and slashed the screens with a knife that appeared out of nowhere."

"What happened then?" Katie asked softly.

"I ran, but he was faster than I was. He caught me." She swallowed hard. "He knocked me to the ground and fastened his hands on my throat. Did you ever feel that you couldn't breathe?"

"No." Katie's hands clasped her throat. "I can't even imagine."

"Well, that day I was sure I would die right there on the spot. I thought he would kill me, he seemed so totally out of control, but suddenly he let me go." As she remembered the sensation, Zoe's face was chalk white and her breath came in gasps.

Katie eased herself to the bench alongside Zoe and put her arms about her mother's frail, shaking shoulders. "I'm so sorry, Mom. Forgive me for pressing you. You don't have to tell me another thing."

But Zoe could not stop. "Once he hit me across the face with the palm of his hand. I was lucky it was only a nasty bruise and not a broken jaw."

Katie could not stop trembling. "If I could, I'd track down that man and kill him."

"And then what? Anyway, he's a horrible, vicious man. He'd kill you." She paused to take a deep breath. "Another time I disagreed with him over the behavior of some stupid politician on TV. He flew into a rage. I ran and locked myself in the bathroom. I yelled at him then to get out of the house." He laughed and flung his full weight against the door. When it failed to break down, he resorted to knocking gently and pleading for forgiveness."

"You didn't forgive him, did you?"

"I'm afraid I did, Katie. I'm afraid I did." Alan's touch had been an aphrodisiac awakening hidden passion long forgotten, and that night their lovemaking had reached new heights of pleasure. The next morning he brought her breakfast in bed, then brushed and braided her hair, ignoring the nasty bruises on her arm and back. Alan knew exactly where to plant his blows so she would never have to seek hospitalization. That day he pampered her, brought iced cloths, and made their meal, all the while saying, "I love you." And fool that she was, she had actually believed him.

Zoe stared into space. "Then, a few days later, he brought that woman home."

"And you hid in the cave?"

"I had to. He might have killed me. Ruben contacted the minister of their church, and they got some men together and went to the house. That's how I knew Alan had gone. He had ransacked the house, taken Grandma Ida's sterling silverware and her jewelry, cut my clothes to shreds, and slashed the curtains and couch cushions. I stayed for days at Olive and Ruben's place. I would have died without them, I'm sure of it."

"They've been good friends, God bless them," Katie said.

Zoe nodded. "Olive wouldn't let me wallow in misery. She set me to sewing new curtains, planting flowers, canning. When I went home Ruben changed the locks and put special clamps on the windows." A muscle in her cheek twitched, and she braced herself. "Alan stole my money, twenty-eight thousand dollars. I didn't squander the money, Katie. It was in a conservative money market account in a bank in Seneca. Mother and Dad left me the money for repairs, taxes, and insurance." *And I was irresponsible, or I would never have given him access to the account. The darkest secret of all is the one thing I cannot tell Katie.*

"Mom." Katie took Zoe's hand. "How terrible it must have been for you. I understand now about the money. It wasn't your fault. I'm so sorry." Then she ventured to say the unthinkable. "Do you think he'll ever come back?"

"Why would he? He got what he wanted." Zoe's bravado was false, but Katie didn't need to live with her fears. They were silent again. "What do you think of your mother now?"

"I love you. I hate him. I'm just grateful you had the cave to hide in, and that he left. I'm glad you're free of him."

If I were truly free of Alan, would talking about him cause my stomach to knot like this and my head to ache? And how do I know he'll never come back?

"It was a terrible experience," Katie said. "But it's behind you now."

It had been terrible. The Holloways had always respected her silence and, bless them, had never asked questions. They had protected her further by telling their minister that she'd had a break-in and theft.

Would it have been different if she'd had a close woman friend to confide in, someone like Maudie? If she had, there would have been impartial eyes to see and to warn her up front about men like Alan. And even if she wouldn't listen, after the first blow, that friend might have taken her by the shoulders and marched her to the police station. If, if—what was the point of *if*s?

"I'm surprised you stayed on in the house alone," Katie said. "You're a gutsy woman. But I also understand now why I hardly saw you during that period, and why, when I called you, you seemed so eager to get off the phone. I thought you were mad at me."

"No, never, my precious. I just couldn't deal with much, and I was ashamed to tell you." Zoe lowered her voice. "I bought a handgun, and Ruben taught me how to shoot it. I hate touching it, I doubt if I could use it, but it makes me feel safer being out there alone."

Katie stared at her, disbelief in her eyes. "A gun?"

Zoe nodded, reached for the oars, and rowed slowly toward the beach. Before they reached the shore, Katie leaned forward and laid her hand on her mother's arm.

"Oh, Mommy, I'm so sorry. You're so gentle. You deserve a good, kind man, like your father was."

Tears filled Zoe's eyes. "Maybe I deserved to be with someone like Alan. Maybe I'm not really a nice person, or how could I have been so taken in by him and tolerated him for so long?"

"Don't even think that, Mom. You made a mistake. Some people are slick and know exactly how to con others, and before they know it, good people are like fish trapped in their nets." Deep lines furrowed her forehead. "There are really bad people in this world. Simpler, trusting people like us don't recognize them, much less know how to protect ourselves from them, at least not the first time. Have you had yourself tested for AIDS?"

Zoe nodded. She'd worried about it day and night until she'd gone into Greenville to a clinic. Thank God the tests, which she repeated six months later, were negative. That she had taken care of.

But since then, there were so many things she had ignored: the accumulating debts, the loans coming due, and now getting down to business with Winifred. It wasn't long before the foreclosure. She hoped it was not too late.

18

A Beginning

That night, dark clouds rolled in. Rain pelted window-panes and sent torrents gushing over the gutters. Maudie prepared corned beef and cabbage for dinner, and after they had eaten, she excused herself to write letters. Zoe, Katie, and Winifred retired to the den.

The uncomfortable silence was broken when Katie looked from her mother to her grandmother and said, "Well, here we are, three Mrs. Parkers."

Zoe decided to start acting "as if." "I'm sorry about the other night," she said to Winifred. "I was startled at the moment." Zoe extended damp hands to Winifred.

Winifred's color heightened. Surprise registered in her eyes, then pleasure as she leaned toward Zoe and clasped her hands. Winifred's palms were dry and cool, and as Zoe's hands closed over the enlarged knuckles of the older woman's fingers, she wondered if her mother-in-law suffered from arthritis as well as Ménière's disease.

Winifred released Zoe's hands and leaned back against the soft cushions of the love seat. This was unexpected! She was certain she could credit Katie with her mother's sudden change of heart. An inappropriate sense of competitiveness stirred in Winifred. She wanted to gloat, to relish the feeling of having won. But weren't these the very feelings that had created the rift between them so long ago? Zoe was making the effort, and she couldn't miss the opportunity to gain what she had really come here for: family, and a place to rest easily.

"I'm sorry too, for everything. It's been my loss, as you know."

"I was thinking that you and I share a common loss in Steven, and we've never talked about it," Zoe said.

"That's true. Perhaps we can sit down quietly and talk about him, soon."

"I'd like that."

Katie beamed. This was going well, better than she'd expected. She moved between them and clasped both their hands. "I'm so happy," she said.

"This may not be the right moment," Zoe said hesitantly, "but time is running out at the bank."

"Yes, I know. Tomorrow we'll go to the bank," Winifred said. "I'll pay off the loan, and we'll go directly to the tax department in Walhalla."

Relief swept over Zoe, and for a moment she could not speak. Finally she managed a "thank you." An awkward silence followed. Winifred rubbed her shoulders. Zoe realized that she too was chilly. She rose and flipped a switch that set the logs ablaze in the gas fireplace. "This should take the chill out of the room," she said. Zoe would have liked to talk more about her debt and express her appreciation to Winifred, but then Katie spoke.

"I'm glad that's settled," Katie said. "I really need support from both of you now. I've been so consumed caring for Laurie Ann that I feel like a phone off the hook, dangling and twisting on its cord."

Winifred said wistfully, "You're feeling a loss of identity. You've been cut off from someone who gave your life meaning and purpose. You need to grieve, of course, but in the end the best thing you can do for Laurie Ann is to carry on with your life."

"You're so wise," Katie said.

Zoe was silent. This same woman could n̲o̲t remember Laurie Ann's name and had spoken of her with contempt when she arrived in Salem. If Katie knew this, would she have granted her grandmother such wisdom and loving kindness? Would she have pressed Zoe to this reconciliation?

Of course she would have. Katie was the forgiving type.

Winifred slipped her feet from her slippers, exposing squashed toes that buckled one atop the other. Zoe, to her amazement, found herself feeling sorry for the woman.

"Hammertoes," Winifred said. "For so many years, I squeezed these double-E-size feet into high heels with pointed toes. I hope neither of you will ever be that foolish. My toes ache so much at night—all because I dressed for a role to satisfy my mother-in-law, whose claim to fame was being the wife of a prominent attorney and a member of the Parker family.

"That woman picked my clothes for years," Winifred went on, surprising Zoe with her honesty. "Designer clothes that never felt right on me and always high heels, even to take Steven to the park when he was a toddler.

" 'We must always be impeccable' was Mildred Parker's motto. That's all she was interested in. I would have died of sheer boredom, had I not cajoled Theodore into giving me space and a desk at his office and a weekly allowance. While my son was in school, I invested my money and made my own small fortune."

She relived in her mind the depth of her disappointment and the pain she had felt at her dismissal from the board. One day soon after that, she had awakened dizzy and had barely made it to the bathroom after bumping against the wall several times. She had become disoriented and nearly fallen when she tried to shower. What horror she had felt when Dr. Lavelle made the diagnosis of Ménière's disease and laid out the prognosis for her!

"You had better get someone to live permanently in the house with you," he had said. "And I would turn that big dining room of yours into a bedroom and bathroom so you won't have to cope with stairs."

"This isn't going to get better?" she'd asked, not yet grasping the full import of his diagnosis.

"Nope, no better. Take care of yourself and you'll not have as many attacks. There are things we can do, including surgery; maybe you'll have to sacrifice the hearing in one ear to avert the dizziness. But all that will come in time. For now, avoid stress."

"You look so pensive. What are you thinking about, Granny?" Katie asked.

Winifred roused herself. "I was thinking that I was very wrong not to have told you and your mother about the Ménière's earlier. I do apologize."

"Accepted," Katie said, and Zoe nodded. What else could she do? She tried to imagine Winifred's life in the stiff formality of the Parker mansion with its huge rooms, its overstuffed, dark furniture, its pomposity and loneliness.

"It's stopped raining," Katie said. She went to the window. "Look at the moon." The sky was clearly visible through the bank of windows. "The way the clouds are, it looks as if they took jagged bites from the moon. The moon looks torn and tattered."

"How very odd," Zoe said.

Winifred shifted on the love seat, and her eyes found Zoe's. "Tell me about my son, please."

Zoe searched for the right words, then said, "You did a good job raising him. Steven was a wonderful man: loving, kind, and generous. He adored Katie." She looked at her daughter. "He'd come home, toss you in the air, kiss your tummy, and you'd laugh and laugh. We would have had more children if he hadn't died; we planned to have four."

The catch in Winifred's throat, almost a gasp, stopped Zoe. "I'm sorry. I didn't mean to make you sad." Should she touch her mother-in-law, smile at her, hug her?

"You had three more years of him than I did," Winifred said. "I've never forgiven myself for that." Tears ran down her face, and she wiped them away. "You'll never know how much I've regretted my behavior. I was foolishly proud and exceedingly stubborn, so stubborn that I couldn't go back on my own words once they were out of my mouth." Her voice was weighted with self-loathing. "Trying to bribe you, Zoe. The awful things I said. They were terrible, and you were so decent despite all I put you through. Zoe, can you ever forgive me?"

Zoe saw the anxiety in her daughter's eyes. *Act "as if."* "I have," she said. Not true, but she might in time.

"Thank you, my dear. Thank you." Reaching for Katie's hand, Winifred looked at her granddaughter. "How sorry I am for everything I missed—your growing up, your high school and college graduations. I should have given you emotional support and money during all those years you were alone, caring for Laurie Ann."

"It's all right, Granny. We're together now." Katie reached over and hugged her.

Zoe took a deep breath. "Steven kept your photograph on our dresser," she told Winifred, and it unexpectedly pleased her to see the glow that suffused the older woman's face.

Winifred lifted a hand to her chest. "My picture?" she asked in wonder.

"Yes. He loved you very much."

"Oh, Zoe, thank you for telling me. It means everything to me." She brushed away more tears. "I was certain he hated me."

"No, he never hated you. Steven had great depths of understanding, and he knew you loved him. He was angry for a while, yes, but he'd say, 'Time will take care of this. You'll see. We'll get it all patched up.'" Zoe turned to Katie. "Your father chose your name and its spelling. He loved the name Kathryn."

"You never told me that, Mom."

Zoe nodded.

Winifred beamed.

Katie smiled a wide, happy smile, and Zoe knew that Steven's choosing her daughter's name, and Winifred's photograph on the dresser were lies sanctioned by heaven.

The next moment Katie brought up the idea of the antique shop and talked about looking at several closed stores on Main Street in Walhalla. Zoe listened and found herself being swept along.

Katie said, "Perhaps we could call it Aladdin's Treasures? I used to wish for a magic lamp to rub and make everything right."

Winifred stroked Katie's arm, the affection in her face obvious. "Aladdin's Treasures sounds perfect, don't you think so, Zoe?"

Zoe stifled the resentment building inside of her. "It's a great name," she said.

"Tomorrow we'll take care of everything," Winifred said. "I'm exhausted now." She stood, a trifle unsteadily. Her blouse had pulled out from her slacks, and she tucked it back in. "The hearing in my left ear has gotten worse in the last few months. I want you to know that, in case I seem to ignore something either of you says to me."

"I'll remember that, Granny." Katie took Winifred's arm and started out the door. "Good night, Mom," she said.

"Good night, Winifred, Katie." Zoe watched them go. Acting "as if" had worked. It had been surprisingly easy, and well worth it. She felt lighter, happier. And tomorrow she'd be free from the threat of losing her home and land.

Settled in bed, Winifred extracted the drawing pad from her end-table drawer and began to sketch. Fifteen minutes later, Zoe's face stared at her from the page. She tipped the pad. Had she gotten the eyes just right? A bit of a line there, a shadow here, and yes, there it was, a fine resemblance. She had captured the mix of anxiety and determination on Zoe's face, the look she wore when she had offered Winifred her hands.

Winifred could read people well. Zoe was a long way from complete forgiveness, but it was a start. Time would take care of the rest.

19

✧

MAUDIE REMEMBERS

While the women talked in the den and the rain hammered the roof, Maudie O'Hara lay in her bed. The rain stirred memories of a night when she was thirteen, a night when fear and a deep sickness in the pit of her belly had accompanied her to bed. That evening she had witnessed her father's drunken rage and the madness in his eyes as he beat her older sister, Emma, over some small infraction. He had never struck Maudie, but Emma seemed to set him off, and nothing her mother did could stop him. No wonder Emma took the fastest way out of that house, getting pregnant and marrying Gerald McEllis before she was seventeen. It hurt Maudie's heart to think how opportunities were cut off for her sister. With her looks and brains, she could have gone far in the world. Instead, she was burdened with seven children and worn out before her time, while Gerald frequented the local pub.

After that fateful night, Maudie walked on eggs around

her father. Why hadn't she, Emma, and their brothers ever fought back against their father? They could have given him a taste of his own medicine and sent him sprawling to the ground. But with the rivalry among the boys, and Emma being as docile as their mam, and she the youngest, they never had.

She had graduated from high school at the top of her class and been awarded a scholarship to nursing school in Dublin. Coming home for holidays, she had been acutely aware of the verbal abuse heaped by Da on her mother and the red marks of a hand on her mother's face. Maudie had tried to spur her brothers to action, but Liam, the weasel, had betrayed them. Da had spent the next few days glowering at her and her brothers, but he had not raised a hand to them or to her. Perhaps he dared not. Either way, she hated him.

Outside her window, the rain eased to a drizzle. Maudie lit the lamp near her bed and rose to open a window. Staring curiously up at her from the patio, the bright eyes of a small red fox glowed in the light from her room. Head held high, it sauntered into the shrubbery. The moon, jagged-edged behind the clouds, would soon be full. At home the leprechauns would dance. As she stood by the window, Maudie ached for the girl she had been, scheming to capture leprechauns and win their pot of gold.

Maudie had seen them, bearded little men in green, dancing in the woods one midsummer's eve, while she was picking wildflowers to make a posy for Mam's birthday. They had regarded her with glimmering, mischievous eyes, and her heart had pounded so loudly it sounded like a drumbeat. Oh, to be home and watch them dance. But she had made the right decision leaving; her life was now in America. Maudie returned to bed.

In her mind, she could hear her mother's voice cajoling her to marry.

"Johnny Garrity's a fine young fella. He'll be working in his father's grocery. You'll never starve."

"I shan't have him," Maudie replied. "I don't like him. He's a bully."

"You're thirty-five, lass," her mother said. "You dunna want to be nursing other folks' wee ones and have none of your own."

Because she loved sweet Mam, with her faded hair and worried blue eyes, she had over the years dated some of the men her mother put forward. None captured her heart, and the very idea of a life like Mam's or Emma's appalled her. She'd broken tradition by not marrying young, by going off to become a nurse, and now she refused to settle down with someone from the village. One day, Da had stared at her with hostile eyes and yelled, "Go live in America with the Yanks, damn you. They're a weird lot, just like you." The idea had taken hold in her mind, and she had done just that.

When she came to Salem, she wrote Mam about the Parker women, assured her that she was happy, that she was no longer minding other people's wee lads and lassies, and that Mrs. Parker senior really needed her. As the weeks passed, Maudie had written Mam about her growing affection and respect for these women, but that most especially she liked Zoe and hoped they would be friends.

"I pray for you every night, and I beg the blessed Virgin to bring you a nice Irishman to marry in America," her mother had replied.

Maudie's eyes grew heavy. Perhaps one day she would marry—but meanwhile, it would be nice if Mam accepted that she had a good life and was happy.

20

LUNCH AT THE
STEAK HOUSE CAFETERIA

Walhalla's Main Street wore its nineteenth-century two-story brick and wood buildings with pride, while new government buildings, offices, and fast-food restaurants pulled the town into the twenty-first century. The railroad tracks that characterized many small towns were no longer needed to link Walhalla to the outside world, and children played a kind of hopscotch on and off the unused, rusting tracks. On the side streets, splendid oaks overhung Victorian houses wrapped with porches and lacy fretwork, and churches whose history dated back to the original German settlers boasted well-kept cemeteries. What had been countryside and farmland was being bought by developers, and new ranch and two-story homes were being built and occupied.

"Who buys these houses? Are they retired or working

people?" Winifred asked, as the three went to Walhalla the next day.

"Some retirees, I think, but also families," Zoe replied.

"I notice that the bank tellers at the Blue Ridge Bank of Walhalla are very welcoming. They call you by your first name after a visit or two, and shopkeepers remember a new face," Winifred said.

"And policemen smile," Katie added.

Any trip to Walhalla included lunch at the busy Steak House Cafeteria on Main Street, which was owned and operated by Gloria and Abed Yassen. "Gloria met Abed in Israel when she traveled there with her church group. They fell in love, overcame immigration problems, and eventually married," Zoe told Winifred. "Their fried chicken is the best. I don't know where they get the chicken, but it's never dry," Zoe said. "I always have it."

They were going to the bank first, then the tax department, and had an appointment with a Realtor about a store on Main Street. "Are you feeling up to so much in one day?" Zoe asked Winifred.

"I feel fine. I slept well last night, and I'll feel even better once we get this business taken care of," Winifred replied.

Zoe would also. After breakfast that morning, she had placed all the dishes in the dishwasher right away for a change. It had taken only a few minutes, and the kitchen looked much better without messy dishes piled in the sink.

Winifred entered the bank armed with a portfolio containing letters of credit, financial statements, and last year's tax forms, and was immediately escorted to Mrs. Tate, who rose to greet them.

The figures were handed to her, and Winifred pulled out her checkbook and wrote a check. Within minutes, the loan papers were stamped 'paid in full' and handed to Zoe. Mrs.

Taft took Zoe's hand in both of hers. "Good luck, Zoe, my dear. I'm so glad you were able to take care of this matter."

They trooped to the courthouse, where Winifred paid the overdue taxes, then moved on to finish their business with a lawyer. Last, they followed the Realtor, a young man named Tom Hinson, in and out of empty stores on Main Street. By one o'clock they were exhausted and in need of lunch. The line at the Steak House Cafeteria had thinned, and they moved quickly to the food counter.

"I like that last store," Winifred said as she placed utensils on her tray. "What do you think, Zoe?"

"It has a good-sized room in front and ample storage area in the back. And the loading dock off the rear alley is a real plus."

Katie was enthusiastic. "They'll let us renovate it. If we hire him, Jon could fix the floor where it sags a bit. He could make it beautiful in no time, I'm sure. He did a wonderful job on the summerhouse."

"Our shop will be a shot of vitamin B_{12} to Main Street," Winifred said.

"Can we have an awning?" Katie asked.

Winifred lay her hand on Katie's shoulder. She seemed to sway a bit, but then grew steady. "Of course, and we must have a logo."

They reached the serving line, and everyone's attention turned to selecting lunch. Katie chose fried chicken, candied carrots, and macaroni and cheese, as did Zoe, while her mother-in-law decided on a vegetable plate.

A booth emptied, and they set their trays on the vinyl tablecloth and slid onto the seats, Katie and Zoe on one side, Winifred on the other.

"I counted seven out-of-state cars parked on Main Street," Winifred said. "Several from Florida. People on their way up

THE THREE MRS. PARKERS   133

or down Highway 28 to Cashiers or Highlands, I bet." She rubbed her hands together. "Potential customers."

Zoe's eyes scanned the room, trying to identify the Florida people. Most people looked the same, in casual clothing and sneakers or boots. A few men, lawyers or salesmen or bankers, wore ties but no jackets. Across the way sat her insurance agent, his wife, and his partner. They nodded greetings. Abed crossed the room and visited a moment at their table. Zoe introduced Winifred, and they exchanged pleasantries. "Send my love to Gloria," Zoe said.

"I will," he replied, and moved away to greet folks at another table.

"You're known in and about Walhalla, aren't you, Zoe?" It was a comment more than a question, and Zoe was pleased that Winifred noticed.

"My family's been around here for a long time," she said. And when Winifred vigorously stirred her iced tea, clinking her spoon against the glass, Zoe smiled at her mother-in-law. For the first time in ages she felt safe, and she marveled that she owed this feeling to Winifred Parker. She silently sent her thanks to Steven as they ate, relaxed, and began to make plans.

"We'll need so many things for the store: crockery, glassware, kitchen utensils, quilts, and furniture," Winifred said.

As Zoe observed the easy flow of ideas between her daughter and her mother-in-law, their rapport amazed her. Theirs was no pretend relationship. Either there was a spark between two people or there was not. These two had it. Their minds seemed synchronized. Winifred began a sentence, and Katie finished it. They laughed at the same things. But best of all, Winifred's idea for an antique shop offered Katie a new challenge and meaningful work to fill the void left by the loss of Laurie Ann.

Loneliness swept over Zoe. If only she were linked to someone with whom she shared sensibilities and interests, like these two.

At that moment, Maudie entered the restaurant. She'd driven into town earlier to see Zoe's dentist, then meet them for lunch. Maudie selected her meal and joined them at their booth, where Winifred slid over to make room for her.

Katie asked, "How was the dentist, Maudie? Did you like him?"

"Yes, I liked him. It feels good to have that taken care of."

Winifred stirred her iced tea again. "We think we found a space for the shop."

"Oh, how splendid. What kind of antiques do you want to sell?"

"A variety at first, then we'll see what the traffic calls for," Winifred replied.

"Where do you buy the pieces?" Maudie asked. "I'd know just where to look back in Ireland."

Winifred said, "You and Zoe might enjoy a trip into North Carolina. I bet you could pick up small pieces of furniture, crockery, kitchen items, things like that."

Suddenly it seemed an interesting possibility to Zoe. Why not try it? A change might be nice, and if Maudie went along with her, they could get to know each other better.

Zoe smiled. "Might be a fun thing to do, but can you cope without Maudie?"

"For a few days with Kathryn here, certainly!" Winifred said.

21

⚭⚭⚭

RENOVATIONS BEGIN

Within three weeks, the renovations at Aladdin's Treasures began in earnest. Air conditioning must be installed; floors repaired, sanded, stained, and polished; and new counters selected and installed. Shelves were added along the walls, and ceiling fans and fluorescent lighting had to be hung. Sunflower-colored paint transformed the walls from dull to bright. With a December opening planned, Winifred anticipated a busy Christmas followed by a slow winter season, during which there would be plenty of time to iron out kinks and hone the system.

The Holloways, swept up by the excitement, stopped in each time Ruben brought a truckload of pigs to the auction or fresh vegetables to the farmers' market. One day Ruben announced, "It's only October, and whatcha know, the frost nipped my toes this morning."

"That's 'cause you won't put on your shoes before you go out," Olive said.

"Six weeks to first snowfall," he predicted.

Zoe believed him. He was a wise man and she'd seen his weather predictions come to pass.

"Honey," Olive said to Zoe, "I got me a friend lives up a holler, Mrs. Stanley Hope. She's ninety-five years old if she's a day, and she's got some things in her house she wants to sell to y'all. When you wanna go?"

"This afternoon's as good a time as any," Zoe replied.

Frail and bent, with bright eyes in a deeply furrowed face, Mrs. Hope planned on entering an assisted living facility. Leaning heavily on her cane, she led them to a room wrapped in floral wallpaper and washed in light from huge bay windows. Once an elegant room, it now served as storage. Furniture was piled tight against every wall and spilled into the center of the room.

"This here's a walnut Queen Anne highboy," the old lady said. "And these chairs goes with it." The curved legs rested on ball-and-claw feet. Zoe saw several beautiful spool-legged mahogany side tables, a round marble-topped table, and a lovely mahogany and satin-wood sewing table.

"You're sure you want to sell all your lovely things?" Zoe asked.

"Atop of goin' to live in that there place," said Mrs. Hope, "I gotta get teeth taken outta my mouth, and that costs plenty." She waved her hand around the room. "These things ain't gonna help me none where I'm a-goin'."

Mrs. Hope hobbled into another room, where piles of toys were stacked on top of tables.

"We never done had no children, but Mr. Hope collected these here toys for our nieces' and nephews' kids to play with when they visited." She picked up a wagon. "Here's a wooden Conestoga wagon. Mr. Hope carved this hisself, and this here tin milk wagon's got a horse and driver good as the day he bought it and brung it home. He made these here whirligigs too." The whirligigs were in the shape of soldiers.

An hour later, when Olive and Zoe bade Mrs. Hope goodbye and wished her well in her new home, Zoe's purchases included furniture, several hand-stitched quilts, a collection of strawberry glass pieces, and a puzzle jug, made, Mrs. Hope had said, for practical jokers like her husband. "Ol' Stanley," she said, "he liked a good trick. He'd fill this here jug with beer so as no one could see the bottom, and he'd come all to pieces laughing when the fella gave one big hoot at that frog a-sitting there in the bottom of that old jug."

Back at the shop, Zoe and Winifred worked late, cataloging, pricing, and storing the pieces, until Winifred sat heavily in a chair and ran her arm across her forehead.

"Ready to go home?" Zoe asked.

"I know you're thinking that if I am tired, I'll get sick, but I tell you, nothing staves off illness like being busy and happy."

Nevertheless, Zoe gathered up their purses and jackets and propelled the older woman toward the door. "Well, I'm absolutely worn out. It's been a very long day."

On the back drive to Salem, Winifred was quiet for a long time. As they neared Amorey Lane, she said, "Zoe, you don't mind, do you, my suggesting that you and Maudie go to North Carolina next week to buy for the shop?"

"It's an interesting idea," Zoe said.

"I was right, you know, about your having a gift for spotting good furniture. You appreciate beauty in any form. The pieces you bought from Mrs. Hope are fine and in superb condition."

"I never would have found Mrs. Hope without Olive taking me there, and if Mrs. Hope hadn't known and trusted Olive, she would never have shown me all her things and let me choose so freely."

"Even so, you and Maudie will do just fine on your own. Is it all right, Maudie going with you?"

"Of course, but are you sure you won't need her? Maudie came here to be with you."

Winifred rested her head against the window of the car. "Kathryn's with me at the shop all day, and Jon and the other men, and I can ask Olive to come in if necessary. Besides, we're closer to the hospital in Walhalla than in Salem, should there be a problem. I'll be fine. Just fine."

And it was settled.

22

REFLECTIONS

Winifred went immediately to her room to rest, but after a quick shower and change, Zoe headed out of the house to walk in the woods. She skirted a patch of rhododendrons, stepped over a newly fallen branch that was too heavy for her to move, and headed directly to the glade of the hero pines. The air was crisp and cool, and the tang of pine filled her nostrils. Some creature of the woods, foraging nearby, scurried away.

Zoe's anxious days lay behind her. Buoyed by a new sense of freedom, she brimmed with high spirits, and she spun around and around, then leaned against the crusty bark of the Agamemnon tree to catch her breath.

This morning the radio announcer had said, "The fall in North Carolina, this year, holds the promise of a brilliant leaf season." Like the year she and Steven had traveled through Pennsylvania at peak leaf season? Nothing she had seen since had ever matched the brilliance of that fall in the

Poconos, when they had lost their way in some small town. On a tree-shaded street of bungalows with tiny front yards, nature sprinkled brilliant autumn leaves onto their windshield, causing Steven to pull the car off the road. They had sat in silence for a long time, and Zoe remembered closing her eyes and resting her head on Steven's shoulder.

"I love you so very much," Steven had whispered.

Zoe thought of Alan, fire, ice, darkness, and it seemed as if the light in the glade dimmed. Zoe wrapped her arms about her shoulders.

Exorcising the remains and reminders of Alan from her house had taken more than a year. For months the kitchen retained the smell of the black polish he had used on his Gucci shoes, and in the bathroom, the scent of musk cologne set her heart thudding with fear that he had returned. She had donated their sheets, pillowcases, pillows, and blankets to the Salvation Army and replaced the mattress. Finally Zoe had moved to her parents' bedroom. Thinking of him even now set her trembling, for she had withheld a piece of information, the most important information, from her daughter, from everyone.

North Carolina would be a delightful change, and Maudie would be a good traveling companion, quiet, sensitive to her moods, never prying. She would show Maudie some of the country: Looking Glass Falls near Brevard in North Carolina, and the Biltmore Estate in Asheville. They would hunt for antiques in small towns in Transylvania County before moving on to Buncombe County, where Asheville was located, and then move on to rural Madison and Yancey counties.

The woods throbbed with silence. It was here, under the Agamemnon tree, that her father had shared a most astounding event in his life, an experience so powerful that it had changed his view of life and death, the world, and his place in it.

"I was a very young soldier in World War II," he told her and her mother. "It was a glade much like this in an ancient forest, a place the local peasants considered sacred. Ear-splitting explosions of shells pounded the earth about me, and the fetid odor of death was everywhere. Our orders were simple: 'You find anyone, man, woman, or child, you shoot them dead.' Somehow I became separated from my buddies. I stumbled through thick brush and finally fell into that glade and collapsed on the ground."

His voice became soft and dreamy. "Everything was silent. The war seemed distant, a horrible dream. I opened my eyes to an incredible white light all around me. I felt safe and loved beyond measure."

Listening to him, Zoe could hardly breathe. She had squeezed her eyes shut, longing for a glimpse of that light, hoping to feel such love and sense of safety. Her father smiled then and drew her close to him, and she smelled the sweet odor of his tobacco on his clothing.

"Total peace came," he said. "I knew I would never shoot a gun again, not at any man, woman, or child, and that I would live to come back home. I must have drifted to sleep, for when I opened my eyes, peasants surrounded me in a silent circle. Like a lamb, I went with them to their village in the forest. I felt no fear. I ate their food without any fear of poison. I played with their children. One day the elders came. They said that the war had ended. I must leave them and rejoin my people. Gaunt and silent, every member of that village, every man, woman, and child, walked me to the edge of the woods, to a narrow dirt road. They pointed south. I looked at the open road ahead of me, and when I looked around, they were gone. I called to them. I wanted to hug them all and tell them, again, what our time together meant to me, for it transcended country, time, place.

"The fields on either side of me were pitted with craters. The debris of war, jagged pieces of tanks lay everywhere. It was quiet. In time I made it to a city where I was welcomed by Americans who assumed I had been a POW, and soon after I was shipped back home."

"Why do you tell that story to Zoe?" Her mother tapped him on the head with her hand, breaking the spell. "It's always seemed odd to me. Are you sure you didn't dream it?"

Her father smiled enigmatically and shrugged his shoulders. Zoe had believed him with her whole heart.

Later, with thoughts of Katie and Winifred tumbling in her mind, Zoe ambled back through the woods to the house. After she had told Katie how cruel Winifred had been to them, why was Katie not angry at Winifred? Winifred had abandoned her only grandchild, been meanhearted and stingy with affection, money, everything Katie had needed. How was her daughter able to forgive the past and care so much for her grandmother? She must talk to Katie about this.

A short while later Zoe left the woods, and when she saw her new summerhouse, genuine gratitude toward Winifred welled up within her—as well as the possibility of a better relationship with the older woman.

Winifred had a passion for gin rummy, and she taught Maudie how to play. After dinner most evenings, they faced one another across the kitchen table, cards in hand. They played for toothpicks, simple wooden ones initially, then moved on to colored ones decorated with plastic frills. Their game tonight offered the perfect opportunity for Zoe to draw Katie off to the living room.

Lamps on a long, narrow table behind the sofa threw soft shadows on the wall behind them, and an accent light Katie had installed behind a tall palm cast webbed patterns on the far wall. They sank onto the sofa.

Tucking her legs under her, Zoe turned to her daughter. "I need you to tell me how your feelings for your grandmother changed."

Katie toyed with the tassel on one of the throw pillows, and her eyes misted. "Losing Laurie Ann made me realize how short and uncertain life can be. Then, out of nowhere, Grandmother was here. It seemed a sign. After the funeral, I started to think about how small our family is. Then I noticed little things: the way Granny looked at me, the way her voice softened when she spoke to me. She seemed interested in me; she cared what I thought and felt. I realized she wanted to mend fences. Bit by bit, she told me things about her life: her awful childhood, her imperious mother-in-law, and how she walked on eggs not to rock the Parker family boat. She stopped being 'that mean old Parker woman' and started being my grandmother, a woman burdened with regrets, suffering from losses, just like you and me. Hearing about Granny's past, how afraid she was of her grandfather, how ignored she was by her parents, made all the difference to me. I think it would have been better, in our family, if we had talked openly and freely about the Parkers."

"What difference would it have made?" Zoe asked curiously. "Would you have phoned her, and would she have told you any of this?"

"Perhaps not. But all the bottled-up anger that was never expressed might have had an outlet, rather than simmering all these years—especially for you, Mom. I guess it would have mattered less to me."

"Why less to you?"

"Perhaps because I never knew her, never experienced the meanness or the depth of rejection that you did."

"That's true. I guess I assumed you felt as I did, that my pain and anger transferred to you."

"If you hated them so much, Mom, why did you keep the Parker name instead of taking back your maiden name after my father died?"

Zoe's voice was clipped. "For Steven, and for you. You're his child. It's your name."

"But it tied you to the Parkers—a bond, of sorts." Katie clasped a pillow to her chest. "Granny said they were the ulti-mate snobs and very condescending. She wasn't well edu-cated, you know, but she was smart and ambitious. She dreaded poverty more than anything. Marrying her boss was a real coup, and she did whatever she had to do to gain his family's acceptance. She hid her background; she claimed to be an orphan. That elicited a more sympathetic response than if she'd said she was raised dirt poor on the coast of Maine."

From the kitchen came the sound of Winifred's voice. "I beat you!"

Maudie laughed. "You beat me."

"She's always got to win," Zoe said.

"I guess so. I don't mind. Ask her about her life some-time; you might find it interesting."

Zoe stretched her legs. "I doubt it."

"I know this isn't easy for you, Mom, and I don't think I answered your question. Basically, as I got to know more about Granny, I began to care about her. Beyond that, I just don't know how it happened." She shrugged and smiled at her mother.

"I hope you understand that I'm acting 'as if,' so don't ask me to like her."

"You've been terrific, Mom."

"But you're hoping it won't be 'as if' forever, aren't you?"

"I guess I am," Katie replied.

Zoe lowered her voice. "She makes me feel incompetent and insignificant."

"Please don't get angry with me, Mom, but I learned in counseling that no one can make you feel anything you don't choose to feel. Maybe in time, if you get to know her better, you'll feel differently."

Laughter came again from the kitchen.

Their discussion tacitly over, they rose and joined Maudie and Winifred for a cup of tea and rum cake made from a recipe from Maudie's mam.

23

҈

Alan Returns

Along with interior renovations and repairs, the façade of the shop underwent a face-lift. Large display windows replaced the narrow, old-fashioned windows, and a pink-and-maroon-striped awning bearing the name Aladdin's Treasures—Antiques extended over the sidewalk.

The day after Zoe and Maudie's departure for North Carolina, Katie was unpacking stock in the storeroom, while Winifred stood at the counter behind the new cash register sorting pens, receipt pads, and credit card forms. When Winifred heard the squeal of a rusty hinge from the front door, she made a mental note to ask Jon to oil the hinge.

A man strode into the shop with an air of confidence, his smile showing perfect white teeth. Under a black jacket he wore a black turtleneck pullover. Black pants hung easily over black Gucci shoes. Of medium build, with hair like a raven's, his skin tan, he was movie-star handsome. Winifred thought he looked overly cool and out of place in Walhalla. Perhaps he was a Spanish businessman or an actor from a shoot somewhere close by, since the area was home to a movie company. An odd thought crossed her mind: *I wouldn't want him as an enemy.*

In the storeroom, Katie was pricing a box of 1940s kitchen crockery she and her grandmother had found at a local flea market. When she heard the door creak, she poked her head into the shop.

The moment she saw him, she knew: Alan Camaro. He was as handsome as Zoe had said, and seductive with his sensuous mouth and intense dark eyes. *Banked passion,* she thought, and rubbed the goose bumps that rose on her arms.

"Good morning, ladies." His voice was deep. "I'm looking for Zoe Parker. Someone suggested she might be here." His eyes scanned the room. "Nice place you've got."

Without time to alert her grandmother, Katie moved closer to the cash register. Soon Jon would be back, but for now they were alone with him, and that frightened Katie.

The man stared at Katie. His eyes traveled the length of her body, and a trace of a smile touched his lips. He raised an eyebrow and nodded slightly, as if he could see through her clothing and approved of what he saw.

Katie went cold. This man was a brute. Why had he returned? What did he want?

The intruder reached in his pocket for a pack of cigarettes. "Mind if I smoke?"

"We would prefer you did not," Winifred said.

"Certainly." He shoved the cigarettes back into his pocket. "Am I in the right place? Is this where I can find Zoe Parker?"

"We own this shop," Katie replied, stepping behind the counter, placing most of her body out of the line of his sight.

Winifred sensed the tenseness in Katie's body, noted her guarded eyes. Something more was going on here than met the eye.

"Does Zoe still live at Amorey Lane? I could just drive out there." His voice purred. "I'm an old friend."

"I am Winifred Parker, her mother-in-law."

He stepped forward and extended his hand. "Pleased to meet you, Mrs. Parker." He looked at Katie. "And you're her daughter, Katie?" He scanned the room and his eyes lingered on the bright quilts from Mrs. Hope's estate, draped now over the Queen Anne chairs. "Antique shop, eh? Nice."

Though her heart beat wildly, Katie managed to say, "The shop's not open yet. In fact, the workmen should be back any minute. My mother's out of town, but if I talk to her, who shall I say is looking for her?" She needed confirmation.

"Just tell her Alan's back."

His smile chilled Katie. "He charmed me, seduced me," Zoe had said. Katie found him unsavory, repulsive, but then, she knew what he was. "I trusted him. When he hit me, I was more hurt emotionally and spiritually than physically." The rage she had felt in the dinghy came rushing back. Below the counter, her fists knotted.

Winifred smelled her granddaughter's fear. Reaching for a pencil and pad, she grasped the pencil hard and wrote his name, Alan. "Fine. We'll let Zoe know. Now, if you don't mind"—she nodded toward the door—"we have work to do."

"I'm sure we'll meet again." With a cocky lift of his shoulders, Alan turned and strode from the store. Through the glass windows they watched him fling wide the door of a black Mustang and slide onto the red leather seat. Then came the roar of the engine, and he was gone.

Katie collapsed into a folding chair. Pulling up a chair beside her, Winifred reached over and cupped her granddaughter's chin in her hands. "What's the matter, Kathryn? Why are you shaking? Who is that man?"

"He's come back. Mom said he'd never come back, but he has."

"Who is he? What is he to Zoe?"

Katie wiped the perspiration from above her upper lip with the back of her hand.

"Tell me about this," Winifred insisted. "Who is he? Why are you afraid?"

Sworn to secrecy, Katie wavered between loyalty to her mother and fear of the danger Alan represented. They would have no more secrets, she resolved; they were a family. Her eyes pleading for understanding for her mother, and with much twisting of her hands, Katie gave her grandmother an abbreviated version of Zoe's relationship with Alan, including the abuse. "She hid for her life in a cave in the woods," Katie finished.

"This is terrible. And now he's here? What for?" Winifred thought a moment. "He wants something. They don't come back unless they want something."

"What can we do?"

Winifred sucked her teeth. "Zoe got away from him that time, but that kind of man detests losing. My hunch is he's come back to finish things with her."

"Kill Mom, you mean?"

Winifred stopped herself. Why make Katie more frightened than she already was? "It's probably not as serious as that. It's a shock though, what you've told me. Who would have imagined that your mother . . . It seems so unlikely." Her jaw tightened. "Well, we'll just have to help your mother get rid of him."

"I don't understand how she could ever have gotten involved with him," Katie said.

"He's handsome and can be quite charming, I imagine. Passion can easily be confused with love. Zoe had been alone for too long, perhaps."

"He hit her. That happens to people you read about in the newspapers, not to your own mother."

"We are none of us, my dear, too far from being 'those people' you hear about on the news or read about in news-papers. I'm trying to decide if we need to go to the police about this."

Katie struggled to get beyond fear, to think more clearly. She searched Winifred's face. "Tell me he'll go away, Granny."

"He will. Now, don't you fret about this, Kathryn. When your mother calls, we won't mention him. She's working and needs a clear mind. When she doesn't come back after a few days, he'll get fed up with waiting and leave."

Winifred had seen this type of man before, smooth as silk, arrogant and mean-spirited, and she doubted he would vanish into thin air. Leaning forward, she kissed her grand-daughter's cheek. The intensity of her love for this young woman was matched only by the love she had felt for Steven. She would fight with her last ounce of strength to protect Kathryn and would die for her if necessary.

"Don't worry, darling. Your mother's not alone this time. This man can't hurt her ever again." Winifred stood and rummaged under the counter for her purse. "Enough of this. I have a small errand to run, and I'll be back in fif-teen minutes. I want you to lock the door, and don't open it for anyone. Jon has his own key. Lord, but I wish he were here."

"Where are you going?"

Winifred lied, "To the bank to sign a paper. Apparently

it got stuck under the others." As she reached the door, she turned. "Kathryn, don't let anyone in before I get back. I won't be long."

Katie nodded and watched her grandmother walk briskly down the sidewalk, then returned to the storeroom. She double-checked the back door and locked the loading dock door. Then, shivering uncontrollably, Katie sank onto a pile of bubble wrap on the floor and waited for Jon or Winifred to return.

Ignoring her dry throat and pattering heart, Winifred walked as swiftly as she could down the block and crossed the street to the police station. A young policewoman, with a square jaw and determined eyes under level brows, sat at a desk behind the wood-paneled front counter. As a man's voice crackled from the microphone in front of her, the desk officer jotted notes.

While the dispatch policewoman repeated street and address numbers into the microphone, Winifred looked about her. The entrance hallway and waiting room were paneled in dark wood, which lent the room a dreary aspect. To the rear, the entry hall opened into a waiting area with wood benches installed along the paneled wall. Most Wanted posters decorated a corkboard above the benches. Winifred walked closer for a better look. Mug shots stared down at her.

Looking at the wall of photos distressed her, yet she felt she must check whether Alan's face was among them. One handsome face sent shivers down her spine, but the man was not nearly as dark-haired or -skinned as Alan, and she returned to the desk.

"Please tell the sergeant that Mrs. Winifred Parker wishes to speak with him."

The policewoman picked up her phone, spoke into it, then motioned to a door behind her desk. As Winifred approached, the officer opened it for her.

"Thank you," Winifred said, before passing into a nondescript room with beige walls. The vinyl floor was scuffed in places and pitted from metal chair legs. Pictures of hunting dogs hung on the wall behind the sergeant's head. A gray metal file cabinet stood near the oversize desk. A large Styrofoam cup of coffee and a small plate of brownies sat near his telephone. Several files, one of them open, lay on his desk. Through a wall of windows, the sergeant—Bill Holloway, his name tag read—had a long view of Main Street in both directions. Was he related to the Ruben Holloways?

Sergeant Holloway half rose from behind his desk, motioned her to one of the two leather chairs, and offered her a brownie, which she declined. He was a solid man with good, clean features. She liked him and felt reassured, just being in this office.

"Howdy, ma'am," Holloway said in his broad drawl. "Weather's holdin' up pretty good, wouldn't you say?"

She nodded, impatient with the necessary niceties that characterized conversation in the South. Mostly it was pleasant enough, but today it annoyed her. She responded in kind, though. "Are you related to Ruben Holloway?"

"Yep." He nodded. "Ruben's my uncle. Seen 'em up at the family cemetery just last Sunday."

"That's nice. Family is so important." Then, with her hands clasped so tightly in her lap that her knuckles ached, Winifred told him about Zoe's relationship with Alan Camaro. She told him everything she knew, including the abuse, and she emphasized Olive and Ruben's protective role. Then she described Alan and told of his visit to the store this afternoon.

"Well, ma'am." Bill's fingers tapped the arm of his chair and his eyebrows met above concerned eyes. "I can see you're right worried and maybe you ought to be. But seeing as this Alan fella ain't threatened none of you, there's nothin' I can do at this point."

Winifred resisted the urge to pound his desk with her fists, to insist that he assign a policeman to stand guard at the entrance to Amorey Lane.

Suddenly Winifred's ear popped and her hearing dimmed for a moment, as if she were a passenger on an airplane making a rapid descent. Stress—and this was surely stress—could catapult her into a full-blown attack. She took several deep breaths and leaned back in the chair.

Sergeant Holloway rose, and his six-foot-four-inch, broad-shouldered frame towered reassuringly over her. "Tell you what I'll do. I'll make a few private inquiries about this Alan Camaro fella. Meanwhile, if he shows up and acts mean or sasses you or gives anyone in your family any trouble, you just give me a ring." He started to hand her his card, then wrote a number on the back. "This is my home phone, if you can't reach me here."

Feeling a trifle more hopeful, Winifred started to stand up, then raised her hand to her temple. She was dizzy. Too dizzy to make it back to the shop alone. "Sergeant, I'm feeling a bit faint. Would you please telephone my granddaughter, Kathryn, at the shop? Ask her to come immediately."

He picked up his phone and punched the number she recited to him.

Katie heard the phone ring and dashed from the storeroom, looking nervously about her as she picked it up.

"Kathryn Parker? This is Sergeant Bill Holloway, Ruben's nephew, at the police station. Your granny's been over here talkin' to me. She's lookin' mighty faint. She needs you. Better get over as soon as you can." He turned back to Winifred, who was very pale. "Can I get you somethin', ma'am? Water, a cola?"

"It's best for me not to eat or drink when this happens," Winifred said. Then she looked at him intently.

Then he asked, "Sure there's nothin' I can do for you, ma'am?"

She shook her head no, and prayed that Kathryn would get there soon.

When Katie hurried into the room, she immediately sank to her knees beside her grandmother and stroked her hand. "Just sit a while, Granny. Take deep breaths."

"I have been." Winifred's shoulders drooped, but her stomach began to settle. The dizziness began to recede. It was amazing how much she trusted this young woman. Tears flooded her eyes at the thought of all the wasted years. She breathed slowly and waited for the spell to pass.

Bill Holloway leaned against the wall, rubbed his chin with his big callused hand, and pondered the way that young woman, Katie Parker, had been able to comfort and calm her grandmother. He'd heard about Zoe Parker's daughter losing her child recently. Sad. *Never mind that the old lady's a Yankee. They're right good folk, and Zoe's a good friend of Ruben and Olive's. Nasty business, this thing with Alan Camaro, though.* He couldn't bear to tell them that over there in Salem, their home was outside his jurisdiction. He would alert the sheriff's department, though.

24

✲

SHOPPING FOR ANTIQUES

Zoe awoke in the motel in Asheville to the sound of Maudie humming in the bathroom. They'd gotten in late last night, had hamburgers at a fast-food place, checked into the motel, and crashed. They'd been too tired to talk or even to phone home. Feeling refreshed from a good night's sleep, Zoe now slipped into slacks, donned a light-weight shirt, and pulled on comfortable walking shoes.

Yesterday, near Brevard in North Carolina, they had enjoyed a visit to falls where the constant mist sent rainbows arching into the sky as the water plunged seventy feet to the pool at the bottom. Zoe and Maudie walked gingerly down the trail and narrow stairs. Halfway down, they joined several photographers on a huge boulder. Spray dampened their faces and arms, and from this vantage point the roar of water deafened them. For a time they had watched younger people roll up their pant legs and wade in the pool below. One woman pulled off her T-shirt—she wore a bra—and sank into the water to her chin.

"It's pretty here, but we're getting quite wet," Maudie said.

Zoe agreed. "Let's go back up." The trek up the steep hillside to the road seemed interminable, and by the time they reached the van, Zoe's legs were cramping. "Why would they cramp? I walk in the woods all the time," she said.

"This is much steeper than your woods," Maudie said, as she helped Zoe massage her calf muscles into a relaxed state.

Ready for the day, Maudie exited the bathroom. "Weren't those falls beautiful yesterday? I'm so glad you took me there."

"I heard someone talking about a place called Sliding Rock," Zoe said. "Water spills over a huge boulder and people slide down on the force of the water into a pool at the bottom. They say it's freezing any time of year but that kids love it. Local camps take their campers there all summer long."

Maudie shook her head. "Not for me. It makes me cold just hearing about it."

"It doesn't appeal to me either."

Soon they were helping themselves to the breakfast buffet in the lobby and discussing their plans for the day.

Zoe extracted a sheaf of notes from her purse. "West of Asheville there's a warehouse, jammed, it says here, with Early American furnishings." She reached for her coffee cup. "We'll go there first."

As they drove west, Maudie spotted the large metal building on the hillside with Packston Antiques in big black letters across the top.

Inside the building, oak and pine tables, chairs, storage chests, and hutches of all sizes were packed tight. Squeezing through the narrow aisles, the women passed footstools, hope chests, sewing tables, shaving stands, cane-back rock-ers, and hat racks. Finally, Zoe purchased a Windsor chair.

"Of all the stuff in here, why did you pick that chair?" Maudie asked.

"Because it has thirteen spindles across the back, which means it's older and more valuable than chairs with fewer spindles." Zoe, who had immersed herself in manuals and handbooks on antiques, had found them interesting.

Since it was a single purchase, the owner balked at ship-ping the chair, and they ended up stashing it in the rear of the van, wrapped in blankets reluctantly purchased from the proprietor.

"He should have given us the wrapping for the chair," Maudie muttered as they drove away.

"I agree," Zoe said. "We won't shop there again. He pretty much ignored us the whole time."

They returned to the main highway. By then it was noon and the vintage diner they happened upon was a welcome sight. The interior gleamed in red plastic and chrome. The young waitresses wore short swing skirts, puffy-sleeved white blouses, and white aprons.

"Let's see if we can find a flea market this afternoon," Zoe suggested once they were seated with menus in hand.

"Good idea," Maudie said.

Waiting for lunch, they spread the local newspaper on the tabletop. The waitress told them about a flea market in the area and provided directions to what turned out to be a hodgepodge of canvas-covered wooden booths that stretched across a dusty field. It yielded astoundingly well preserved blue and white willow pattern cups, dishes, and bowls. Zoe knew willowware. Years ago, she and her mother had occasionally shopped for serving pieces. She held up a plate to the light, then handed it to Maudie.

"You can recognize willowware by the design on it: a Chinese landscape, a bridge, monks walking across it, and doves, trees, a pagoda. Doves represent the souls of slain warriors, while the bridge offers an escape route for monks after a failed rebellion. The pagoda symbolizes shelter. Their version of a safe house, I imagine." Turning over a plate, she searched for an artist's mark that would indicate the age of the piece, but found none.

Maudie examined a water pitcher of the same pattern. "Mam had a pitcher like this once, only we didn't know that it had a name." Her mother had sobbed when her father, in a drunken rage, had smashed it to bits. Maudie hugged the pitcher to her chest. "I'm going to buy this for Mam."

From among the mishmash of items piled on tables, Zoe extracted a graceful Meissen gravy bowl. She turned the bowl over and smiled with satisfaction, knowing that the letters KPM on the bottom indicated a valuable piece.

The young woman behind the table shrugged when Zoe asked if there were other pieces to go with the gravy bowl. "I'm just minding the place till Miss Findley gets back," the young woman said. "It's her booth."

As they walked away with their purchases, Maudie said, "Mrs. Parker senior was right about you being good at finding antiques. You have a knack for spotting the best things."

"And I'm enjoying myself." Zoe stopped in her tracks and turned to Maudie. "You know, Maudie, it's been a very long time since I've enjoyed myself so much. Part of it's the fun of being an antique sleuth, but the other part is that we're getting to know one another, and it's much more fun to drive around and shop with someone, don't you think?"

"Aye, I do think it's better than traveling about alone. It's sure a pleasure getting to know you too."

By day's end, they had added several pitchers to their stash. One had a banded design and another, more valuable, had the design of a tree.

"By what name do you call these pieces?" Maudie asked.

Zoe said, "This is café au lait mochaware. It's a special type of heavy pottery with colored decorations that was sold in America in the eighteen hundreds. The older the piece, the lighter the color of the clay."

"You know so much about it all."

"I've been reading and studying pictures. I'll share the books with you. You'll soon know as much as I do."

Back at the motel, they unwrapped and examined each piece carefully before repacking it for the trip. Then they ordered in a pizza and discovered that they both liked pepperoni, onion, and mushroom toppings.

"This has been one of the nicest days I've had in America," Maudie said.

Zoe yawned. "It was a great day, and productive too. I'm so glad we came."

When Zoe called home the next morning, Katie raved about the milk glass, toby jugs, and cranberry glass she and Winifred had found at a local flea market, and Zoe spoke enthusiastically about their purchases.

Then Zoe asked, "Shall we come home? Do you need us at the shop? I think we could find more if we stayed on a bit." She was enjoying herself and loved getting to know Maudie. "There are so many terrific flea markets here, and they seem to all have valuable pieces in good condition."

"Don't hurry back," Katie said. "Keep shopping and bring back lots of wonderful items. Take some time and enjoy the fall."

Katie had wanted to say, "Please *don't* come home, not

now, not next week, not next month." But Zoe would have to return eventually, and Katie feared that Alan, who drove down Main Street every day and blew his horn to annoy them, would still be here. The moment Katie hung up, she called Olive. She told Olive about Alan's sudden appearance at the shop and how he taunted them with his daily drives past it.

"We'll be over this afternoon after we tend the animals and stay the night. I'll see Ruben brings his shotgun. We'll stop over as long you need us."

Katie heaved a sigh of relief. She told her grandmother, "The Holloways will stay with us a few nights until that man leaves town."

"I doubt he'd come out to Salem, but if it makes you feel better, why not? They're good people. I didn't think there were folks like them left in this world."

The hands of the clock had barely touched five in the afternoon when the Holloways arrived at Amorey Lane. Olive lugged a yellow-and-brown-checkered cardboard suitcase dating from the 1950s, and a sober-faced Ruben carried a shotgun slung across his shoulder and another suitcase of the same vintage. Katie settled them in her rustic bedroom it being, as Olive said, "plainer and more normal-like" than Maudie's room, and Katie moved into her mother's room.

"I've got dinner made," she said.

"Well, from now on I'll cook us supper. I'll make you some right good corn bread, and Ruben's got to have his greens."

They would divide their time between their own farm and land and Zoe's place.

25

JON AND KATIE

Katie couldn't shake the sense of impending doom that had settled over her with the appearance of Alan Camaro. Jon's presence in the shop lifted her spirits, but renovations were drawing to an end: the shelves in place, the painting done, the floors sanded, stained, and coated with a hard finish, and the face-lift of the front complete. All that remained were light fixtures to be hung, and a door that needed sanding and rehanging in the small back office.

Rain dripped from the awning, and Katie watched people dodge the drips as they hurried by. Alan drove past and honked: psychological warfare, Katie called it. What would she do when the work was done and Jon and his men packed up their gear and moved on to another job? Maybe if she confided in Jon, he would linger. Or maybe if he went to the police, they would put more stock in a man's perception of the threat.

Because she trusted Jon, Katie decided to once again

break her mother's confidence and tell him about Alan. Then she hesitated. Why? Was she afraid to become too close, too intimate, with him? When she caught him looking at her, which was more and more often now, her knees went weak. Winifred, a sharp observer of human nature, had said to her, "That boy's eyes tell me he cares a great deal for you, Kathryn. I cannot imagine why he hasn't declared himself."

Katie nearly laughed. Declare himself? Surely Granny didn't mean that Jon should formally request her permission to date her granddaughter?

"Granny, you're being silly. We're friends, that's all." Katie turned pink even as she protested. "Jon's shy." *But, darn it, why can't he ask me to have lunch with him?*

Finally Katie decided to invite Jon to have lunch with her.

With all but two of the fluorescent lights hung, Jon called lunchtime for the men. They climbed down from their ladders and removed their tool belts.

"You coming?" one asked.

"You guys go ahead," Jon replied.

Kibitzing among themselves, Jon's men walked out. Only then did Jon climb down from his ladder.

An awkward silence followed.

Winifred said, "Why don't you two young people go to the Steak House Cafeteria for lunch? You can bring me back chicken and macaroni and cheese." She wiped her hands on a flannel cloth tucked into her waistband.

Jon looked at Katie. "Would you like to do that?"

"Yes, I would."

He extended his arm to her. "My lady?"

She slipped her arm through his, and smiling, they left the shop.

*   *   *

Winifred locked the doors and watched them from the window. They looked so good together, arm in arm, ambling down the sidewalk. *They're supposed to be so modern and so open, these young people, and I had to get them started.* She chuckled. *Kathryn needs someone to love, and we could use a good man in this family.*

Her mind drifted down memory lane to her late husband, Theodore Parker. She saw herself, young again and in love with her unattainable boss. And he had noticed her too but was shy at first, like Jon. Emboldened by his frequent glances, in small ways she had let Theodore know that she was intensely aware of him and interested.

People at the office gossiped. They whispered that she was after his money and called her a social climber. How dare she flirt with Theodore Parker? Winifred recognized the envy and resentment in their eyes. How little they knew! She loved him and would have married him had he been a poor man with a limited future. But he wasn't poor, and he had a splendid future. Embedded in the equation, however, was the fact that marrying Theodore meant marrying his mother.

Winifred sighed. She'd been young and willful, and after they were married, she had made many faux pas, which had further damaged her tenuous position with her mother-in-law. Many a night, while Theodore slept, she had cried herself to sleep, until slowly she had learned how to play the game.

The lunch crowd at the Steak House Cafeteria was thinning. As they finished their desserts, Katie noticed Alan sitting kitty-corner from them, staring at her. When had he come in? The pie on her fork toppled to the plate, and her arm hit the glass, spilling her iced tea onto the table and her lap. "I'm so sorry." Flustered, she dabbed at the tea with her napkin. Alan, she could see, was grinning.

A waiter hastened over, mopped the table dry, and refilled her glass.

"You're pale as a ghost, Katie. What's wrong?" Jon asked. "Your hand's trembling."

"I'm sorry," she said. "That man's staring at me."

"I noticed. Do you know him?" Jon tipped his head in Alan's direction.

"He came to the shop the other day," she said.

"I don't like the way he's staring at you either."

"He gives me the creeps. He makes me want to dash home and take a shower."

"If you're finished, let's get out of here," Jon said.

Outside the wind gusted, sending leaves swirling in eddies alongside the street. The wind outlined Katie's breasts beneath her T-shirt and tickled her nose. She sneezed.

"Bless you." Jon reached for her hand.

Behind them, the door of the Steak House Cafeteria swung shut behind Alan. His footsteps sounded on the pavement as he sauntered behind them.

Katie walked faster and tightened her grasp on Jon's hand.

"That guy really spooks you." Jon slipped an arm about her waist. "Wanna go steady?" he asked.

"Sure." He was joking, surely, but for one sweet moment, she recalled a scene from an old black-and-white cowboy movie she had watched on AMC recently. The hero, who had actually looked like Jon, wore a holster with a gun and a wide-brimmed cowboy hat shoved back on his forehead. Reins dangling, his horse following him down a dusty street, the cowboy strode to meet a woman in a bonnet and long skirt. After mounting his horse, the cowboy bent, offered her his arm, then swept the woman up to sit before him. They had trotted off into the sunset, into happily ever after.

If only movies were real life and Jon would swoop her up and ride away with her, far from Salem and the encounter with Alan that seemed inevitable when Zoe returned.

Jon stood high on a ladder and handed up the last of the fluorescent lights to Billie, his electrician, when the front door of the shop swung open. Alan Camaro, every hair in place, hands shoved deep into the pockets of his black slacks, stepped inside.

Winifred had gone out of the shop for a moment, and Katie's heart skittered in her chest. Jon started down the ladder as Alan walked past it and pretended to stumble. With a crash, the ladder bearing Jon toppled to the floor.

Alan reached down and offered Jon a hand up. "An accident. Sorry."

"That was no accident," Katie said tightly.

All conversation stopped, and the air seemed to thicken. When Jon declined his hand, Alan's eyes narrowed. Katie rushed to Jon and knelt beside him. "Jon, are you hurt?"

Jon struggled up, clasped his right side, walked unsteadily to the counter, and leaned against it. In that moment, before Jon's men gathered around, it seemed to Katie that all their lives were as fragile as crystal goblets and destined to shatter, crushed by fear.

"I'm all right, Katie." Jon faced Alan. "This shop's not open yet." He looked at the door, indicating that Alan should leave.

Alan's affable smile faded, replaced by grim-mouthed defiance. He spread his feet and his hands tightened into fists. Then Jon's men formed a circle around him.

The bellicose look on the intruder's face evaporated. He smiled and held his hands up, palms open. "An accident, really. Sorry." Alan saluted the men, turned, and sauntered from the shop.

Katie crumpled against the counter.

Jon said, "What's going on?"

Taking him aside, Katie told him everything. "My mother's lived with the fear that he might come back some-day, and now he has. We don't know if we ought to tell her he's here and insist she stay away for a good long time."

"I'd tell her the truth," Jon said, "and tell her to remain in North Carolina. That man's capable of anything." He shook his head. "Who would ever think that Zoe would fall for a man like that? I'll be darned."

"I don't know what to do, Jon."

"Let's begin with going to the police."

"Granny's already done that. Sergeant Holloway, Ruben's nephew, said he'd do a check on Alan Camaro, but he had no cause to arrest him. I guess someone has to be killed be-fore anyone pays attention or gets involved."

"Let me see what I can do. Two complaints may carry more weight than one." Jon turned to one of the men, the one built like a wrestler, Larry. "Do me a favor. Mrs. Parker's at the florist shop down the street. Pick her up, and run her and Katie home in their car. I'll be out to pick you up." He took a step and winced. "I know Bill Holloway. I'm going over there now to talk to him about this episode."

"I'm so sorry. I'm *so* sorry," Katie said.

"Don't be upset, Katie. You didn't do anything. That bastard." Jon stopped. "Ted, finish up here, will you?"

Ted nodded.

"Chuck," Jon said, "gimme a hand to my car. You'll have to drive. First stop, Sergeant Holloway, then we'll head for

Doc Franklin's office." He turned to Katie and gave her a kiss on the cheek. "I meant what I said about us going steady. Go on home. Larry'll stay till I get there. Lock everything up. I'll be there as soon as I can."

"Olive and Ruben Holloway are staying with us," Katie said hoarsely. "Ruben brought his gun last night."

"It's that bad, eh?" Jon said. His face was grim.

Up in North Carolina, Maudie and Zoe had gone to Boone, where they'd spent the day scouring antique stores and flea markets. Now, in the motel, Zoe was unable to sleep. Lying with her head against the high back of the tub, she soaked in a hot bath and tried to make sense of the feelings of anxiety that had haunted her all day. Something was wrong at home; she felt it. Her father used to say she had inherited "the gift" from her mother. Ida always knew when something was going to happen, particularly something unpleasant.

Her mother suffered from prophetic dreams that arrived with headaches that lasted for days. She'd once told Zoe that she hated knowing things before they came to pass.

"There's going to be a dreadful earthquake," she'd said, wrapping her arms about her shoulders and shivering. Sure enough, a few days later a quake resulting in serious damage and loss of life made the headlines.

Now she wished she saw things as clearly and specifically as her mother had. Mom could home right in, pinpoint things. *I'm never sure. It's like I have half her gift. Or maybe I don't trust it in myself.*

Zoe shivered. She turned on the hot water again and slipped low in the tub. Too bad her "gift" hadn't warned her about Alan.

26

AT AMOREY LANE

"I cannot," Winifred argued with Doc Franklin on the phone.

"You must, and you will."

"I will not. I must go to the shop and help Kathryn."

"When your granddaughter picks you up off the floor, then, I'll see you at the hospital."

Silence, then a resigned voice. "I'll stay home," Winifred said. "I'll rest."

"Good. Now put Katie on the phone."

After he hung up, Doc Franklin bandaged Jon's sprained ankle and instructed him to rest and allow the bruised ribs to heal. "And stay off that ankle for a few days."

Jon nodded agreement, but when he left the office, he instructed Chuck to drive him to the house on Amorey Lane.

"Doc says you oughta go home and get off that leg," Chuck said.

"I will. But I have to go out there first."

"You're a stubborn son-of-a-gun, you know that?" Chuck said.

"Just drive."

Katie and Winifred felt safer with the Holloways living there, and now Jon was ensconced in Maudie's room. "You will stay with us," Winifred said. "We'll take care of you. You can't go home and try to hobble around an apartment by yourself."

In the morning Olive, commander of the kitchen, announced, "I'm making y'all start-from-scratch pancakes." She concentrated on beating the batter in the yellow crockery bowl.

Ruben sat comfortably at the kitchen table with the gun braced against his leg, hands folded in his lap. "Morning," he said to Katie.

"How are you today, Ruben, Olive?" Katie asked. She kissed them both on their cheeks.

One hand on her hip, the other brandishing the spatula, which dripped batter, Olive said, "I certainly hope Mrs. Parker senior is staying home today. Doc Franklin said for her to rest. And it's time you took a day off yourself, Katie girl. Stay home with your granny."

Jon limped into the room and agreed. "This leg's pretty useless, and Katie, you shouldn't go to the shop alone." He started from the kitchen. "Be back in a minute."

"You can all stay home one day and rest yourselves. Nothing but work, work, work since you got the idea to open that shop." Olive set out syrup, butter, and fresh-baked biscuits and began to flip pancakes on the griddle.

"Olive," Ruben said, rising, "I gotta get back to the haying. A storm is predicted, and my old bones tell me the weatherman's right this time. I gotta get that hay under cover, get the cows in the shed."

As he went toward the back door, Olive called after him, "Git you back here by noon sharp for dinner. Git some of those no-good cousins of yours to give you a hand with that hay and the animals."

"Can I help you with anything, Olive?" Katie asked.

A stack of golden-brown pancakes sat in the center of the table, and the comforting smell of fresh-baked biscuits permeated the room.

Raising the kitchen window, Olive yelled, "Ruben, you get back in here and get some breakfast before you go." She put her hand to her head. "Lord, Katie, I forgot he ain't ate this morning." She waved Katie to a seat, pulled out and sat in the chair next to her, and leaned close.

"I like that young man of yours, that Jon." She lowered her voice. "Ruben don't like me talking about this, but I always knew that Alan was no good. Lord, I worried so about Zoe. Little tyke of a thing, living out here with that monster. I wasn't surprised it ended like it did. I ain't surprised he's come back, either." Olive shook her head. "Terrible time that was, believe me. Terrible time." She glanced at the door and lowered her voice. "First time I seen that Alan fella, he like to scared me to dead." She wiped her hands on a towel. "Your mama was so stuck on him, I couldn't tell her what I seen in that pretty face of his." Her face grew grim. "Meanness. That's a real bad 'un. I know the likes of him. Somebody always gets hurt. Lucky your mama knew where to hide, and he took off."

"But now he's back."

"You tell your mama, when she calls, to stay put wherever she is."

Then Ruben walked in, and his wife motioned him to

the table and rose to serve him. "I near forgot you ain't had no breakfast. Shows where my mind is. Now eat up, Ruben." She turned back to Katie. "Lord, one day we came a-looking for your mama, and that Alan was screaming and cursing. I ain't heard cursing like that in all my born days. Maybe we should carry y'all off to our house and not stay here, any of us."

Katie smiled at them. "I felt safe enough last night just knowing you had your gun, Ruben."

The look Olive cast her husband surprised Katie, and she said, "Gun's no use. He's done forgot to bring bullets."

Ruben's face fell. "I'll get 'em when I go about the haying."

"Good," Olive said. "Don't you forget 'em. If that Alan shows up"—she set her hands on her hips—"you can shove that loaded barrel in his face while we wait for the police to come."

But what if Alan showed up with his own gun? They could all be wounded or dead before the police got here. "Maybe we ought to pack up and stay in a motel in Walhalla or Seneca," Katie said.

"Pack up?" Winifred, dressed in a blue silk robe and slippers, stood in the doorway. Jon stood behind her, one hand supporting her arm, his other hand pressed firmly against his side.

"Come and sit, Granny and Jon. Olive made a great breakfast."

"I am not leaving this house," Winifred said. "The only thing I ever ran from in my life was my ignorant family in Maine." She lifted her chin. "I'm a trifle weak right now, but with this cane I'm fine." It was sturdy walnut, with a solid silver knob.

"Are you sure you shouldn't have stayed in bed?" Katie asked.

"One must stand up to bullies," Winifred said.

Olive shook her head. "He's worse than a bully."

Katie agreed, and fear caused her stomach to knot.

And now the weatherman had predicted a drop in temperature and an early ice storm, as well.

"You know," Katie said, as they helped themselves to pancakes, "when I was little, the storms at night scared me. They still do." Even now, she never slept in the dark, but kept a small light on in her room.

"No need to be scared now we're here," Olive said. "You can just come crawl into bed with Ruben and me."

Katie grinned. "Thanks, Olive. I may just do that."

"We'd be right glad to have you, sugar," Olive said.

Katie said, "Not only was I scared of storms, I was scared of other things, and superstitious. I never walked under a ladder, and I was certain that black cats were bad luck. I wouldn't go away to camp in the summer because I was scared of bugs." She paused. "And I was as shy as can be when I went off to college. Meeting Hank and marrying him helped, and I started to gain more confidence. Then Laurie Ann was born and Hank left, and I couldn't afford the luxury of being shy. I realized it was up to me to advocate for my child, or I would never get the services I needed for her."

"I can't imagine you being shy, Kathryn," Winifred said.

"I was." She remembered how it had seemed like sheer magic when Hank Iverson stepped out of her dreams and asked her out in her senior year, and even more magical when several months later he proposed marriage. When he'd left, at first she had run to Zoe, but deep within her she'd known she must begin to stand on her own two feet. Hidden courage had come to the fore, and she had developed into a fierce advocate for her child, demanding the best care, schooling—whatever the city, the county, the state could provide. She'd become so versed in advocacy for the handicapped that other parents sought her out for advice and information.

Winifred's words pulled Katie back into the present, with pancakes growing cold on her plate. "Things were going so well at the shop, and out of nowhere comes this awful Alan."

Katie shivered. "We can't let Mom come home. Maybe if she stays away, he'll give up and leave."

Clasping her hands in prayer, Olive said, "I'm gonna pray on this." Her lips moved silently for a moment, then she lowered her hands and smiled. "The arm of the Lord is mighty. We'll put our trust in the Lord, sugar."

27

BILTMORE ESTATE

Back in Asheville, with the temperature in the mid to high sixties, Zoe and Maudie had decided to take a day off to tour the Biltmore House gardens. They drove through the grounds past tangled clumps of ferns and majestic evergreens; maroon- and plum-leafed dogwoods and fire-bright shrubs glowed in patches of open sunshine.

They parked below the walled garden and strolled past sweeping beds of chrysanthemums: orange, rust, yellow, and stunning vermilion. Ornamental grasses grew along the gray stone walls, some tall as Maudie, some short with rust red stems.

"I was here with Steven once in May," Zoe said softly. "There were roses everywhere. I remember their fragrance. In April it's azaleas, some the color of your hair, Maudie."

They followed the road that bordered the French Broad River, then drove across a narrow stone bridge to the lake. Reflected in the water were peach, gold, and mauve trees.

The sounds of birds filled the air, and as their dark bodies rose, their tapered wings beat against the cerulean blue sky.

By a willow tree near the water's edge, Zoe opened their folding chairs and set out the sandwiches they had brought along. Across the lake on a hilltop, the gray stone walls and towers of Biltmore House looked like a fabled Bavarian castle.

"It's been such a nice and productive trip," Zoe said. "We've gotten so much done, yet I hate to go home."

Maudie popped open the tab of her cola and drank. "It's lovely here. Reminds me of home. 'Tis one old castle after another in Ireland, you know."

They ate and watched a family of ducks waddle onto the edge of the bank, slip smoothly into the water, and glide away. Maudie studied a line of ants carrying off tiny bits of crumbs. "Hardworking wee chaps." Zoe smiled. They watched the determined bugs maneuver around obstacles, over obstacles, retrieving whatever they dropped, moving ever onward.

"I remember a childhood story about ants, about how industrious they are. I used to wonder if ants think like we do, or if it's instinct that drives them," Zoe said.

"You've always been a thoughtful one, haven't you?" Maudie asked.

"I guess I am." A twig fell, rippling the colors reflected in the water. "I guess being an only child, with parents who discussed every issue you can imagine, made me thoughtful and serious. Too serious for a child, maybe." Zoe stretched her arms above her head. "It's so peaceful here. I could stay forever."

"Forever is a long time. Forever is boring."

"You're practical and down-to-earth," Zoe said. "I wish I were like that."

"You're fine the way you are. Maybe we're opposites, but opposites can be great friends." Maudie rubbed her arms. "Notice it's chilling down?"

"It sure is," Zoe said.

They stood, folded their chairs, repacked the basket, and returned it all to the van. Minutes later they stopped at the winery and gift shop, where Zoe chose a bottle of chardonnay for Katie, a floral-pattern umbrella for Olive, and a jar of Biltmore Estate grape preserves with an elegant label for Winifred. Maudie bought a teacup with Biltmore House painted on one side for herself, a bright blue silk scarf for her sister, and a book with glorious photographs of Asheville and Biltmore Estate for her mam.

28

❧❦❧

NOT HERE. NOT NOW.

In Salem the next morning, sleet beat against the windows as the wind turned to a driving gale. Trees swayed and moaned; doors and windows rattled. The extreme drop in temperature turned the rain into ice that hung from leaves and branches. On the radio, a somber-voiced announcer reported that cars and trucks were skidding on black ice on the roads. Power failed in some areas, and in Walhalla a child broke his leg sliding down an icy slope behind his house on the top from a metal garbage can. Business-as-usual came to a halt.

Katie was surprised that the phone worked, but not surprised when Olive's voice said, "We can't get up our road, sugar. Ice is forming on the ground. We got no electric. You okay?" She had gone with Ruben to help with finishing the hay and to make sure their animals were dry and safe.

"We're fine. Jon's here. We still have power. Don't even try to get back here. Are you all right?"

"Ruben's done made us a right warm fire in our fire-place. Remember, your mama's got plenty of firewood in that old shed behind the kitchen, if you need it."

The fireplace in the den used propane gas, but as a backup, Zoe had installed a potbellied wood stove in the kitchen.

"We'll be fine," Katie said. "You take care of yourselves, Olive, and thank you and Ruben for staying here with us."

"Why, sugar, that's what neighbors do. I wish we could be with you tonight. We'll be back soon as we can."

As she hung up, Katie wondered about the weather in North Carolina, and where her mother and Maudie were. The thin layer of ice on the patio had fractured, and as a ray of sunshine found its way through the clouds, the ice glis-tened, throwing off flashes of light. Then the sun vanished and the world went gray.

From a drawer in the hutch, Katie selected a sunflower yellow tablecloth and three napkins and began to set the kitchen table. She chose plates that Zoe had hand-painted with wildflowers, then added blue water tumblers. Using a majolica teapot as a centerpiece, Katie filled it with chrysanthemums she had gathered only yesterday from the garden. The teapot was heavily decorated with fruit, flow-ers, birds, and a twisting tree. She stood back. The table looked bright and cheery and inviting.

Then Katie set out all the ingredients for Mexican omelets: eggs from her mother's six chickens and spinach, tomatoes, green pepper, and onions grown in Zoe's kitchen garden, which had surely been withered by frost. On the counter she placed olives, bits of ham, and chunks of cheese. With a spring in her step, she walked down the hall and poked her head into Winifred's room. "I'm making omelets."

Propped in bed, her sketchpad open across her knees,

Winifred looked up. She closed the pad, as she did whenever anyone came upon her sketching. This latest sketch could serve as a wanted poster for Alan Camaro, she remembered him so clearly. She smiled at Katie, thinking how much like Steven she was. "I am absolutely ravenous this morning. I'll get up and dress and come to the kitchen."

Katie knocked on Jon's room. "Breakfast. Mexican omelets?"

"I'm just about to take a shower. Give me ten minutes."

"Okay."

Ten minutes later Winifred entered the kitchen, with Jon close behind. "My, how cheerful," her grandmother said.

"This is a treat." Jon pulled out a chair for Winifred.

"You've set a charming table, my dear." Winifred picked up a plate and studied it. "Do you know who painted this?"

"Mom did."

"Zoe?" A look of surprise crossed Winifred's face, followed by one of appreciation. "Really? A hidden talent."

"Mom's good at decorating pottery. She used to paint pictures."

"Interesting. And that outrageous teapot," Winifred continued. "My Lord, how many years has it been since majolica earthenware's turned up on any table I've sat at? Whimsical. Popular in the eighteen hundreds. We must find some majolica pieces for the shop."

"Maybe Mom'll bring some back," Katie said. "By the way, Olive called. They're iced in."

"The ice can be pretty bad on those narrow, twisting roads." Jon took a gulp of coffee and sat back. "Well, we can't get to Walhalla."

"Good day for gin rummy," Winifred said.

"The weatherman says that everyone should stay put. Everything's a mess, with car accidents and trucks in ditches," Katie said.

"Well, my work ethic allows time off in weather like this," Jon said.

"I've always hated," Katie said, suddenly serious, "that you can be on the verge of emotional collapse, yet it's not okay to your boss, or even to yourself, to stay at home unless you're sick or the weather is foul."

Winifred said, "I've been guilty of coming down on employees and questioning if they were really sick when they took off a day."

"That's one reason I work for myself," Jon said. "Nobody can dictate when or how I work."

"You're your own slave driver, right?" Katie asked.

They laughed and set to eating, and when she was finished, Winifred eased up from her chair and carried her empty plate to the sink. Returning to the table, she rested both hands on Katie's shoulders. "That was delicious, Kathryn, dear. A treat. There are so many things to love about you, and you're a gourmet cook too." She patted her granddaughter's shoulders. "My bed and book await me."

A deep quiet fell on the kitchen. Katie waved away Jon's offer to help stack the dishes in the dishwasher. When she rejoined him at the table, she said, "I want you to know how much I appreciate your being here. I'm always afraid that *he* might show up."

"How long will your mother be gone?"

"Mom said they were going to Micaville, northeast of Asheville, and to a place called Spruce Pine. Then they'll go to Johnson City and Jonesborough in Tennessee. They've had a hitch put on the van and rented a ten-foot U-Haul."

Jon sipped his coffee. "You need to tell her about Alan. She should stay away until he leaves the area."

"If he leaves, she'd never have to know," Katie said.

"What's the point of hiding this?"

"She's been through enough with him."

"Things are better out in the open, Katie."

She looked away. Were things in the open with them? Did he feel about her the way she did about him? He had joked about going steady that day in Walhalla and said nothing since. But would he be here with them if he didn't care? He was a good man, and reliable. But Jon was a man who did not need to be in love with a woman to offer his help if she were in trouble.

"Well." Jon set both palms against the edge of the table as if he was about to get up.

"Don't go, please, Jon."

He pushed back his chair on two legs. "I'm not going anywhere. I'm not going to leave you out here alone. If Alan shows, I can handle him."

You're bandaged and limping, Katie thought. She took comfort in the knowledge that the doors and window were secured. If anyone tried to break in, they would hear him and have time to dial for help.

Jon patted his stomach. "I'm afraid I overate."

Again, silence. Why? They usually had so much to chat about. The tingle in her spine, the warm liquid feeling in the pit of her belly when she looked at him scared her. She couldn't handle rejection, especially so soon after losing Laurie Ann. She fought the wild impulse to shove back her chair and slide onto his lap. It seemed a shame to be so young and to have no love or affection from a man in her life. Jon appealed to her. Whatever happened between them, it was nice to know that she could still tingle.

Katie leaned across the table. Their conversations had been light and easy, filled with jokes and laughter, but she knew little about Jon's life or his deepest feelings. "Why did you come to this area, Jon? Where were you born? Do you have a family?" She repressed the urge to ask if he had ever been married or had kids somewhere.

He chuckled. "In what order do you want the answers?"

"Tell me about your family."

"My family. Well, I was born in Idaho, a change-of-life baby to older folks. No siblings. Dad died when I was nineteen. I was needed at home, so I quit the state college and enrolled at the local community college for building trades. That was practical, and it pleased my mother. She never understood my desire for a doctorate in anthropology. I took care of her until she died two years ago."

"Your mom was lucky to have you."

"I was lucky. She was a wise and good woman, a great mother. We weren't wealthy, and she needed me. I guess I needed her too."

Zoe had said to Katie, "Pay attention to the way a man treats his mother. That's how he'll treat you." Katie's heart grew warm, listening to Jon. "Do you like your work, Jon?"

"Most of the time. I like people, like being involved with them. I think of each project as a joint venture between me and the customer." He leaned forward. "I pay close attention to body language and what people do, rather than what people actually say. I try to figure out, early on, how they're gonna be to work with.

"Take your mom. Now, that lady's afraid to get involved. You get the message fast: don't violate my space, and don't touch me. With her, I had to resist my natural impulse to draw the client into the project. A polite distance was what she wanted. After that first day when she fell into the pond, your mother hardly came near the summerhouse while I was working, and if she did, I'd greet her respectfully and go on working."

Katie smiled. "Mom told me about that. She felt so embarrassed about falling into the pond, but by the time you finished the summerhouse, she'd grown comfortable with you. She trusts you. She likes it that you're doing the shop for us."

"I like your mom too." He turned his spoon over and over before setting it on the table. "Zoe's cautious, like a doe you happen upon in the woods."

"You're right. She's hard to get to know." Katie poured herself another half cup of coffee and offered him some.

He shook his head. "I can see why she'd be gun-shy, after her experience with this Alan."

Katie switched the topic back to Jon. "So how'd you end up in Walhalla?"

"Providence? Accident? After a winter to freeze your buns off in Idaho, I sold the family estate, which was comprised of one small brick house and five acres, packed my tools in my truck, and headed south. The truck broke down as I was coming down the mountain from Cashiers. The wrecker hauled me to a garage off Main Street in Walhalla. They had to order parts, so I stayed a couple of days. I got to chatting with Abed at the Steak House one afternoon, and he made a good case for my staying a while. He's been great. He sent me my first three jobs." He looked at her and his eyes grew soft. "I'm glad I'm here. I like the area. Couldn't find better people anywhere." He reached across the table and laid his hand on hers. "Especially the Parker women."

Her face grew serious. "And now you're out here with a bandaged rib and a sprained ankle because some sleazy character my mother knew showed up out of nowhere."

Jon smiled. "The rib only hurts when I stretch a certain way."

Katie's eyes clouded. "Jon, do you think he'll come here?"

The smile on his face faded. "No. I don't."

Through the slightly open kitchen window, a gust of wind delivered a whiff of wood smoke from some distant chimney. Katie's brows drew together and she moved to close and lock the window. As suddenly as it had come up, the wind died down, and the driving sleet ceased. For a moment there was a clarity to the air that snapped details into focus. Etched in light, the icicle-jeweled trees sparkled against a deep blue sky wedged between steel gray clouds.

"How lovely it is, though the ice is so dangerous," she said as Jon joined her. "Look at the patio. All ice and debris blown from heaven knows where: grass cuttings, an old paper cup, that dogwood branch."

"That's what we can do today—clean up the patio."

"Oh, sure." She punched his shoulder lightly. "What about Doc Franklin's order to rest?" She turned and walked to the hutch, opened the bottom drawer, and removed a Monopoly game and a game of Clue. She held them up. "Which one?"

"Monopoly."

She set the box on the table.

"Monopoly's a poor substitute for what I'd rather we do," he said.

"And what's that?"

Slowly he came to her, tousled her hair, and drew her gently to him.

She ached for him, but this was hardly the moment, with Winifred reading just down the hall. "Not here. Not now, Jon. Later."

He kissed her softly. "Yes, later."

Katie set out the game board. "I'll take the shoe. What do you want?"

"The hat." He looked at her with a tender smile. "Later?"

"Later." Feeling totally happy, she threw the dice.

29

THE ATTACK

Katie and Jon played Monopoly until she owned nearly
all the land and he paid rent at every throw of the dice.
Good-naturedly, he threw up his hands and declared bank-
ruptcy. Lunch was spaghetti with meat sauce from a jar. Jon
chopped onions and green peppers, which they added to
the sauce. He was as fastidious in the kitchen as he was at
work, where he swept up after himself and placed his tools
neatly in his toolbox at the end of the day. Winifred
remained in her room resting, and Katie brought her lunch
on a tray. That afternoon, Jon trounced Katie at gin
rummy.

"You'd be a good match for Granny."

"I'll challenge her sometime," he replied.

Olive called at six o'clock. "Ruben tried to take the truck
out," she said. "Sun never did come out over this way, so
the ice don't melt, and he's stuck in a ditch halfway up our
hill."

"We're fine," Katie assured her.

After an early dinner of leftovers—cold chicken and potato salad from the night before—Jon and Katie ended up in the den sitting before the fireplace. Although the freezing rain had ceased, the sky was banked with threatening gray clouds. The wind played tricks, hiding, then rushing out with a roar. Jon drew her close on the love seat. "Tell me about your little girl," he said.

Katie's eyes misted. "I loved her so much. Laurie Ann was so helpless. I'd look at her and just know deep inside of me that there was an intelligence trapped inside of her that she had no way of expressing."

"How frustrating for both of you. How sad that she could never tell you how much she loved you, as I'm sure she did."

Katie nodded. If she began to cry, she would never stop.

Jon waited for her to collect herself, and when she seemed in control of her feelings, he cradled her hand in both of his.

Good hands, she thought. *Firm yet yielding, like a willow tree. A good man.*

"Jon," she said, "that was nice, what you said about Laurie Ann loving me. A lot of people saw her as hopeless. They pitied me. Many people wondered why I didn't put her in a home. Sometimes I thought Mom felt like that, but she never said so." Katie snuggled into his arms. "I couldn't do that," she said. "There were moments when I felt her frustration so acutely, I hurt for her. All I could do was hold Laurie Ann and love her."

He waited a moment. "Your husband?"

"When she was born, he couldn't deal with it. We divorced."

"I'm sorry." Jon stroked her hair.

She reached for and kissed his suntanned hand. "It was long ago," she whispered.

Jon drew her closer. They slid from the love seat to the floor, his arm about her, her head against his chest, their feet stretched toward the fire. He placed his lips on hers and their kiss deepened.

But it was not to last. A moment later they drew apart, alarmed by the crackle of gravel in the driveway. Moments later, a firm knock sounded at the front door.

"Who's there?" Jon called when they reached the door.

"Sergeant Holloway from the Walhalla Police. Thought I'd stop and check on you folks."

Katie flung the door wide. "Sergeant Holloway, I'm so glad to see you."

"How you folks doin'?" he asked.

"We're fine."

"How's Mrs. Parker feelin'? I was right worried about her the other day in my office, when she took a spell."

"She's better. She's resting, and I'm sure she'll be fine in a few days. Come on in. Can I get you something?" Katie asked.

Bill's reassuring presence filled the doorway. Dressed in jeans and a ribbed sweater under a leather jacket, his hair windblown, his cheeks and nose red from the cold, he looked younger than in his uniform. "No, ma'am. I'd best be gettin' along. I'm on my way to help Ruben get that old truck of his outta that ditch. Olive's been givin' him the devil for goin' out when the road's so icy." He shuffled from leg to leg. "Well, I gotta be off now. Best to your granny."

"Thanks for stopping by. Tell Olive we're fine."

She watched the policeman step over the dogwood branch on the patio and felt a pang when he revved up his solid four-by-four Ford and crunched down the road. A flash of something shiny in the bushes off the driveway caught her eye. Dismissing it, she closed and locked the door.

They hadn't moved ten feet toward the den when the door-knob rattled, a scratching noise was heard, and the door opened. They turned and were horrified to see Alan Ca-maro, dark and sinister in black, standing in the doorway.

"Aren't you going to invite me in?" he asked. The smirk on his face terrified Katie.

"How did you get in?"

He waved a long, slim tool. "There's isn't a lock around I can't open." He closed the door and locked it behind him.

Jon took a determined step toward him. "Get out of here."

A black handgun was leveled at Jon's chest. "Where is she. Where's Zoe?"

Katie's legs turned rubbery as she stared at the gun. When he was sure Zoe was not here, would he rob the place and leave, or hold them hostage until she returned? And then what? There'd be no time for warning, for Zoe to run, to hide. The image of a graveyard flashed before her eyes: six headstones with a sign above the entrance that read Amorey/Parker Cemetery. She clung to Jon's arm.

Pools of water, bits of melting ice, formed around Alan's well-shined ebony shoes. "Where's Zoe?" he asked again.

Katie imagined a scenario: the wet tile floor was slippery. Alan would slip and fall, Jon would grab the gun, she would dial 911.

"Okay, baby," Alan said. "Let go of your boyfriend." He motioned with his head. "Into the kitchen, fast, both of you."

Once in the kitchen, he pulled a chair away from the

table and said to Jon, "My business isn't with you. I don't need you interfering. Sit down. You, Katie, tie him up."

Katie shook her head and drew back. Her eyes fell on the thin, coiled rope hanging from a silver clip attached to his belt, and she shivered.

With his gun leveled at Jon, Alan grasped her wrist and yanked Katie forward.

"Ouch! You're hurting me!" Katie said.

"You think that hurts? Just wait. Tie him up—tight, now. We don't want your boyfriend making some stupid move and getting himself shot, do we?"

Please, God, she prayed, *let this be a dream.*

"Do it," Alan ordered, his voice cold and harsh.

Katie looked at Jon, who nodded slightly. *He must have a plan.* Functioning like a robot, Katie took the rope Alan thrust at her.

Suddenly Jon leaped from the chair and threw himself at Alan. The gun fired into the ceiling. Alan kicked out and the toe of his shoe smashed into Jon's injured ribs, bringing him to his knees.

Alan pressed the gun to Jon's temple. "Now, you listen to me, asshole. Get back in that chair or I'll put a slug in your gut and let you bleed to death. And you—" He grabbed and twisted Katie's arm. She gave a sharp cry. "Tie him up, dammit."

Katie could not look at Jon as she wound the rope around and around his body, fastening him to the ladder-back chair. "I'm sorry," she whispered. Her hands and body trembled violently.

Alan moved behind Jon and whipped out a handkerchief from his back pocket. "Bite me and I'll put a bullet in her neck." He nodded toward Katie. Jon opened his mouth to accept the gag that would silence him.

"Please; don't hurt him. What do you want? Money?" Katie managed.

"Money? Most assuredly, we do not hoard cash in this house," a voice from the doorway said.

With a sneer, Alan snatched Katie about the waist, jammed his gun into her back, and turned to face Winifred Parker.

Winifred stood erect in the doorway, her eyes burning coals of anger, her knuckles white from gripping the silver head of her cane. Leaning against the wall, she unclasped the treasured pearls from about her neck. "Take these," she said. "They're worth ten thousand dollars. Let my grand-daughter go."

"Where's Zoe?" he asked. "I got business with her." Any semblance of charm or politeness had vanished; now a brute with malevolent eyes and a gun in his hand stood in the kitchen.

"Zoe's out of town."

"Well then, old biddy, I'll just wait here for her, and I'll have those baubles." He thrust Katie forward, the gun poking into her back. "Get 'em."

With quavering hands, Katie took the pearls from her grandmother and handed them to Alan. He shoved them carelessly into his back pocket.

Winifred winced.

Alan kept his gun trained on Katie. "I don't bargain," he said. "Now, both of you, walk."

A gun at one's back is persuasion enough, but still he held Katie in a tight grasp. He knew exactly where the den was, where the lights were. "Sit down." He shoved Katie into one of the love seats and motioned for Winifred to join her.

Grandmother and granddaughter pressed close. Winifred

held Katie's hand tight in hers. Concentration was hard. *Dear God, please don't let an attack of Ménière's start now.* It occurred to her that this might be her final hour. Perhaps if she offered him money . . . Everyone can be bought, her mother-in-law and her husband had believed. Just find their emotional Achilles' heel—greed, or need, or revenge. What would it take to buy off this madman?

Why, Katie wondered, with Jon tied up in the kitchen, did Alan need to threaten them with a gun? Was there something she could do or say to appease him, so that he would at least allow her grandmother to go to her room? Perhaps if he knew how sick she was. Her mind raced, trying to think of some ruse, some trick to divert him, to kick away his gun. But Jon had tried that and failed. Katie's heart sank.

"It's damn cold in here." Alan rubbed his right shoulder. "Don't you know you've got central heat in this house? Damn control's in the hall still, I imagine?" He took a step toward the door as if to leave them to raise the temperature on the heat gauge, then swung about on his heel, and headed for the fireplace. "Tricked ya. Thought you had me there, eh?"

"What is it exactly that you want?" Winifred asked.

Alan slouched against the fireplace wall. "Zoe. She belongs to me. I've come to claim what's rightfully mine." He looked at their appalled faces, burst into raucous laughter, and slapped his thigh. He stepped toward them, leaned forward, and lifted Katie's chin. Venom lurked behind his pitch-black eyes. "What the hell. You mean the bitch never told you?"

Repulsed by his touch, Katie shoved his hand away.

Alan's laughter filled the room. "Easy, baby, you don't want to piss off your stepdaddy now, do you? That's right,

I'm your stepfather. Your ma and me, we tied the knot. We hardly had time to celebrate when she up and ran away, damn her." His eyes clouded. "Now, why would she do that?" He stared at them and took a step forward. The gun waved crazily in his hand. "Answer me. Why would she do that?"

Katie ventured a hesitant, "I don't know."

Alan paced. His eyes never left them. "Don't none of you move." He lit a cigarette. The room filled with acrid puffs of smoke. Winifred coughed and coughed again. He blew one last puff in her direction, then stubbed out the cigarette on a rosewood table. The blackened wood smoked, giving off the sharp acrid odor of its lacquered finish.

Alan rubbed his right shoulder again, then returned to stand near the fireplace. The fire's red glow against his dark clothing reminded Katie of Dracula.

A clap of thunder shook the house as the wind rattled the windows, and rain struck the glass. Then the lights went out. Katie tensed to rise and felt Winifred's hand holding her back.

Alan lit his cigarette lighter and held it close to his face, distorted and twisted in the flicker of flame. "Move and I'll shoot you dead on the spot."

Katie felt Winifred tighten her hold on her arm. Lightning brightened the room for a moment, amplifying the bizarre gothic atmosphere and Alan's rage-filled face. Then the lights came on, and Katie saw him blink and blink again and his right shoulder slump. Maybe he's sick, she thought hopefully, or he's getting tired.

"You don't need to hold us at gunpoint, Mr. Camaro, if what you want is a divorce and a reasonable settlement," Winifred said. "I'm sure Zoe—"

"What the hell do you know about what I want?" Alan

appeared outraged. "All my life, women've taken advantage of me, starting with my ma." His voice was hard, his eyes a mix of rage and sheer meanness. "A parade of men in and out of the damn house. 'Get him a drink, Alan.' 'Run and buy condoms.' 'He wants coffee, Alan. Get it. Fast.' Drunken bitch in heat's what my ma was. Afterward she'd say she was sorry and cry, and next thing you know, she'd have another jock between those filthy sheets." He spat into the fire. "Damn, I hated her."

His eyes fell on a framed photo of Zoe on the mantel over the fireplace, and for a moment his face softened. He caressed the edge of the frame with one finger. "Now, Zoe here was one sweet, compliant woman. You know how she is." He grinned knowingly and glanced at Katie who, not knowing what else to do, nodded. "Looked like Ma, small and delicate, only Zoe was a quiet one, obliging and docile." His voice hardened again and he glowered at Katie. "Zoe did what I said. The minute I saw her, I knew I had to have her." His chin tilted up. "I know how to butter up a dame. She was ripe and tumbled right into the sack."

He glared at Zoe's picture and for a brief moment desire smoldered in his eyes. "She was real good in bed." He smirked. "But she started asking questions: 'Where you going?' 'Tell me about yourself.' Making demands: 'Take me out for dinner. She started expecting things from me, just like Ma did. I had to discipline her, keep her obedient, you know?"

Any hope of reasoning with someone this dangerous and unpredictable vanished. Katie's breath came rapidly. They were trapped and powerless and terrified. Could her grandmother tolerate this stress? What would the maniac do if she collapsed?

Suddenly Alan hurled Zoe's picture to the stone hearth,

and glass shattered. "Damn," he said, kicking pieces of glass into the fireplace with his toe and smiling crookedly. He picked up a piece of glass, fingered it, and studied Katie. "You a hot little number like your ma?" He threw the glass fragment to the floor. Two quick strides brought him to stand in front of Katie. "Bet you're a hot little number, eh, baby? Give your new pa a kiss." He bent toward her.

Katie's fist met his nose.

Alan covered his face for a moment, and blood trickled between his fingers. The gun thudded to the carpet. In an instant, Katie was up and running.

But he was too fast for her. His arm circled Katie's waist and crushed her to him even as he bent to retrieve the gun.

"Let me go!" Katie screamed. "Let me go!"

Laughing, Alan twisted her to face him, bent her back, and clamped his mouth to her neck, the barrel of the gun pressing against her back. His eyes glazed, he seemed more animal than human.

"No! Stop!" Katie fought him with fists as useless as a baby's against his hard muscles. She twisted, squirmed, and tried unsuccessfully to wedge her knee into his groin. That further enflamed him. The buttons of her blouse clinked against a wall as he ripped them away and buried his face in her breasts.

Sweat dripped from Winifred's face, stained her armpits, and dampened her blouse between her breasts. It was all happening too fast. Kathryn striking out at the monster, running, being overtaken and attacked. Waves of nausea threatened to incapacitate Winifred. She could hear the monster's breathing, raspy, hard; he was a rabid creature intent on hurting her Kathryn. Well, not so long as she breathed.

Summoning all her courage and stamina, Winifred heaved herself up from the sofa. Alan was bent over Katie, his shoulders straining, muscles knotted hard. His body pressed into her, and Kathryn's blouse hung in tatters. The monster's mouth was fastened to her neck even as he reached to unzip his pants. Kathryn, gasping for breath, continued to pummel his chest with her fists and screamed for him to stop, to let her go.

Lust is his Achilles' heel. He has no eyes or ears for me, or anything else now. Now! Strike now! Winifred drew the sleeve of her bathrobe across her face to clear the sweat that filmed her eyes. *I must not fall. I must do this. I will do this.*

With the grit and resolution of a lifetime, Winifred's arms rose like the powerful wings of a giant condor. The hard silver knob of her cane struck Alan's head with a loud crack. Blood gushed, streaking his thick, dark hair, and the gun clattered to the floor. He sank to his knees, clutching his head with both hands. Then he toppled forward onto the rug. Blood trickled from his nose, down his cheek, and along his neck onto the Persian carpet.

Terrified and confused, Kathryn turned toward her grandmother, covering her breasts with both hands. Her face was streaked with tears.

On the floor, Alan twisted and raised his head. Black eyes, puzzled, then enraged, met Winifred's. "Goddamned stinking bitch," he muttered.

The gun lay close by his hand. One lunge and he would have it.

As he struggled toward the gun, Winifred lifted the cane with shaking hands to strike his right shoulder, to incapacitate him. But the blow missed his shoulder and struck his head, the sound of a hammer on stone. His body flattened, and he lay still.

Enormous silence filled the room, broken a moment later by a thud from the kitchen. Jon had freed himself and staggered into the room, one hand pressed against his side, the other brandishing a long kitchen knife. He stared from Katie, to Winifred, to Alan, and back to Winifred. Katie, huddled in a corner of the room, wept with her head between her knees, her arms covering her chest.

Winifred stared at Jon with unseeing eyes, uttered a cry, and crumbled to the floor.

30

❧❧❧

THE AFTERMATH

From the corner, Katie lifted her head and looked about her. All was still, too still. Something had happened—what? On the hearth, broken glass sparkled like diamonds. Then she saw Alan lying facedown on the carpet, his blood soaking her mother's rug. Crumpled against the love seat, her grandmother lay with her eyes closed, her head toppled forward. Oh, God, had Alan killed her?

Low keening sounds issued from Katie's lips as she staggered to her feet and made her way, stepping over Alan's body on the floor beside Winifred. She cradled her grandmother's head in her lap and rocked back and forth.

Jon was bending over Alan's still form. "He's dead. I'm going to call 911 and Dr. Franklin," he said.

"Dead?" Katie felt numb and terrified. None of this seemed real.

A dark stain seeped in an ever-widening patch around the body. The beautiful Oriental was irretrievably destroyed.

The lights flickered, went off, and come on again. The fire flickered in the fireplace. Was Alan really dead? Fearfully, Katie stared at the body on the floor for signs of life. He was tricky—maybe he was faking, intending to spring up and shoot them all. She could see his gun, black and shining in a pool of blood. His hand rested close to it; she must get it. Gently laying Winifred's head on a pillow, Katie crawled toward the gun.

"Don't touch it." Jon kneeled beside Alan, his fingers once more on Alan's neck. "He's dead, and you don't want your fingerprints on that gun." Jon pressed his hands against his own ribs.

Winifred stirred and moaned.

"It's over, Granny," Katie whispered. "It's over." Was it, really? She looked at Jon to confirm her words.

He nodded. "Yes, it's over. The bastard's dead."

Katie began to shiver uncontrollably. Jon removed his long-sleeved shirt and helped her to shove her arms into it, then he wrapped her in his arms and held her.

Someone pounded loudly on the front door. "Salem Fire Rescue," a man's voice called.

"In here," Jon replied.

The front door pushed open, and four EMT-firefighters in helmets, heavy jackets with reflective stripes on the sleeves, and high rubber boots walked into the den.

"Granny, help's here, thank God," Katie said.

"Let the EMTs work," a tall man said. "They need space."

Two of the men went immediately to Winifred while another checked Jon, and yet another gently escorted Katie to an ambulance in the driveway. There a female EMT put a blood pressure cuff on her arm. Her partner questioned Katie as he checked her arms, legs, back, neck, and throat for scratches and bruises. "Does anything hurt? Did you hit your head? Were you unconscious at any time? Are you on any medications? Do you have any conditions we should know about? Tell us what happened."

A police officer stood close at hand, a notebook and pen in hand.

"He broke into the house," Katie said between sobs. "He tied up Jon in the kitchen. He attacked me."

"Did he rape you?" the women asked.

"No, but he was trying to. My grandmother hit him with her cane. Then he was on the floor. He was bleeding and reaching for his gun." She shuddered. "That's when my grandmother hit him again. Then she collapsed."

One of the EMTs tore open an instant ice pack and placed it on Katie's back, where nasty bruises had begun to swell.

At that moment, through the small crowd of firemen, EMTs, policemen, cameramen, and reporters in the driveway, a policeman escorted Ruben and Olive Holloway to Katie's side.

"Her neighbors," he said to another policeman by way of explanation. Katie buried herself in Olive's wide arms and broad, soft chest.

"If she isn't hurt bad, and doesn't need to go to the hospital, they're gonna take her to their place over on Holloway Road," the policeman said.

"Doesn't look like she has to go to the hospital," the female EMT said.

While Katie had been relating what she could of the events of the evening, Jon had been carried out on a stretcher to another ambulance, questioned, and ministered to by EMTs, who had cut off his T-shirt to examine his side. "Where were you when this happened?"

"I was tied up in the kitchen. When he first came in I tried to get his gun, but he shot at me and kicked me in the side, right where I'd been injured in a fall. The bullet's probably still in the ceiling."

"Let's get him on a backboard," one of them said to his partner. "And to the hospital."

Back in the den, another team worked on Winifred, who lay with her eyes closed, looking more dead than alive. They took her vital signs, lifted her onto a gurney, and hooked her up to a cardiac monitor, then took her by ambulance to the hospital in Seneca.

Another team had focused on Alan. One person began CPR while others checked his vitals and focused on his head injuries. After a time others arrived with a body bag, and his body was zipped up, put on the stretcher, and carried away.

Several hours later, when the forensics team had collected and removed evidence—the bullet shot into the kitchen ceiling, the gun, Winifred's cane, the shattered glass, and other items—the house was secured against break-in and the driveway emptied of all vehicles.

"You're comin' back to the house with us, sugar." Olive put her arm around Katie's shoulders and in the light from the fire department trucks led her down the hill to their car, which was parked on the main road. "The policeman who brought us to you, he gave me a name of someone who'll come right out and clean the place, so it'll look good as new."

Katie heard her voice but not the words. "Why can't I stay at home?"

"'Cause the place has gotta be cleaned up good first."

Katie leaned against Olive. "What about Granny? She needs me now. Oh, Olive, will she be all right? She was already sick, you know. She saved me, maybe saved my life too. Where did she find the strength?"

"Love and fear lend us strength where we thought we had none," Ruben said.

"Amen to that. Winifred's safe and sound at the hospital by now, and Jon too," Olive assured Katie. "And Doc Franklin's with 'em, I'm sure. Don't you worry, now. They'll be all right. You're gonna be all right too."

Katie was crying softly.

"You go ahead and cry, sugar. After what y'all have been through, a good cry can't do a bit of harm."

"I was so terrified, Olive."

"There ain't none of us ignorant of fear." Olive squeezed Katie's hand gently. "When we get home, I'll run you a nice, hot bath."

"I don't want a bath."

"What can I do for you, then, sugar?"

"Just be with me."

"That I will," Olive said.

31

TELEVISION NEWS

Olive made tea for herself and Katie, and coffee for Ruben. As they sipped in silence, she said, "Now, sugar, don't you keep worrying about your granny. She's gonna be just fine, and your mama'll be here soon."

Katie jerked so fast, she spilled her tea. "How do you know that? Did she call?"

"No. I feel it in here." Olive tapped her chest.

Ruben flipped on the TV. The national news came first, then the local anchorman said, "And now, Fred Yurly in Oconee County. Fred, what's going on there?"

Fred Yurly had close-cropped blond hair, watery blue eyes, and a thick neck. He stood at the entrance of the house on Amorey Lane. "I'm standing in front of the home of Zoe Parker in Salem, where one man has died from what police preliminarily call a blunt force trauma."

Next came quick shots of the sheriff's vehicles, lights flashing, crime scene tape, and an ambulance pulling away.

The house looked bleak in the glare of the television lights. Then it was back to Fred Yurly.

"According to the on-scene commander, an elderly woman was defending her granddaughter from an attack by the victim. We will update this story as information becomes available. Back to you, Tom."

"Thank you for that report, Fred."

Katie threw a magazine at the television screen. "That's it? That's all? What about saying that Alan broke into our house? And he didn't mention Jon."

"Those reporters say whatever they want," Olive said, taking the remote from her husband and clicking the off button. "You don't need any more upset tonight. Don't you mind what they say or don't say, sugar."

Katie shivered. Even with the blanket Olive had wrapped about her, she was cold.

When the phone rang, Ruben picked it up. "Zoe? How are you? Yes, Katie's here. No, she's not hurt bad, just some bruises and scratches. She's gonna be fine." He handed the phone to Katie. "Your mom."

Tears rolled down Katie's face. "Mom. Come home right away." She couldn't go on, but handed the phone to Olive and curled up in a corner of the sofa.

Olive walked from the room with the phone. "It was right terrible, Zoe. Alan broke into your house, and from what I can tell, he went after Katie. Winifred hit him twice with her cane and he's dead." They talked for a time, Olive relating what she had gleaned from her nephew and Katie, and explaining that Jon and Winifred had been taken to the hospital. "I'm gonna see that Katie takes some nice, hot milk and goes to bed. I'll sit with her all night if I have to," Olive said.

"Your mama's comin' home tomorrow," Olive told Katie when she hung up.

"I couldn't talk with her. I feel like I'm never going to be able to talk about any of this."

"Don't matter if you do or don't. What you got to do now is go to bed. And I promised your mama that I'd stay in your room till you fall asleep."

The next morning, the local newspaper headline read, MAN KILLED IN SALEM. It went on to say

> A man alleged to be Alan Camaro was killed last night in Salem in the home of Zoe Parker. It is alleged that Camaro attacked one of the women in the house and another woman struck him twice with the heavy silver knob of her cane and killed him. Neighbors said they heard nothing and were shocked to hear of this kind of incident happening in this quiet rural area.

Just after noon, Doc Franklin called to say that Winifred had stabilized and that they could visit her at the hospital in Seneca that evening about seven o'clock.

At three in the afternoon, a car wound its way down the driveway. Moments later, Zoe, followed by Maudie, raced to the door of Olive's farmhouse.

Katie rushed to open the front door and threw her arms about Zoe. "Mom!" Katie nearly brought Zoe to the floor with her embrace.

"It's going to be all right, darling," Zoe whispered.

Katie clung to her mother as if she were three years old and cried.

"I'm so sorry," Zoe said again and again. "This was all my fault."

Katie buried her face in her mother's chest. She couldn't bear to let her go.

"Praise the Lord, you're home." Olive reached to help Zoe remove her jacket, while Zoe held on to Katie.

"We heard the television report. What a shock that was. Then an accident on the road today sent us on a detour that took forever. I was such a wreck. Thank God, Maudie drove. When we got to our house and saw the police tape, we figured you'd be here."

Maudie stood to one side, not wanting to intrude. "What can I do to help?"

"You could make us a pot of nice strong, hot tea," Olive said. "Let me show you where the kitchen is."

"Have you some tuna fish, or maybe some cream cheese and jelly? I'll make some tea sandwiches, with the crusts cut off. Small, soft eats will help to soothe us all, and they're nice with tea," Maudie said.

"I got both. Bless your heart, Maudie."

When the phone rang Doc Franklin suggested that Maudie come to the hospital. "Winifred's asking for her," he told Zoe.

"Jon? Is that Jon on the phone?" Katie called from the living room.

"It's Doc Franklin."

"Ask him to ask Jon to call me here."

"How is Jon?" Zoe asked. "Is he well enough to talk to Katie?"

"Jon's got broken ribs and they're gonna take time to mend. The bastard kicked him good. I'm keeping him another night, then he can go home."

"Thank Jon for me, will you, Doc? For everything he's done for Katie, Winifred, and me. I'm so sorry he's been hurt."

"Jon's young and strong. He'll be fine. One other thing." His tone became more serious. "We know it's clearly a case of self-defense, but Winifred did kill a man, so there's procedure to follow. Weeks from now, there could be a preliminary hearing to decide if they're going to charge her. But if it comes before the judge, he'll probably throw out the whole thing."

"*Probably?* And what is a preliminary hearing?"

"The way I understand it, it's simply a presentation of the facts to the judge to see whether there's cause for the arrest of a person."

"*Arrest?*" Zoe felt afraid and out of control.

"Listen, Zoe, probably nothing will come of this. It's not murder, after all; it's involuntary manslaughter at the worst. Don't worry about it. They'll probably drop all charges, if there are any, and that'll be the end of it."

"What's involuntary manslaughter?" It was an effort now for Zoe to keep her voice down.

"That's when someone kills someone without planning to do so."

"You've given me something to worry about that I never would have thought of," Zoe said. "I wish you hadn't said anything about any of this. Don't tell me any more, please." Zoe's head felt muddled; she needed time to think, to sort things out before she visited Winifred. *It's all my fault, and I don't know what to do, what to say, how to handle anything.*

"Pull yourself together, Zoe," Doc Franklin said. "Winifred and Katie are both in shock, and you owe it to them to be calm and strong."

"I understand that. I just need a little time. I'll be fine, don't worry."

"Good. I'm signing off now."

Olive was immediately at Zoe's side. "What is it, honey?"

Zoe walked to the table and pulled out two chairs. "Sit and I'll tell you, but let's keep it between us." Zoe repeated what Doc Franklin had said and finished, "He says they'll probably drop the whole matter."

"Well, I surely think they will," Olive said.

"How's Mrs. Parker?" Maudie asked from the doorway. "Are we going in to see her tonight?"

"Come, sit," Zoe said. "That was Doc Franklin. He gave Winifred a sedative. He wants you to come to the hospital tomorrow."

Olive rose. "I'll clean up this kitchen." She began to fill the dishwasher with their plates and cups.

"I'll help you," Maudie said.

"No need. It's about done."

"I need to be busy," Maudie said.

"Why don't you and Zoe take a walk down to the barn? It's still light. Ruben's down there with the calf that was born two nights ago. A sweet little thing. And you could bring up some potatoes." She handed Maudie a straw basket.

As she and Maudie walked toward the barn, Zoe thought of a time when she had been called to the principal's office and accused of cheating because she had shared a test paper with another girl. The teacher, the principal, and Ida had reprimanded her. But once away from the school, Ida had gently cupped her daughter's face in her hands.

"We all use poor judgment and make mistakes sometimes, Zoe dear. I have. Your dad has. It can be very embarrassing. But there's always a lesson to be learned from it."

"Maudie," Zoe said, "Do you think there's always a lesson to learn when we make a mistake, a really big one, like I did with Alan?"

"Aye, I do."

"My mother used to say nothing was accidental, not even our mistakes. She had this idea that people did what they did because either they felt safe and secure, or they were fearful and insecure. Secure, I believe she meant, referred to all those things that give a person a sense of well-being: self-confidence, security, love. We're afraid of things because we lack confidence and feel insecure, she'd say, or because we are ignorant about them."

"I never heard it put quite like that," Maudie said. "I have to give it a wee bit more thought."

Zoe looked at Maudie. "When Steven died, I stopped trusting life and especially God. It was easier, with Katie, to live with my parents rather than face life as a single mother. For a very long time, the pain of losing Steven was like a knife slicing my heart. My parents helped keep me going. My mother was infinitely patient, and we grew closer with every week that passed. It got easier and easier to stay with them, to lean on them." She kneeled alongside the bin of potatoes stored in the barn.

"I don't see how my mistake, and all that's come from it, has taught me anything except to be distrustful of men. How could what's happened to my Katie and Winifred have any value? What could they learn from such a thing?"

Maudie shook her head. "I don't know."

As they returned to the house, Zoe said, "Someday I'd like to show you the cave that saved my life."

"I'd be honored if you did."

The next morning, after breakfast, Katie walked over to Zoe and rested her head on her mother's shoulder. "I'm so glad you're here." She looked into her face. "I'm just so tired. I sleep and sleep, and I'm still tired."

"Don't underestimate the enormous stress you've been under. Your body needs all the rest you can give it." Zoe ran her hand over Katie's hair. "Take a magazine or a book, lie down and relax, even if you don't sleep."

The cleaners were specialists in crime scenes.

"When we're done, you'll never know anything happened here," Jake Flurry assured Zoe, as he and his two helpers unloaded pails and a variety of scrubbing and cleaning products.

"What about the rug in the den? Can you get those stains out, or will I have to get rid of it?"

"We'll have it looking like new," Flurry said.

"We're going to take a walk in the woods, maybe for an hour. Will that give you enough time?"

"That'll be just about right for us," Jake said. "It's just the den and kitchen and in the hall, where they tracked mud."

Zoe and Maudie left the cleaners to their work and headed into the woods. Leading Maudie over bits of broken branches and earth that was thickly covered with leaves, Zoe avoided thorny branches of wild roses and blackberry bushes. After negotiating a particularly large clump of berry bushes, she said, "My mother used to say that guilt was an excuse for doing nothing. I think she was right." After hearing the news report on their motel room TV, she had shared the story of Alan with Maudie.

"I've felt so guilty about Alan and what it cost me in pride and money, and it's been debilitating."

"Guilt also leads to depression, and depression thwarts action," Maudie said. "People need help to overcome depression. I know; I was like that once. Purgatory's what I call it."

"What were you depressed about?" Zoe asked.

"Things in my family, the way my father drank. He beat my sister. I hated him." They walked on for about ten minutes.

"Where is this cave of yours?" Maudie asked. "I'm going to go to the hospital soon."

'It's well hidden. Let me show you."

The cave, tucked in a thicket of rhododendrons and veiled by vines, was invisible. Zoe stretched out her hands and parted the tangled vines.

Maudie gasped. "I could have come this way a hundred times and would never have seen it."

"Go ahead. Look inside."

Maudie bent to look and pulled back. "It's so dark. Quite a fearsome place, it is. How far in does it go?"

"Not far at all, maybe four feet." Zoe dropped the vines and the cave vanished.

"And this is where you hid from that terrible man?"

Zoe nodded. A wide, flat boulder nearby offered a place to sit, and they settled onto it.

"Thanks for coming here with me and for listening to me," Zoe said softly.

"Friends listen," Maudie said. She checked her watch. "Doc said for me to come to the hospital at noon."

"We'll be back at the house in plenty of time. Thanks for being my friend after all that's happened."

"Surviving the bad times with someone is what makes a friend. Having a friend is important, very important. Life's too lonely without one." Maudie thought of Mam and Mam's friend of a lifetime, Megan O'Callahan, and she knew that it was the strength and constancy of their friendship that had sustained both women over long, hard years.

Zoe drew her knees up and hugged them. "I've spent a lot of time trying to understand what I was so afraid of, that I let a man like Alan into my life."

"Come to any conclusions?"

Zoe's shoulders rose and fell in a shrug. She could think of Alan more easily now that he was really gone. "I'd started menopause. I was moody and feeling tired and old. I wasn't sleeping well. Sometimes I'd wake up from a nightmare absolutely terrified, and I'd turn on every light in the house and sit up all night, as if that made me safe. Before that, I'd never been afraid out here."

"Sweats, insomnia, and panic attacks can come with menopause," Maudie said.

Zoe sat silent for a moment or two, then shook her head. "No. I can't really blame menopause for Alan. Even when I knew what he was, I did nothing. It makes me crazy thinking about it." She turned to Maudie and gripped her arm. "Maudie, he could have killed Katie, Winifred, and Jon. If my parents had been alive, I would never have had dinner with Alan Camaro, never brought him into my life and my home. None of this would have happened. It was loneliness." Zoe began to cry. She hid her face in her hands, then lifted her head and looked at Maudie. "I thought he'd change because I loved him. And I was too ashamed to go to the police."

"You had no support system, no one to talk to. Women get trapped in bad situations with bad men." Tears brimmed in Maudie's eyes.

"Like your mother?" Zoe asked gently.

"Like my mam, yes."

"One day after Alan was gone, I was sitting by the pond, and it struck me that underneath the loneliness, I was afraid of life itself and terrified of growing old alone."

"We all feel that sometimes, don't you think? Mam used to say she worried about her older days. I was too young then to understand. I do now."

"My parents had one another to share their feelings. They were very close."

"To live without meaning is what really frightens me," Maudie said. "And to be without a friend." She slid from her perch on the boulder and extended her hand to Zoe. "It must be close to an hour. Jake may be finished and waiting for his check."

A tiny white flower in a crevice in the rock caught Zoe's attention. She plucked it and handed it to Maudie. "Thank you for being my good and wise friend."

"Aye. That I am, your friend."

"And I am yours." They moved homeward among the trees. "Now I must find a way to stop blaming myself and forgive myself. That way I can truly forgive Winifred, and not just because she saved Katie."

Maudie said, "Anger and blame are things that hurt the one who feels them."

"You're so right. I see that now."

After a time, Maudie said, "Zoe, Mrs. Parker adores Katie, and I believe she cares for you very much. She's sorry for all that happened."

Zoe did not reply as they moved out of the woods.

Maudie spoke again. "Winifred's love is so big and so strong that she risked her life for Katie."

"And I will value her for that forever," Zoe said. "Since she's been here, I've had moments of great tenderness for her, like the night of the tornado when she was hurt by a piece of glass, and when I saw her toes all twisted over one another. Perhaps in spite of myself, I do care for her." She could almost feel Steven nearby, saying, "Good for you, Zoe."

As they hastened down the hillside and across the pasture to the house, they saw the men waiting in their truck.

Inside the house, all looked the same as it had before Zoe went to North Carolina. There were no bloodstains on the rug in the den, no hole in the kitchen ceiling, and the entrance foyer floor was clean and shiny. Everything smelled fresh.

"Thank you so much, Mr. Flurry," Zoe said. "This is wonderful. Now I'll be able to bring my daughter and my mother-in-law home."

At Olive's, everyone was waiting for her.

"You're just in time. We were about to leave for the hospital without you," Katie said. At that moment, the phone rang, and Katie picked it up. When she hung up, disappointment showed in her eyes. "That was Doc. Granny's asleep and he says not to come, not even Maudie. Do you think he's hiding something from us?"

"Your granny had a terrible strain. It will take time for her whole system to stabilize," Maudie said. "I don't work at that hospital, and she has private nurses. I'll be there for her whenever I'm needed."

32

❧⟐❧

RECOVERING

Good heavens, I'm still alive, Winifred thought when she opened her eyes. Confused for a moment, she wondered where she was.

The gentle voice of a woman asked, "Can I get you anything, Mrs. Parker?"

Winifred turned her head. "Maudie, is that you? Who are you?"

"Alice Janson." The pretty blond nurse rose from the leather chair near the curtained window and came to stand beside Winifred's bed.

Winifred lifted her hand as if to shake the nurse's hand and winced. "Why am I hooked up to this?" She pointed to the intravenous needle, then her eyes followed the plastic tube to the bag of clear liquid suspended from a metal frame. "I'm in a hospital?"

"Yes. You came in last evening suffering from shock. The drip into your arm helped stabilize you."

"How long have I been here?"

"Since about ten thirty last night. It's four in the after-noon now."

"And you are?"

"A private duty nurse. Your doctor ordered nurses around the clock."

Winifred's eyes grew frightened. "Kathryn, my grand-daughter—is she all right?"

"Yes. Dr. Franklin said to tell you that your granddaugh-ter is fine. He ordered her to rest in bed today. They'll be coming to visit with you soon."

"That horrible man didn't hurt her, then. Thank God, he didn't hurt her." Tears welled as she remembered Alan pouncing on Katie, Alan on the floor bleeding, his hand reaching for the gun, her cane descending, the awful crack-ing sound like a huge clay pot breaking. Winifred closed her eyes. "He would have killed us." She did not ask about Alan, preferring not to know.

The nurse said. "You try to rest now." She rubbed Winifred's unfettered hand gently.

"I'll just close my eyes. If there's anything you have to do, Miss Janson, go ahead and take care of it."

"I'll just sit over here and read in case you need me."

Winifred turned her head. The nurse had said her family would be coming, so Zoe and Maudie must have returned. She'd be so very glad to see them all. The taut chin, the tight muscles about her eyes and mouth began to relax, and Winifred closed her eyes.

Time welded the past and present together. She had gone from rags to riches, but she had paid a price. Her hus-band, she discovered soon after they were married, pre-ferred the company of his mother. Every day after work he visited her to discuss his problems and his triumphs, while she paced the floor at home in frustration and silent rage. Then there were those awful years after Steven married Zoe. She and Theodore had sat at opposite ends of the long dining room table and eaten their meals in chilling silence.

She didn't often think about the two miscarriages she had had, crushing losses followed by soul-stifling depression, but she did now. Except for Ellie, the black cook who had comforted her, cajoled her into eating chicken soup, and held her when she wept, she had suffered alone. Years later, their butler, Lewis Treadwell, would become a friend, playing cards and games on long winter evenings. But essentially she had been a very private woman, not given to confiding in people.

And then the miracle: after nine years of marriage and nine interminable, anxiety-filled months, Steven had been born hale and hearty. His birth precipitated her move into his nursery, and then into the guest room across the hall. It seemed natural then that physical contact with Theodore should diminish and finally cease. He had protested initially, but only mildly. Had he taken lovers? She did not know and did not care. He had his heir, and Steven filled the emptiness in her heart.

When Steven started school, boredom drove her into community service work with homeless children, and her organizational abilities surfaced. She began to invest and make money, and she found that she loved the adrenaline rush of buying and selling stocks. In time she gained the respect of her husband, and they developed an amicable business partnership, even a friendship. There was respect, and that, Winifred thought, counted for a great deal between two people.

Something stirred in the room. Probably Nurse Janson, getting up or doing something. Winifred opened her eyes.

Sunset filtered through the window slats. How nice that they had painted a hospital room a cheerful yellow and hung prints of flowers on the walls. Closing her eyes again, Winifred slipped back into her past.

She could still gloat about the day when Theodore, his father and mother, and fourteen-year-old Steven sat in the audience as she, Winnie Oxnaur from Goose Cove, Maine, stepped to the podium to receive the Woman of the Year Award from the mayor of Philadelphia. Looking out into the crowd, she saw only Steven, her beautiful boy with her green eyes and his father's red hair. An A student, a prize-winning swimmer, ambitious and kind, Steven had shown so much promise. Winifred pressed a hand against her heart, remembering Steven's graduation from college. He had stepped forward in cap and gown to receive his diploma. Phi Beta Kappa. Law school lay ahead.

But then there was Zoe. Her heart skipped a beat. She'd been a foolish, inflexible, arrogant woman. She was responsible for her separation from her son and his family. Even after all these years, remembering Steven created a burning ache in her chest. Why was she alive, and Steven gone?

To save Kathryn's life. The words seeped into her brain, and she opened her eyes and looked about her. The nurse lifted her head and smiled. Winifred moved restlessly and closed her eyes again.

She saw herself in the drawing room of the Parker House in Philadelphia, where Parker ancestors stared down at her from gilded frames and mocked her. When his father died, Theodore insisted that they move into the family mansion so that Winifred might more easily supervise the care of his mother, Mildred Parker, who by then had Parkinson's disease. Long days provided the opportunity for reminiscences, and her mother-in-law spoke of her own rigid upbringing (children should be seen and not heard), her arranged marriage, which had joined two eminent and affluent Philadelphia families, and the loneliness of life with autocratic and indifferent Theodore Parker Sr.

Winifred had softened toward the sick old woman, and they had come to understand and appreciate each other. It had pained Winifred to see her mother-in-law decline and to witness her anguished frustration at the loss of her powers, her failing mind, the uncontrollable body movements. When Mildred died, Winifred missed her more than Theodore did.

The nurse spoke softly. "They've brought dinner. Can you try to eat a little?"

"I'm not at all hungry," Winifred murmured. She felt the bed being adjusted, her torso rising. "I guess I should try to eat a little," she said, opening her eyes. She managed the pudding and toast and butter with jam. "My daughter-in-law makes wonderful fresh jam."

Then she lay back, her hand heavy across her eyes and forehead. A quote from Saul Bellow came to mind. *"Everybody needs his memories. They keep the wolf of insignificance from the door."* She had good memories of the homeless children she had helped, of the twenty underprivileged young men and women she had sent to college and graduate school, one even to medical school. Several of them still remembered her with a card at Christmas.

She had raised a fine son, been a faithful wife, and raised funds for good causes, but she had also exhibited false pride, which had led to the alienation of her son and his family. She had antagonized and rejected her cousin, Emily. How she missed her. *Please God,* she prayed, *let me find Emily and apologize, and let me honestly accept and love Zoe. Let me live long enough to make up the lost years with Kathryn.*

It seemed as if a soft hand touched her cheek. Was that Steven, standing in the shadow? "Come closer," she called softly.

The nurse stirred at the sound of her voice. "Is there something I can get you, Mrs. Parker?"

"No, nothing." The image vanished, but it was enough to have sensed her son's presence. Winifred smiled and fell into a deep, restorative sleep.

When she awoke, it was dark. Miss Janson stood alongside the bed, and a man stood at the foot. Miss Janson seemed to be arguing with him.

"Good evening, Mrs. Parker. How are you feeling?" he asked.

Winifred lifted her head and squinted to read his badge. "J. P. Simpson. Who are you?"

He smiled. "Staff, ma'am, just checking on you. How are you feeling?"

Staff? He looks like a real con man. Winifred's skin prickled. "I'm fine. Now go away." *Where is Miss Janson? Gone? Why?*

Simpson pulled a straight chair alongside the bed and flipped open a black notepad. "I'd like your version of the events of last evening, ma'am."

"You'd like what? What are you doing with that pad and pen? Who the devil are you?" She squinted again at his badge. "J. P. Simpson. None of my doctors is named Simpson. Shoo! Get out of here."

Ignoring her, he crossed his legs and prepared to write. "Now, how about telling me about the events of last evening."

"I'll tell you no such thing. Miss Janson, where are you?"

He started to rise but kept on asking questions. "Were you fearful for your own life? You killed a man, after all."

"I did what?"

"Alan Camaro is dead."

"Dead?"

The shock on her face gave him his answer. "I see you didn't know."

Winifred's heart raced, and her vision blurred. The familiar buzzing started in her ears. "Please, go away," she said. "I'm not well."

"Are you certain you did it? Dr. Graine, the pathologist, says that whoever killed him must have been very strong, and you don't look strong to me." He was backing toward the door. "Was it your granddaughter who did it? Are you taking the blame for her?"

"I struck the blow," she said, a look of triumph in her eyes. She turned her head away.

Miss Janson and a tall, heavyset orderly stood in the doorway. The orderly approached Simpson. "How did you get in?" he asked. "I recognize you, you're press. Get out of here, right now." He fastened a large hand on Simpson's shoulder and propelled him into the hall.

Miss Janson said, "If anything happens to Mrs. Parker, you're responsible." Then the voices moved away.

Mists began to close in, yet in her mind Winifred continued the conversation with Simpson. "He went down after I hit him. I saw him reach for the gun." Then in a blur of background sounds, she heard her husband's voice, loud and angry.

"How dare he come in here like that and harass her?" A pause. Whispers. Then a male voice said, "This woman's been through the worst experience of her life. Who let that man in here? I'll have an answer, and damn fast."

Theodore was here—he had come to help her. *Good for you, Theodore!* She wanted to laugh but was too tired.

"This is an outrage. An absolute outrage, and heads will roll for this, I guarantee it," the voice said.

I could never kill anyone in cold blood. You tell them, Theodore. She could hear him explaining to someone. "Whoever sneaked that damn reporter in here, I want him or her fired. I'll take this to the top. He could have sent Mrs. Parker into a relapse."

Winifred floated. Theodore would handle this. He would see to it that the intruder went to jail.

She wanted to ask Theodore if he'd seen the whole thing. Had he seen her fight to protect Kathryn? Wasn't Kathryn a beauty? His voice was moving away from her, growing dimmer. *Theodore, don't leave.*

With great effort, Winifred opened her eyes. Miss Janson stood by the bed with a syringe in her hand. "You were dreaming," she said, "calling for someone named Theodore."

Winifred jerked her arm away. "Theodore? Where is he? What are you doing?"

"Your doctor was here. You were asleep. He didn't want to wake you, but he wants you to have something to make sure you rest easy tonight."

Nausea overcame her and she heaved, barely missing Miss Janson. After that, Winifred remembered nothing until late the following day, when once again she awakened to Miss Janson's ministrations. The nurse handed Winifred a pill.

Winifred pushed her hand away. "What is it?"

"A low dose of Valium. Dr. Franklin prescribed it."

"Valium, eh? Well, I'll take that. I don't take any medication that hasn't been on the market for at least five years. I'm nobody's guinea pig." She swallowed the pill and drank the water the nurse presented, then, exhausted, she lay back. "There was a man, an intrusive man here asking questions, am I correct, Miss Janson?"

The nurse nodded. "I'm so sorry about that. I ran out to call the charge nurse since I have no authority here."

"Who let him into the hospital?"

"I don't know. Dr. Franklin was very angry. He's looking into it."

"I hope he finds out and fires the person who would do such a thing."

"I hope so too."

"Thank you for going for help. I appreciate that. Now, when will Dr. Franklin be back? I want you to page him in case he's still in the hospital. If he isn't, then call his office and tell them I want to see him. He's to wake me up if I'm sleeping, no matter what time it is. Thank you."

Later that afternoon, Doc Franklin waited for the family in the lobby of the hospital. They could see him pacing, checking his watch, dabbing his forehead. Zoe, Maudie, and Katie hurried to his side.

"Is Grandmother all right?" Katie asked.

He exploded. "No, she's not all right! Some damn reporter managed to sneak into her room, asking a lot of questions. I had to sedate her last night and again this morning, but she may be awake now."

"A reporter?" Zoe clutched Doc Franklin's arm.

He nodded. "I'm hell-bent on finding out who let him in and then firing that person."

"How could he do that?"

"Some reporters are sharks. They'll stop at nothing to get a story," Doc said.

"I'd like to see Granny. Can we go up?"

"Yes, but don't stay long."

But when they entered Winifred's room, she was asleep. The three women tiptoed out and left the hospital, deeply concerned.

33

In the Days After

Detective Harry Mason found Katie sitting on the edge of the dock, her bare feet dangling just above the water. She was older than he expected, or was it her white hair and her lack of makeup that belied her youth? Her green eyes, weighted with sadness, were striking—the kind of eyes that made a man stop dead in his tracks and stare.

"I'm right sorry to bother you, Ms. Parker. I wonder if you might be kind enough to answer some questions. I'm trying to get up to speed about what happened the night Alan Camaro died."

She turned away from him and concentrated on the leaves in the pond. "Must I talk to you?"

"No. You don't have to, but sooner or later you'll have to give your account of the event. Mrs. Parker, your grandmother, isn't well enough, and Mr. Bickford wasn't in the room when the incident occurred."

"This is so hard. I just want to forget about it."

"It's been tough on you ladies, and I'm right sorry to bother you."

Katie recognized empathy in his eyes. It's his job, she reminded herself.

Mason said, "My work often gets a negative response from folks. There are days when I go home, stand in front of the mirror, and remind myself that I'm not a bad guy."

He sounded honest; she felt she could trust him. "What do you want to know?"

"Whatever you can recall about the evening, from the time Alan Camaro entered your home until he died."

Katie swung her body around to face him. "We might as well go sit in the summerhouse. It's cold out here in the wind. Would you like a Coke or Seven-Up?"

"I'd appreciate a glass of water."

They walked up the bank and were soon seated in the summerhouse, with a Coke and a large glass of cold water. "You just go ahead and tell me whatever you remember," he said.

Katie started slowly, with a low voice that grew louder and more agitated as she recalled the disbelief and confusion she had experienced when Alan walked into the house. Then her shock when he drew a gun, and increasing dread as he talked about her mother. She told the detective about her alarm when he approached her, the terror she'd felt when he grabbed her, her attempt to struggle, uselessly, against his strength, and finally the relief she felt to see him lying still on the Persian rug. "I didn't realize at first that he was dead. My first thoughts were for my grandmother. I wasn't sure if he had killed her."

Mason listened attentively. When she had finished, he asked, "Did you see Mrs. Parker strike him the first time or the second time?"

She did not speak immediately.

"Take your time," he said.

Midway out in the pond, a fish leaped into the air and plunged out of sight, stirring ripples. "Look," Katie said, pointing across the pond. "A deer." The young deer stood with its head high, alert, then bent to drink.

"Must feel pretty safe, coming so close with people about," Mason said.

"All animals feel safe on this property, thanks to my mother." Katie closed her eyes.

He waited.

"This is very difficult," she said. "I remember falling hard when he let go of me." She paused.

"It's over now," the detective said quietly. "He can't hurt you. Take your time."

"He did hurt me—not by raping me, but by violating my space, my privacy, my being. He would have raped me, maybe killed me." Her hands crossed over her chest. "Funny, the things you remember—the *ping* when he tore my blouse and the buttons popped off and hit the fireplace wall. I remember thinking they sounded like BB shots."

"Try to remember what happened *after* he let go of you."

"When I got up from the floor, I turned around. He was on the ground. I kept thinking how the blood would ruin the carpet."

"Did you see the gun?"

"No. It was on the other side of him. I heard him call Granny a damned bitch, so he was still alive, but then he moved, trying to reach his gun, I think. If he'd gotten the gun, he would have shot Granny, and God knows who else. I saw my grandmother lift her cane and hit him. That's the only time I saw her hit him. Afterward he just lay there." She shivered and began to tremble. "Then Granny collapsed, and Jon was there. I remember crawling over to her. Jon said he'd call 911." She turned dull eyes to Mason. "Jon said he—Alan—was dead."

"That's all I needed to know: he was alive after that first blow and still threatening you and your grandmother. Look, Ms. Parker, you don't have to be afraid any longer. Camaro's dead." He drew a deep breath. "I'm sorry you went through such a terrible ordeal, and I'm sorry to have intruded on you."

When he was gone, Katie slipped out of her shoes and her dress, and in her underwear, cold as it was, dived into the pond. Long, powerful strokes propelled her halfway across. Overhead, puffy white clouds formed faces: a dog, the craggy visage of an old man, a woman with long, streaming hair.

Too cold to swim. And as she headed for shore her mind raced. If they had heard Alan before he'd broken in, they would have had time to call 911. But they had been as helpless as babies. For the first time in her life, Katie was angry with Zoe. Angry that Zoe had not told her about marrying Alan. Angry that her mother had not installed an alarm system. That might have stopped Alan and at least given them time.

Katie could not remember feeling this angry since Hank abandoned her and their child. It had taken years with a therapist for her to gain perspective on why people do what they do, and on her expectations of others. When she had finally reached a place of detachment and freed herself from Hank, life had changed for the better in every way. When someone cut her off on the road, or a salesperson was inordinately slow or stupid, or the wait was excessively long in a doctor's office, she no longer fumed inside but took things in stride. But this was her mother, whom she had always trusted. What Zoe had done and not done defied comprehension, and these thoughts plagued Katie as she dashed to the house to warm herself.

The days after Detective Mason's visit were cold and rainy and confined everyone to the house, where they trod gingerly, as if afraid to make noise or disturb one another. Katie avoided Zoe. It was easier that way, and Zoe seemed to understand and stayed mainly in her room, or played cards at the kitchen table with Maudie. Katie resented the way Maudie stayed close by Zoe. Did Maudie suspect that she needed to protect Zoe from her own daughter?

Then Katie noticed that the U-Haul they'd brought back from North Carolina was still sitting in the yard, and she exploded. "Isn't it costing money every day you keep that U-Haul here? It's probably full of things that should be taken to the shop!"

Zoe slapped her cards hard on the table. "Don't you talk to me like that, Katie. I'll get to it when I'm ready."

"And when will that be?" Katie asked.

"When I'm ready." Zoe brushed past her daughter and exited the kitchen.

Maudie began to take dishes from the dishwasher and place them in the cabinet. She looked at Katie. "Be patient with your mam, Katie. She's blaming herself for this whole thing."

"She *should* blame herself. We could have been killed." The wind went out of Katie, and she sank into a chair. "Oh, Maudie, Mom and I've never had such a barrier between us. If I don't talk to her and tell her how I'm feeling, I think I'll go crazy."

"Then get her off alone and do what you must, lass." Maudie closed the cabinet door.

"I'm sorry. My nerves are raw from that detective coming here and questioning me. It brought the whole thing back so vividly, it really upset me."

"Aye." Maudie sighed. "'Tis some rough sailing for this ship."

"I have moments when I'm really angry at Mom, and that scares me, Maudie."

"I can see it might. And your mother is stricken with guilt, she is. She knows what she did and didn't do. Try to understand. She was humiliated, Katie girl, and ashamed and terrified that Alan would come back."

"She told me the story, all but the part about marrying that man. I thought I understood—but what happened was so horrible."

Maudie put her arm about Katie's shoulders. "Everything takes time. You talk with your mam." She left the kitchen, leaving Katie alone with the ticking of the clock and the hum of the refrigerator.

That night, Katie knocked on Zoe's door. "May I come in, Mom?"

"Certainly."

"I think we need to talk." Katie declined the place on the bed that her mother patted and chose the chair at the vanity. "I'm troubled, Mom. I understand your falling in love with someone, and him turning out to be a bastard. I even have a grasp on what it must be like to be a battered woman, and afraid. But why didn't you have an alarm system installed or have dead bolts put on the doors. Why in God's name did you marry him?"

"I've asked myself all those questions a million times."

"And the answers?"

Lying in her bed, Zoe looked small and frail and vulnerable. "He insisted, and I was afraid not to marry him. I was completely immobilized for a long time, and didn't even think about the locks. It was Ruben who changed them. And Alan had cleaned me out financially. I couldn't afford to have an alarm system installed. I called a locksmith to put in dead bolts, but he wanted two hundred dollars to install four dead bolts. I was reeling from my losses, and I didn't have the money. Time passed, and Alan didn't come back. I just wanted to forget, to pretend it never happened. That was an unforgivable error." Tears spilled from Zoe's eyes and she dabbed at them with the edge of her sheet. "I am so sorry, so very sorry. You're my life, Katie, and my negligence could have cost you *your* life. My heart breaks over what's happened, and Winifred being ill. I owe her an eternal debt for saving you."

"Granny and I shall never forget that night. Perhaps we'll never get over it, either," Katie said.

Zoe sat up and leaned forward, her hands outstretched to her daughter. "Katie, please, please try to find it in your heart to forgive me. As you've said, we're such a small family to hurt or blame one another."

Katie stood and shoved the chair back under the vanity. "I do forgive you, but I also need time to think, to understand it all."

"Just remember how much I love you. Never in a million lifetimes would I deliberately hurt you." She was crying as Katie walked from the room.

And then Jon arrived. He was walking straight again and the limp was greatly reduced. "You're better," Katie said, hugging him gently. *Physical injuries heal faster than emotional ones,* she thought.

"I came to tell you we're just about done at the shop."

He stood in the hallway and rubbed his hands together. "That U-Haul's costing you gals money. I'll drive it to the shop and get it emptied."

"That would be wonderful," Maudie said.

"Good. Then I'll need you to follow in my truck, Katie." She hung back.

"What's the matter, Katie?" Jon asked.

"I feel uncomfortable going into town, being seen. I haven't been in town since that night, except to go to the hospital to see Granny."

"All the more reason to get out of this house. Anyone you might meet knows what you've been going though. Let them see that life hasn't beaten you down."

"I don't want to see anyone, or for them to see me."

Jon tipped Katie's face up and looked deep into her eyes. "I know it's hard, but you're a brave woman, and you can do it. Just hold up your head, go on with your life, and before you know it, the gossips will be talking about someone or something else. That's the way with people."

"Can't Maudie drive your truck?"

Jon hugged Katie. "She could, but I'd like you to come with me."

Thus persuaded, Katie sat behind the wheel of Jon's big truck and followed the U-Haul to Walhalla. Her spirits lifted when the barber down the street from the shop hastened toward her.

"Katie, how good to see you. We were all concerned for you. Are you all right? How is your grandmother and Zoe?"

Sergeant Holloway appeared and hugged her. "So glad to see you back. How is Mrs. Parker senior? Rumor has it she's on the mend."

Katie nodded. "She's recovering."

"Good."

Katie looked at Jon and smiled. "I'm glad you made me come." She stepped inside the shop. Sunshine poured through the new glass windows and door, and freshly painted shelves lined the walls. "It's beautiful," she said. "You've done wonders here."

With the help of Jon's workmen, they unloaded the U-Haul and began to unpack the cut glass, as well as the pottery and china, including a nearly complete set of Wedge-wood. From boxes waiting in storage at the back of the store, they unpacked quilts and quilt stands, old lamps, and lanterns. Katie marveled at the fairy lamps, popular in the 1870s, and painted tinware pieces, including an old deed box, as well as pewter mugs in fine condition and dishes with the touchmark of Joseph Danforth, dated 1758–88. There were pans of brass and iron. A hundred-year-old type-writer was in mint condition. The shelves began to fill. As they worked, they stopped periodically to exclaim over a piece that neither of them had noticed earlier.

"I'm impressed," Jon said. "You're off to a fine start." He walked over to where she was unpacking a china bowl, and he took her face in his hands. "And I'm most impressed with your courage. It touches me, seeing you and your grandmother to-gether. That old lady loves you from the depths of her soul."

"I love her too." Through her tears, it was all Katie could say. She clung to Jon.

"I understand how hard this is for you, especially with your mother right now. It's going to work out, you'll see." He wrapped his arms about her and held her to him. "I'm here if you need me."

It took twelve seemingly interminable days, but finally Winifred's blood pressure stabilized and the debilitating dizziness vanished.

"You can go home today," Doc Franklin said.

"Just like that? Today?"

"Yes, today. I've called Maudie to drive in and pick you up. I'll sign you out. Can you dress yourself, or should I send someone in to help you?"

Winifred swung her legs over the side of the bed. "Dress myself? Just watch me."

But coming home meant remembering. The den, though it had been thoroughly scoured, was a place no one wanted to go into. Winifred picked at her food the first evening, though Maudie had made her favorite, crisp fried chicken. She drummed her fingers on the tabletop, bit her lip to fight back tears, and squeezed her hands into tight fists.

Zoe was particularly kind. "Try to eat a little," she urged. "You have to keep your strength up."

Winifred took one more forkful of chicken. "Believe me, if I could, I would. Maybe tomorrow. I'm so tired."

Later, in bed, she lay awake thinking how ironic it was that she had killed a man, even in self-defense. Was she no better than her father's cousin, a violent man who had murdered another man in a drunken brawl? All of Goose Cove spoke of him with contempt, and the family had been shamed.

What nonsense! The comparison to Cousin Arnold was hardly worth the time it took to remember him. But she *had* killed a man, and though, in the circumstances, she would do it again, issues of right and wrong, good and evil troubled her. *If I were a Catholic, I could go to confession. The priest would listen and grant me absolution, and I would be at peace.*

But not being a Catholic, she faced the dilemma of how to resolve the nagging sense of having committed a grievous crime. Who would she, could she, talk to? Who did she respect enough to discuss this with, to bare her soul to?

Theodore would say, "Purely a case of self-defense. You're not at fault. You committed no crime, and no one would say that you did."

Logical? Yes. Had she intended to kill Alan? No. She had not. Her intent had been to immobilize and render the monster incapable of hurting Katie, herself, Jon, and Zoe.

"Well then," her pragmatic husband would say. "What's your problem, my dear?"

"My problem," she said aloud, "is that although everyone is very kind and supportive, it's forgiveness I crave, from God himself."

"Well, then," the voice of her husband in her mind said, "ask him for forgiveness. You don't need an intermediary. If anyone understands, God does."

Katie hovered about her grandmother. "Can I get you anything, Granny?" "Time for your medication, Granny." "Are you sure you feel well enough to go outside?" It brought a lump to her throat to see her grandmother's worried looks and furrowed brow, and Katie wondered what she could do to ease Winifred's mind. Katie waited for her to express an interest in Aladdin's Treasures, but she did not. When Katie spoke of the shop, of the items she and Jon had placed on display, her grandmother smiled vaguely and said, "That's nice, dear."

"What shall I do?" Katie asked Jon. "Granny stays in her room most of the day and evening and mopes."

"Nothing," he said. "Your grandmother's mind and body are still in a state of shock. Give her time to sort things out. She's a brave, strong woman, and she'll come around."

And then Detective Mason phoned. "How is Mrs. Parker?" he asked Katie. "When can I visit her?"

"Visit Granny? For what? Hasn't she been through enough?" She slammed down the phone.

From her bedroom, Winifred heard her granddaughter's tirade and the phone slam. She knew that the policeman was simply doing his duty. A man had been killed, and they must gather the facts as best they could for their report. A final report, she hoped; she wanted to put it behind her.

Maybe I should go away for a while, take Maudie and go on a cruise to the Caribbean, where all my needs will be tended to and no policeman will call . . . But what am I fussing about? What needs of mine are neglected here? None. I would only return to the same unfinished business.

When Kathryn brought two cups of steaming hot tea for them, Winifred decided to share with Kathryn a court scene she had witnessed many years earlier. "Once I went to court to see your great-grandfather defend a woman who had, according to the prosecutor, murdered her husband in cold blood. Hospital records stated that he had beaten the woman severely and repeatedly. In those days the courts were not sympathetic to a woman who killed her husband, even in self-defense." She sipped her tea. "I can still see that woman, so frail, with stringy hair and eyes sunk deep into her face. She took ill in that courtroom and threw up all over my proper, meticulous father-in-law's shoes." Her eyes clouded. "Not only was it most unpleasant, but rather than gain her sympathy, it turned the jury against her. I couldn't bear to humiliate myself like that, especially not in public." Her clenched fists lay in her lap. "I'll talk to the detective who called earlier. We'll do it in the living room, not at the courthouse or the police station, you understand?" She paused a moment. "Is it the same detective you spoke to?"

"Yes."

"What kind of person is he?"

"He was very kind, like Bill Holloway."

Winifred sighed. "They have to close the case, and I can do it. Set it up for me, will you, Kathryn? Tell him I'd be happy to speak with him any afternoon this week at two o'clock."

"I'll call him." Katie started for the door and turned. "Granny, there's something else. My mother. Are you angry with her? None of this would have happened if she hadn't messed up so badly."

Winifred beckoned Katie to her side and took her hands in hers. "Beloved child, I'm too old and ill for anger and resentment. I think how dreadful it must be to be beaten and abused, how terrible to live in fear. How many nights did Zoe jerk awake at the sound of a branch falling or an animal rooting in the trash bin? I empathize with her." Winifred shook her head. "She understandably tried to forget. It must have been hell."

"You don't hate her?" Katie asked.

"Not at all, and I'm not angry with her. Catch your breath. Wipe your eyes. No more tears now, my girl."

Katie quieted. A sense of peace eased its way into her heart. "I love Mom. I've been angry, and I don't want to be."

"It's easy to blame. Let it go. Forgive her. You've been through quite a bit: losing Laurie Ann, deciding to settle here rather than go back to Greenville, and then Alan. It's going to take time."

Later the night, when the house was dark, Winifred lay in her bed in the dimly lit room. Memories she hadn't the energy to control pressed into her mind. As a child and adolescent she had been labeled "foul-mouthed." Her mother would scrub her mouth with a rough cloth and nasty-tasting laundry soap. Her mother's hands had smelled of onion and garlic mixed with lye from making soap. Her sisters had snickered and rubbed the finger of one hand over a finger of their other hand in a "shame on you" gesture that had enraged her more than the disgusting taste in her mouth.

Her mother had been an austere and bitter woman. Born poor to rigid and abstemious parents, married into a penurious existence with a fisherman who spent much of his life at sea, what comforts did she enjoy? Tilling the rocky earth by hand, she had raised, canned, and stored much of their food. Winifred had come upon her weeping once, because the land yielded fewer potatoes and smaller vegetables and berries with the passing years. And there was that time when her mother fell plowing and crushed her arm, and her father jeered at her and called her stupid and a clumsy fool. Winifred had watched her mother pick herself up and go on working. Her arm, healing without benefit of a doctor's care, remained crooked and forever caused her pain.

Years later, when she was wealthy, Winifred attempted to atone by sending money to her mother. Her father, that bastard, returned her checks, continuing to deprive her mother of a modicum of comfort.

"I'm like my mother," Winifred whispered into the darkness. "I never cried when my sisters drowned, nor did she. My father called me a coldhearted bitch. 'Just like your damned mother,' he said." The truth was, she'd been too shocked and devastated to cry. Perhaps it was to mourn for them, to say good-bye, that she had returned to Goose Cove just before getting Zoe's call.

How Goose Cove had changed. Now it was a tourist

mecca with inns, guesthouses, even a hotel, and no familiar faces. She had carefully edged her way down to the sea and sat upon a damp, rugged boulder. The ocean slipped from shore. She stayed to watch it return, then hastened, her heart hammering in her chest, back up the hill to avoid the incoming waves. She had wept, then, for the hard mean years, for sisters lost, for her mother and her sad and miserable life. Soon after, she had decided that she must come to Salem. Perhaps, deep inside, she'd hoped that she and Zoe could patch it up. That maybe she could find some measure of peace and family, even in that god-awful place, Salem, South Carolina.

And she had found Kathryn, blessing enough, and now no longer felt alone. A fish in a picture caught her eye. Puffing out her cheeks, she pursed her lips and mimicked the fish. She was even getting used to this silly room.

Before she'd left home, Dr. Lavelle had suggested that she rent comedies on video. "Laughter heals," he said. "And you don't laugh nearly enough."

When was the last time she'd really laughed?

Suddenly, the fish seemed ridiculously comical. Winifred chuckled, then broke into a full belly laugh that carried across the hall and brought Kathryn running to her room. When the phone rang, they were laughing and making silly fish faces.

"What fool's calling after eleven?" Winifred asked, still smiling.

"I'll get it. Hello?" Katie listened, smiled, looked at her grandmother, and covered the mouthpiece. "Guess who's on the phone?"

"The man in the moon?"

"No. A lady who says she's your cousin, Emily."

Winifred's heart caught in her chest. "Emily." Tears sprang into her eyes.

"Shall I get her number and tell her that you'll call her back?"

Winifred hesitated. She needed time to collect herself. She nodded.

"Emily, this is Kathryn, Winifred's granddaughter." She smiled at Winifred. "Granny's in the bathroom. Can she call you back?"

At that moment, Winifred blew her nose.

The raspy voice on the phone said, "No, she's not, the old hellcat. I know her. Now, you hand her that mouthpiece right now."

Katie covered the phone with her hand. "She knows you're here and insists on talking to you." She untangled the cord and handed over the receiver.

"Well, so it's you, is it?" Winifred said.

"Oh, Winnie, I nearly died when I heard the report on the television. Are you all right?"

Winnie! The name she had hated now sounded so comforting. "Emily." Winifred's voice cracked. "Where are you, Emily?"

"Living right up here in North Carolina, near Hendersonville. Been here six years now, since I married a good man from these parts."

Light filled the shadowed corners of Winifred's soul. She laughed. "Married, eh? That's fine. Well, well." She sat straighter. "You're close by, then?" Emily was all that was left of her past. The longing to see Emily, to hug her, to apologize for her behavior, grew by the moment, and Winifred waited, hoping and yet afraid to ask Emily to come to her.

"I want to come see you, Winnie."

Winifred took a deep breath. "I wish you'd come," she said. "I've missed you so much."

Katie patted her grandmother's shoulder and tiptoed from the room.

"And I don't mind you calling me Winnie, Emily. After all, it's who I am."

There was silence on the other end, then a cough, then the sound of Emily blowing her nose.

She's crying, Winifred thought in wonder. *She's crying about me, about us.* "Please come, Emily. It would mean everything to me."

"I'll leave George at home and come for a few days. Your daughter-in-law, what's her name? It's a funny one."

"Zoe."

"Zoe? Will she mind having me?"

"No, she'll be glad to have you. That was Kathryn who answered the phone. Oh, Emily, she's such a fine girl, so like Steven. She has his eyes. You'll love her. She's got plenty of grit too, like her granny, and . . ." She hesitated a moment. "And in some ways she's like her mother. Zoe's been through hell, I must say. She's got to be gutsy, or she would have curled into a hole and died long ago. Anyway, you just come. When?"

"I'll pack a few things and hit the road tomorrow. Is that okay?"

"Yes. Wonderful. Kathryn's gone to her room, so if you call again in the morning, I'll have her give you directions."

"Will do. See y'all soon, then." The *y'all,* though southern, had a decidedly New England drawl to it.

Winifred set the phone on its cradle and brought her hands into a position of prayer. "This was absolution. Thank you, God," she whispered. "Emily's coming tomorrow."

She began to make plans. She would put on makeup, a nice dress, and she'd ask someone to take her to the market for corned beef and cabbage, carrots and potatoes. It had been Emily's favorite meal too. Her heart swelled because now Emily would be in her life again.

34

❧❦❧

Cousin Emily

Sunshine filtered through billowing clouds, and the air bore the scent of honeysuckle with a dash of fresh-mown grass. Winifred awakened early. A trifle unsteady on her feet, she walked carefully across the bedroom, remembering Doc Franklin's admonition to move slowly.

By eight, she had completed her toilette. Her hair was brushed back and sprayed in place, and she had applied a creamy base to hide the brown age spots near her nose and on her forehead. Tilting her face upward, she added a light blush and lipstick. Using the handrail that now ran along the hallway wall, Winifred made her way to the kitchen, where weakness forced her to lean against the door. Maudie helped her to a chair.

"How quickly one relapses, and how slowly one recuperates," she said to Maudie.

"Aye. In my experience, patients who take it slow and are patient with the process recover more quickly. When you push yourself and overdo it the minute you feel a bit better, it takes longer."

"I've never had much patience for long recoveries," Winifred said. "But now I don't seem to have much choice, do I?"

"That's right, you do not. Toast and jam with your eggs?" Maudie asked.

"I'd love that. Hospital food's miserable reputation is well deserved."

When the eggs were cooked, Maudie set the frying pan in the sink and joined Winifred at the table. "Katie told me about the phone call from your cousin. Emily got directions early this morning, but I think she won't arrive until after lunch. How long has it been since you've seen her?"

"Too many years. To tell you the truth, Maudie, I'm all a-jitter. What am I going to say to Emily? That I killed a man?"

"She knows that, and she knows you didn't intend to kill anyone. Just you keep a positive attitude."

"True. Your optimism is good for me." Winifred finished a slice of toast. "I won't bring it up unless she does. I need to rest and not worry myself into a snit before she arrives. I wonder how she looks after all these years?"

It was the middle of the afternoon when Emily's red Ford Escort pulled into Amorey Lane and crunched up the gravel driveway.

She sat behind the wheel for a moment, taking in the wheat-colored pasture, the glistening pond and the summerhouse, before looking toward the main house. Her apricot cable-knit pullover sweater hung well below her hips over a lightweight brown cotton skirt. She wore high-top sneakers and socks. She rolled down the window. It was at least ten degrees warmer in South Carolina than up in the mountains. "Nice in winter, hot and muggy in summer," she'd heard said about this area.

She pulled the sweater over her head and dropped it into the backseat of her car. It was cooler in just her blouse. She took a slow, deep breath that she hoped would quiet the jitters in her stomach. *It's going to be all right between Winnie and me. I could tell by her voice on the phone.*

Just before she had left the house, her husband had said, "They're gonna charge your cousin with murder, I bet."

"Not on your life. Winnie might be a cussed old thing, but never a murderer—or she'd have done in her grandfather and her father years ago."

As Emily procrastinated, a pretty woman, too young to have hair so white, stepped from the house and moved swiftly toward her.

"Cousin Emily." The woman embraced her. "I'm Katie. Granny calls me Kathryn. Welcome."

"So you're Steven's girl, her granddaughter?" Emily stepped back and studied Katie. "You look like your father."

"Thank you. It pleases me to hear you say so. Granny's so eager to see you. Let me take your suitcase. She hasn't been well, you know."

Emily nodded emphatically. "Being accused of killing a man's plenty reason not to be well. She's no murderer, though. That's not in her nature."

"No, the radio and TV really distorted the story. Please, Cousin Emily, don't bring it up unless Granny does. This whole business has been devastating for her—for us all." They started toward the house, Emily toting a large canvas bag, Katie carrying the lightweight gray suitcase. "She's been ill for a while, even before she got here, did you know that?"

"Ill? With what? She's a tough one. Nothing can keep her down."

"It's called Ménière's disease, and it's a middle ear imbalance. She can fall or become dizzy and nauseous. It happens fast and is quite frightening for her."

Emily stopped walking. "She look funny, act funny?"

"No. It only happens when she has an attack."

"Attack? Like epilepsy?"

"Different, but just as debilitating. Why don't I let her tell you herself?"

"So how does she look? Tell me, so I won't drop my jaw from shock."

"How long since you've seen her?"

"Seven years maybe."

"She looks tired, I'd say, and probably older than you remember her," Katie said.

They started onto the patio. "That's to be expected, what with all that's been going on. How come she's living here and not in her fancy mansion in Philadelphia?" Emily asked.

"Mom invited her to come. She'll tell you," Katie said.

"I didn't like how she treated your mother, right from the start."

"That was a long time ago. Things are different now."

As they reached the house, Zoe, in khaki pants, a dark blue denim shirt, and hiking boots met them at the door. "Welcome." She extended her hand to the small woman whose short hair was the brown of seaweed washed ashore on the beach in summer, and whose pale blue eyes studied her with curiosity from behind wire-rimmed glasses.

"How good that you could come. It means so much to Winifred. This is Maudie O'Hara, Winifred's nurse, though *companion*'s a better word."

"Emily Kelley. My husband's George Harrelson Kelley from Long Dry Creek." She lifted her chin with pride. "His family's been there six generations."

"We're pleased to have you," Zoe said, waving Emily into the house.

Sitting at the end of the couch, Winifred waited in the living room. When Emily appeared in the doorway, they appraised one another for a long moment. Then Winifred lifted her arms, and Emily hastened to embrace her.

"Winnie, Winnie. Lord, it's good to see you."

"Let me have a good look at you, Emily. You look wonderful. Marriage agrees with you."

"I've got a good man this time, Winnie."

"Come." Winifred patted a cushion. "Sit on the couch with me and tell me all about you, your husband, your home."

Katie appeared with a tray of finger sandwiches and a pitcher of iced tea. "You two have plenty to catch up on. I'm going to the shop with Mom, but Maudie's here if you need her, Granny."

"What shop?" Emily asked.

"We opened an antique shop in Walhalla. We'll take you to see it."

Emily laughed. "You, a shopkeeper? Well, that's something." She slipped off her shoes and curled her legs up under her on the couch. She gazed around the room, finally settling on the fireplace. "Plenty of stone in that fireplace wall, ain't there? That's quite something."

"Zoe's parents built this house. Wait until you see my bedroom. It's decorated in so-called Caribbean style, with the silliest-looking fish picture on the wall."

"Our church sponsored a trip one time to the Caribbean. George and I went. Lord, that water was so blue, and all that sky, and those big old towering clouds. I'd stand at that ship's rail and feel like I was lost at sea. And all those fancy shops and tourist things to buy on the islands, and people getting all dressed up for dinner like they were going to a funeral."

"Did you buy things?" Winifred asked.

"Mugs from different islands and T-shirts for all the grandkids. I inherited seven grandkids when I married George." Emily rose and walked to the windows, lifted the end of a curtain, and rubbed the lace between her fingers. "You figure this is handmade lace or machine-made, Winnie? So many beautiful things are made by machines these days. Up near Asheville, on the Blue Ridge Parkway, they've got a lovely shop called the Folk Arts Center. They've got exhibits—ironwork, furniture, quilts, things like that—and there's a gift shop with handcrafted items: baskets, blown glass, jewelry, ceramic dinnerware, and lots more. Expensive too."

Before Winifred could respond, Emily continued. "I have a full life now, Winnie, what with church, the family, and I belong to the Red Hat Society. You ever hear of that?"

"No, I haven't."

Emily rejoined her on the couch and made herself comfortable. "Well, we wear red hats and purple clothes and meet once a month and go out for lunch or dinner, and like last week we went to the Folk Arts Center. Once we went all the way to Cherokee, to Harrods, to gamble. Ever gamble, Winnie?"

"No. I never have."

"I only did it that one time. We each took five dollars in quarters and played the slot machines. I won two dollars and fifty cents. Most everybody lost money. But we had a good time, and people kept coming up to us and asking about our red hats."

"Is there some purpose to this organization?" Winnie asked.

"It's to have fun. We laugh a lot at the silliest things." Then Emily was back to the subject of handicrafts. "Aunt Lucille spent all those hours trying to teach us handiwork: tatting, knitting, crocheting, embroidery. Remember, Winnie?"

Winifred smiled. "And you learned them all. One year you knitted purple booties for every baby in Goose Cove."

"I had no choice. Aunt Lucille only had purple yarn."

"I couldn't manage those needles. I was all thumbs, dropping stitches, with some rows too tight and some too loose," Winifred said.

"You did most other things so good, it made me proud to be better at handiwork than you were. Did you know that?"

"I can't say that I did, but you were sure good with those needles."

Emily peered out of the window. "Nice place, here. George's got five hundred acres that go from the river to the top of the mountain." She helped herself to several of the sandwiches Kathryn had left for them, and drank her tea. "I just love sweetened tea, don't you, Winnie? That's one thing the South invented that I just love."

Winifred said, "Emily, I detect a bit of a southern twang."

"Got it the same place you got your fancy Philadelphia accent—husband and his kin." Settled on the couch, her legs tucked under her like a hen who had just laid an egg, Emily went on talking. "When in Rome—isn't that what you used to say? Hardly a trace of the old Pine Tree State left in either one of us now."

Winifred said bluntly, "I went home, Emily."

Emily lowered the sandwich she was about to bite into. "To Goose Cove? Whatever for?"

"I had to see it again. But it's gone. Everything we knew—the houses, Mrs. Elk's grocery—and the old cemetery's overgrown. I hired a man to cut the weeds and to take care of the place, but you never know what'll happen if you're not watching."

"True. True." Silence followed. Then Emily said, "Winnie, I never wanted to go back home. I didn't think you did either."

"Until this last year, I never did. Then suddenly I had to go back, and I'm glad I did. It seemed to settle a lot of things in my mind, but don't let's talk about that now."

"I'm *so* happy to see you, Winnie, I could just pee in my pants!"

Winifred smiled and felt her chest, her shoulders, even her stomach relax. It was just like old times. Emily was good medicine.

On the second day of Emily's visit the sun shone bright, and Winifred stood on the patio and lifted her face to the sky. How good to have a lovely, warm day this time of year. The transitional periods between fall and winter, winter and spring were hard for her. Temperatures shifted as much as thirty degrees in a day, and deciding what to wear was always a problem. But today the air was crisp, not cold, and for the first time since that dreadful night, Winifred was glad to be alive, and to be here in this house on Amorey Lane.

Maudie appeared and pulled two chairs and a small round table under the dogwood tree. "For a change, I think you'll be too warm in the sun today." She helped Winifred to a chair. "Cup of tea?"

"No. I'll wait for my cousin." Saying "my cousin" made her happy.

Moments later Emily appeared wearing a pinstripe shirtwaist dress and lavender bedroom slippers. "Corns," she said, pointing to her feet. The dress had long sleeves and Winnie was going to suggest she change into something lighter, cooler. But then she remembered that Emily had very particular ideas about her clothes and had always preferred long sleeves to short, so she refrained from commenting.

Maudie lifted the tea cozy from the teapot and removed the doily from the wicker basket, exposing a variety of tiny homemade muffins. She removed the glass dome from the butter and the quilted dome covering a pot of Zoe's homemade blueberry jam, then spooned fresh fruit salad into small glass bowls. "How do you take your tea, Cousin Emily?"

"Cream and plenty of sugar," Emily replied, smiling up at Maudie.

Maudie filled their cups. "I'll be leaving you two ladies now."

They watched her walk away with long, firm steps and close the door of the house behind her. "She seems like a fine young woman" Emily said.

"She is. She's been a blessing to me."

There was a moment of silence before Emily said, "George and his kin are good people. Not fancy, but solid, honest folk."

"How did you come to meet him?" Winifred asked.

Emily laughed. "The good Lord had a hand in it, for sure. I was on vacation in Asheville and went to the Apple Festival in Hendersonville. I wasn't paying no attention to where I was walking and ran smack into George's booth. Blacksmithing's his hobby. He had plant stands, doorknockers, wind chimes, stuff like that for sale. I near to knocked his display table down. He helped me straighten everything and didn't get upset or make a fuss, and then he offered me a glass of fresh apple cider he made from his own apples. He's the best man I ever knew." She sat quietly for a moment, then said, "This place reminds me of home."

"Of Goose Cove?"

"Not in looks. Maybe it's just being here with you. We have no other kin now. Seems to me the folks here like you, Winnie, and that makes me feel good. There's a comfort in that when you grow older—having good people about you. Most of George's kin stayed near the homestead. Only one of his children moved away, and she didn't go far, just to Forest City, a bit down the mountain. These days, with all the ideas they get from TV and movies, many of the younger ones leave. They'll regret it, though—only a matter of time until they find their way back home. All of George's children have been real nice to me, even though I'm new in their family and not really their mother. She passed away about ten years ago. I think they were happy to have someone to look after their father, though Lord knows, George doesn't need anyone looking after him. That man is active! He fishes and hunts in season, and he whittles wooden dolls for the grandkids. He's never idle."

"I'm happy for you, Emily. It's good not to have a man underfoot all the time, and depending on you for his entertainment."

"Right you are about that, Winnie."

They sat and sipped their tea for a time, and then Winifred said, "You mentioned people moving away from home. It's a shame, really. In this world, too many of us older folk live far from relatives. There's too many lonely people."

Emily buttered half a muffin and smeared it with jam. "What was the best thing about going home, Winnie?"

"The ocean. I found it so frightening as a child. It's still vast and wild and cold. I went down into the cove when the tide was out and sat there, and I really said good-bye to my sisters." She shrugged. "I guess I just needed to see Goose Cove one more time before I died. I was having dreams about the place, Ma especially."

"Tell me what it was like."

"The cove's much smaller than I remembered. The tide doesn't go out nearly as far as I remembered. I stayed at a new bed-and-breakfast built right into the cliff, and I walked up to the knoll where our houses used to be. They're gone. A family from Portland was having a picnic under a tree. You remember any trees being up there?"

"Not a one. Meet up with anyone we knew?"

"No. I went on over to Stonington, and it looked like something out of a movie. Fishing boats were fresh painted and piles of lobster pots were piled near the docks. Renovated houses and tourists taking pictures. All kinds of new restaurants had been opened, some in new buildings they built to look old, and others in storefronts. I felt like a stranger everywhere except at the graveyard. Mary's and Bethany's markers were gone, but the other graves were there—your folks and mine. The place is sad-looking. They've got a new graveyard now, and that's well kept up. It was a hard life back then. Ma was so scared of Pa."

"Why?"

"Pa drank. Didn't everyone know? Weekends when he was home, and especially if the catch hadn't been great, he'd tie one on, yell and scream, and sometimes he'd hit Ma."

"Me and my brothers were scared of your pa, the way he looked at us, mean-like," Emily said. "But I didn't know he hit her. Did he hit you?"

Winifred shook her head. "He yelled a lot, but he never hit me. Ma made us keep our mouths shut about how he treated her. She said it was family business and no one else's. I wanted to tell you, but . . ." She shrugged. "People stayed out of people's business, as you know." Winifred was silent for a moment, then smiled and touched Emily's hand. "All the years growing up there, I haven't one happy memory except for you."

Emily laid her hand over Winnie's. "I was scared of both your ma and your pa, Winnie."

"Ma had a hard hand, but looking back, I understand why she never smiled and was so quick to anger. Hers was a life of deprivation and loneliness. She worked the land while Pa was out to sea fishing, and she had to deal with Grandfather. The house—everything—stank of fish. I wonder if it repulsed her. And if Grandfather repulsed her as much as he did me."

Emily rubbed her arm. "It gives me the willies to think of him."

Winifred stared at her. "Did he . . . ?" Winifred wondered how she could ask the question. She plowed on. "Did he try to touch you?"

"Sure he did. But my ma saw him, and she threatened to beat him with her iron skillet till he was senseless. She screamed at him, 'You touch her, and they'll find you dead in that cove at low tide, old man, if the sea don't get you first.'" Emily looked at her cousin shyly. "He try with you?"

Winifred nodded and shivered, remembering. Who but Emily would understand? "When I was ten, he came to live with us. After a time, he said he'd hurt Mary and Bethany if I didn't do what he wanted. I was scared out of my mind, but I told him to just try, and I'd scream until everyone living on the hill came running. I kept a good eye on my sisters too."

She was proud of that, of taking care of them. "What made the old man like that, I wonder?"

"I can tell you." Emily folded her arms over her chest and looked smug. "I heard Ma telling Pa about how Grandfather's father, another boozer, used to sneak into our grandpa's room at night. Everyone knew, but they were too scared of him to say a word or try to stop him. And he beat him too."

"That's just awful," Winifred said. "Just awful that people do things like that to children. It scars them for all of their lives."

A visible tremor went through Winifred. "What hell Grandfather's childhood must have been. Sins of the father passed along to the next generation, wouldn't you say?"

Emily nodded. "Amen. So he never got you?" she asked hesitantly, flushing.

Had Emily wondered about this all their lives? "No," Winifred said. "Maybe if I'd been younger, but even at ten I knew about things." Her brow furrowed. "I don't know how I knew, but I just did, and somehow I knew I couldn't give in to his threats."

"You were always a clever one, Winnie. Had your eyes wide open."

"We might have fought plenty, me and my sisters, but when he threatened them"—Winifred's tone became defiant—"I knew I'd fight him even if I died." *Love gave me power, like it did for Kathryn.*

A heavy silence lay between them for a time. "He never got me, but I never felt safe when he was about," Emily said.

There was silence again. As hard as it was for them both, they needed to speak of that which they had never shared with anyone else.

Winifred said, "I'm glad we're having this talk, Emily. I've always thought he was responsible for Mary and Bethany's deaths, that they went out on those rocks to escape him. They never went out that far before."

"Nasty old man. Ugh." Emily made a face.

"We could be kind and write it off as his being a victim of his own childhood," Winifred said. "I don't want to, though. He was a nasty, mean old man. But he's gone, and we've done well for ourselves, wouldn't you say?"

"I most certainly would." Down at the pond, a fish jumped and struck the water with a plop. "Look at that, will you?" Emily leaned forward in her chair. "That fellow has to be big, for us to see him from up here." Suddenly the air was filled with the chirps and trill of birds. "And listen to the birds."

"Carolina wrens," Winifred replied. "Hear the *tweedle, tweedle* call? Kathryn bought me binoculars."

"How do you know about birds? I can't for the life of me remember you ever being interested in birds."

"Kathryn's a bird-watcher, and she's been telling and showing me. The Carolina wren's a red-brown bird with a white line over its eyes. And I recognize the cowbird, too."

"Cowbird? What a funny name."

"They're odd birds. They lay their eggs in other birds' nests, and those birds raise the cowbirds' young. You see cowbirds in the fields with the cattle."

"Well, I never," Emily said. "Don't even raise their own young. So how do the young 'uns know they're cowbirds? You think they just know?"

"Must be."

For another hour, their talk drifted from their present lives, to Goose Cove and childhood, and back to today. Emily spoke of her life with George, and Winifred of her coming to Salem, and of her love for Kathryn.

"It would have been nice if someone had loved us like that when we were young, don't you think, Winnie?"

"It certainly would have."

They strolled slowly down through the pasture to the

pond, and took turns swinging in Zoe's hammock. They rested, and walked, and talked some more, and Alan Camaro's name was never spoken.

They were all in the kitchen when Sergeant Bill Holloway stopped by the next morning. Emily was introduced.

"Howdy, ma'am. How's the weather up in your parts?"

"Lots colder than down here," Emily replied. "We had morning frost on the grass last week."

"We had a spell of ice not long ago," he said. "That's unusual for us that early in the year."

"Coffee?" Maudie asked.

"Sure could use a cup." Holloway pulled up a chair, straddled it, and brought his arms around the back of it. After a long drink he set the cup down, raked back his hair, leaned toward Winifred, and patted her hand. "Well," he said, "this ain't official yet, but I know you're worried, so I stopped by to tell you that they ain't gonna charge you with anything. Not manslaughter, nothin'."

Katie moved beside her grandmother's chair and circled Winifred's shoulders with her arm.

The older woman leaned against her. "That's wonderful."

"But that Mason fellow's still got to get out here and talk to you, Mrs. Parker, so he can close the case right proper."

"I'm prepared to speak with him any afternoon."

Holloway rubbed his chin. "They were talking for a while about calling a grand jury."

"What is a grand jury, anyway?" Katie asked.

"A grand jury is no big deal; it just sounds grand. It's twenty-three folks who listen to the facts in a case and decide whether someone should be charged with a crime. But no one thinks Mrs. Parker set out to kill that Alan person, so there's no need to call a grand jury."

A buzz, followed by the sound of distant thunder, started in Winifred's ears. Holloway's words hardly made sense, but the faces around her were smiling. Even Theodore stood there. She could see him, tall and elegant in his dark blue suit, briefcase in one hand, *The Wall Street Journal* tucked under his other arm. Then he was gone. Winifred shook herself. Was she going crazy?

Holloway looked from one to the other and smiled. "Detective Mason will be over in a day or two, then, to go over the facts. Based on the information he had from Katie, he presented the case to the D.A. in such a manner that there was no need to carry it a bit further. Good man, Mason. I'm glad he was assigned the case."

"He was very kind when he came to talk to me," Katie said.

Holloway tapped the table with his fingers. "Camaro had a rap sheet the length of a telephone pole." He stood. "Glad to bring good news. I reckon I'll be headin' home now."

Winifred lowered her head onto her palms. Her body quivered. Everyone cried and hugged one another, and gradually, as she relaxed, the humming in Winifred's ears subsided. She had beat an attack of Ménière's again, thank God.

What a healing thing joy is, she thought.

35

PROPOSAL

Later that day they took Emily to Walhalla to see the shop.

"It's wonderful. I just love it," she said. "What a fun idea." She hugged Winifred.

Soon everyone was at work unpacking more boxes that were stacked in the storage room. Katie insisted repeatedly that her grandmother not bend, reach, or lift. "You sit in that chair and tell us where to put things."

Winifred complied, until some vase on a shelf looked off center, or her keen eyes detected a twist in the way a quilt was folded. Then Katie had to take her arm and steer her back to her chair.

"Some people never learn, do they?" Katie asked in mock exasperation, her hands on her hips.

Winifred smiled and promised to stay put, but she only did so when Emily came to stand beside her chair. "You really like it, Emily?"

"I sure do, Winnie." Emily looked at her cousin and smiled. "Imagine going back to work at your age. I'd never believe it if I didn't see it with my own eyes."

"I'm not doing this alone, as you can see. It would be impossible without each of these dear people."

Zoe and Kathryn looked at her from across the room and smiled. Katie blew her a kiss. Warmth and love spilled from their eyes. Content, Winifred folded her hands in her lap.

"No, you are not alone, and I'm glad for you," Emily said.

Back in Salem, when she kissed Winifred and the others good-bye, Emily said to her cousin, "Looks like you've got yourself a whole new family, Winnie."

Jon arrived as Emily drove away, and he joined them on the patio, where he stood looking awkwardly at Katie.

Winifred said, "I'm going to sit here and count the number of times you and Jon give one another that puppy-dog, lovesick look. Why don't you two get married? We could use a good man around the place, and not just in times of crisis. I want to see my great-grandchildren, and I'm not getting younger."

Katie gasped. "Granny, how can you? Jon, please excuse her."

"What for? I think it's a great idea." He put his arms about her and kissed her. "Will you marry me?"

Katie moved away and wiggled her shoulders playfully. "Of course I will." She took off running down into the pasture, and he followed, laughing and calling her name.

Some men can be so slow getting on with things, Winifred thought. In the pasture Jon caught up with Katie, and Winifred watched with satisfaction as they kissed. "Good."

She rose and, feeling stronger than usual, walked unattended into the house.

Down in the summerhouse, Jon said, "I haven't much to offer. I'd wanted to wait until I'd built a home for you, but your granny is right. Life's too darn short to put off matters as important as this." He sank to his knees. "This is my official proposal. Marry me, and I will love you, Katie, with all my heart, forever."

"Officially, yes, I will marry you." Katie leaned forward, and he rose to kiss her. "I love you too, Jon, with all my heart." When he released her, Katie spun around and around. "Look, Jon, how beautiful the world is."

"Love will do that," he said. "It colors everything brighter and clearer."

"If Mom should want to give us a piece of land for us to build a home on as a wedding present, would you accept it, Jon?"

For a long moment he stared out across the pond. Katie put her arm about his shoulder. "I'd like it if you said yes. I know you're proud, but after what we've all been through, can't you think of us all as family now?"

Jon sighed, then swept Katie in his arms. "I'd be happy to be a part of this family, and yes, if you want to live out here, I'd accept the land and build us a home on it."

Katie wanted to dance with happiness. "There's a piece of land I've had my eye on for years. It's got the greatest view. Want to see it?"

"Sure. Now?"

"Why not?" Off they went, around the pond, and up toward the woods, taking a trail that skirted the trees. The land dipped and rose. Finally they came to a clearing where they could see one hundred eighty degrees around.

"This is it," Katie said. "What do you think?"

"It's gorgeous. Are you sure Zoe'll part with this?"

"Mom'll be thrilled to have us nearby." Katie hugged him. "I do love you, Jon, so very much." For a tiny moment apprehension crossed her heart about the issue of children. She must share her concerns with him, but not at this lovely, special moment.

"When should we get married?" she asked. "What date?"

"Our home will take at least five months to build," Jon said.

She mentally counted forward. "I'll give you six months. May. Okay?"

"May sounds fine."

"May it is, then."

Later, when Jon had gone, Katie found her mother reading in the living room. Zoe set the book aside and held her hand out to Katie, who took it. She drew her daughter down on the couch beside her. "Darling, Winifred told me. I am so happy about you and Jon. It seems so right."

As if she were a child again, Katie rested her head on Zoe's shoulder. All her anger had evaporated. "I'd like to be married down by the river, where the two forks join. When I was little, I'd sit and daydream that one day I'd be married there. What do you think?"

"It sounds beautiful," Zoe said. "And I want you to pick out a piece of land. That is, if you and Jon want to live out here. You might not."

"Oh, yes, we do. I hoped you'd say that. You know the piece that I love—past the cave, around the hill. We'd be close but not in your face. And Jon will build us a house. We'd like to be married in May."

"A bit over six months. I think that gives us enough time to get ready for a wedding."

"Not a big formal wedding, please."

"Hardly a formal wedding, when people have to walk down across a pasture to get to the ceremony." They laughed and held each other.

But the sense of unease Katie had felt with Jon found a foothold in her mind again, and she knew she must speak her deepest fears.

"Mom, something's bothering me. In the midst of being so happy, I get this sense of apprehension. Am I so accustomed to stress and responsibility that I don't believe happiness is possible?"

"What is it, Katie?" her mother asked.

Katie flashed back to an astrologer she had visited during a period when she had been desperate for answers. The woman looked like anyone's grandmother, but the way she scowled at the lines and angles crisscrossing Katie's chart had frightened Katie.

"For you, happiness comes late, after much trouble," she had said. Then she had looked Katie squarely in the eye. "Then suddenly, poof, all your troubles are gone, like the sun comes out after a storm."

Was this after the storm?

"What if Jon wants children, Mom?" Katie reached for Zoe's hand. "Older mothers run a greater risk of having a child like Laurie Ann. I can't go through that again. What shall I do?"

"Have you talked to Jon about this?"

"No. Maybe if I can't or won't have a child, he won't want me."

"I think you ought to talk to him sooner, rather than later. See where he stands on this issue. Has he ever talked about children?" Zoe asked.

"No. Granny mentioned great-grandchildren today, and he didn't blink an eye or react one way or the other."

"Well, he's a good man, and he loves you. Talk to him, Katie. One handicapped child doesn't mean you'll have another. Take the Kennedys—they had a retarded daughter and several children with no problems at all."

"I can't risk it." Katie leaned against her mother.

Zoe put her arm about Katie. "There are tests, amniocentesis, sonograms. If anything were wrong, you wouldn't have to go on with a pregnancy."

Katie huddled against her mother. "I don't know if I could do that. I couldn't abandon Laurie Ann."

"You were young. You did what you felt was right at the time. You didn't understand the full impact of your choice, and certainly none of us, not even the doctors, really knew the degree of her helplessness."

Katie remembered feeling that it was imperative to stand up to Hank. When she left the hospital with Laurie Ann, she'd felt superior to him, and certain that she could handle anything and everything that life dished out.

Katie looked at her mother. "I doubt if I could handle such a thing now."

"We do the best we can with what we're given. And Jon loves you. So talk to him."

"Thanks. I love you, Mom," Katie whispered.

"I love you too, Katie." After a time Zoe said, "So many changes are happening, and all at once. I need to make some changes myself. I'm reorganizing my room. I've bought baskets to store things in, and I'm finally sorting things. I'm going to get rid of my parents' big bed and get something smaller, and I'm changing the color scheme and those heavy curtains. The house has been a shrine to your grandparents for too long. I'm going to suggest to Winifred that she redecorate her room any way she'd like."

"But she's just come to enjoy those fish." Katie laughed.

"It's also time to change the love seats in the den and get a firm, comfortable sofa so that Winifred won't have trouble getting up and down." She nibbled her lower lip. "I know it's been well cleaned, but I can't look at that Persian rug. I want to change that too."

"I'm amazed at you, making all these changes," Katie said.

"It's time!" Zoe rumpled her daughter's hair. "And maybe, since you're going to have a whole new life, you'd consider coloring your hair. I miss those copper curls of yours."

In the past this comment would have elicited an argument from Katie, but now she said, "I just might do that."

Zoe smiled. "All three of us Parker women have embarked on new paths, haven't we?"

36

※

ALADDIN'S TREASURES

Aladdin's Treasures held an open house on December ninth with punch, coffee, and finger food. Because the day was balmy, in the sixties, refreshments were set on tables on the sidewalk under the awning. A flutist played popular classics from a corner of the shop, and Olive stationed herself off to one side with her arms crossed.

"I'm keepin' my eye out for thieves," she informed Zoe, then assigned Ruben to the front door, saying, "We're not sellin' today. Keep your eyes open and make sure folks leave as empty-handed as when they come in. Now, you smile and act friendly-like, so as no one will guess you're checkin' 'em out."

Everyone came to the opening: Mrs. Tate from the bank, Zoe's insurance agents, Gloria and Abed, owners of the Steak House, the garden shop owners from Seneca. Sergeant Holloway brought his family, and Detective Mason showed up with his wife, mother, and mother-in-law.

Newspapers in Seneca and Clemson carried notice of the opening, and the next day summer people, returning from Highlands and Cashiers to their homes late this year, stopped and bought all the Wedgewood pieces and many of the quilts. A couple bought Mrs. Hope's toys for their grandson in Savannah.

The next week a major promotion for Keowee Key Development brought a busload of women who spent hours shopping and gave the shop the biggest sale day of its short existence.

On Christmas Eve, as they closed and locked the doors to Aladdin's Treasures, Zoe looked at Winifred. "This was a truly great idea. And you were right about me too. I do enjoy ferreting out the best items at a flea market or antique wholesaler, and I got to know Maudie a lot better. She's a terrific person."

"She strikes me as the kind of woman who's a good, solid friend."

"I think you're right, but we haven't had a major disagreement yet. I always think you really only know if a new friendship will survive and grow after you've had a serious disagreement. It tests the waters."

"Then I wish you a disagreement, a happy resolution, and a long friendship," Winifred said.

As they headed for the car, Zoe squeezed Winifred's arm. "I've been wanting to thank you for everything you've done for me and for Katie. You're quite a splendid woman. What you did that night . . . How can I ever thank you?" Her voice choked. "I owe my daughter's life to you."

"I love Kathryn. I would have died rather than see her harmed."

As Zoe unlocked the van and opened the doors for them, Winifred continued, "I want to thank you, Zoe, for taking me into your home. Initially, I wasn't easy to have around."

"In these few months, so much has happened." Zoe helped Winifred into the front passenger seat. "So much has changed."

At nine p.m. Main Street was empty, the stores closed, few cars passing. Heavy clouds hid the stars, and the smell of snow hung in the air. Christmas lights, white and yellow, red and green, twinkled from light poles and signs, and framed the windows of stores.

"There's something very special about a small town at Christmas," Zoe said.

"Maybe it's because at Christmastime, the Main Streets of small towns come alive with light and good cheer." Winifred looked down the street. "That Christmas tree in front of City Hall is lovely, and the carolers who came by were quite wonderful too—so much cozier and more heartwarming than in Philadelphia."

Later, as they sipped spiced cider and watched the news on TV, the weatherman announced, "Well, folks, we're going to have a white Christmas."

And indeed, by two in the morning the snow began its gentle drift to earth, and it did not surprise Zoe when a soft tap on her door brought her face to face with Maudie.

"I saw your light on again," Maudie said. "I'm going outside. Want to come? It's beautiful."

They bundled into coats and boots and stepped onto the carpet of white covering the front patio. All about them snowflakes wafted to earth, stuck to their hair, landed on their shoulders, and wet their cheeks. Snow snuggled into the crooks of branches, and in the distance, the pond seemed a circle of dark mink in a sea of white ermine.

Zoe thought of her parents and Laurie Ann under blankets of white. "I think my parents would be pleased with how everything's turning out here." She smiled.

37

THE WINTER MONTHS

Bitter cold January days slowed the construction on Jon and Katie's home, but by the end of February the walls rose above the foundation and the roof was on. Space heaters warmed the interior so that the men could work, and the air around the clearing resounded with saws, hammers, and a radio playing country music.

Katie and Jon had talked and agreed that they needed no children. He'd never wanted any, he assured her, and looked forward to their life together. Katie briefly regretted not giving her grandmother a great-grandchild, but it was the right decision for them.

In March Katie shopped in Greenville for a simple wedding dress. Simple was hard to find. "Something," she told the saleswomen, "appropriate for a May wedding in the country, down by the river." After three such trips, Katie had found nothing that pleased her.

Olive came to the rescue. "Get me a picture of what you

want, sugar, and the material you want, and I'll sew you up a dress."

In a magazine Katie found an ankle-length dress in a light, flowing fabric with a square neck and puff sleeves, trimmed in scalloped lace. "This is what I want," she told Zoe and Winifred.

Maudie, shopping with Katie, spotted a bolt of antique handkerchief linen from Ireland. She fingered an end and closed her eyes. "So soft," she said. "Near my village, they spin this linen. It's the finest in the world. It comes from flax plants, linen does. Did you know that?"

Katie shook her head.

"The stalks of the plants are soaked in absolutely pure water, free of minerals, for seven whole days. When the gum dissolves, the fibers are pulled out. It's hard work, and labor-intensive."

Even the saleswoman was looking at her with interest as Maudie unrolled a yard of fabric and held it against herself. "The fibers are broken up, cleaned, straightened, combed, beaten, bleached, and then doubled into fibers strong enough for yarn."

"How do you know all this?" Katie asked.

"My mother's family worked with linen for generations. Their exact process is a well-kept secret. I only know what I've told you."

Katie held the material to her face. "It's wonderful."

And so the cloth was purchased, along with lace for the trim, and taken directly to Olive, who exclaimed on its softness and took Katie's measurements.

By April first invitations were mailed to Katie's friends and former colleagues in Greenville, to Emily and her husband, and to all their friends in Salem and Walhalla.

Winifred helped address the envelopes. One she hesitated over. It was the only person other than Emily whom she cared to invite. Should she include him? Why not? Impulsively, she sealed the envelope and wrote the address of her former butler, Lewis Treadwell.

Eight days after his invitation was mailed, she received a note thanking her for thinking of him and accepting. He offered his help with food and drinks, and it was arranged that he would join them as soon as possible and that he would stay in Walhalla with Jon.

Jon asked Ruben to be his best man. Katie asked her mother to be her matron of honor and asked Winifred to give her away.

Winifred said, "Give you away, child? But I'm not a man."

Katie said, "You're my father's mother. I know he would want you to stand in for him."

A great happiness welled in Winifred's heart, and tears of joy filled her eyes. "Of course, if you want me, I will happily walk you down the aisle."

Later that evening, Winifred reflected on the way the events and people in her life had been portrayed in her sketches. No longer did she draw her sisters' tight faces, their tense bodies and anxious eyes, or her mother's bent back, or her grandfather's clutching hands, or Steven walking away. Since coming to Salem, her sketches showed the summerhouse, Jon, and Kathryn: Kathryn, her face flushed, the wind blowing through her hair as she ran up to Winifred from the pasture; Kathryn in pensive mood, reading and cutting pictures of tables, couches, and colors she liked from magazines. Winifred never tired of sketching her granddaughter.

There was a sketch of Olive, smiling, and Ruben, somber with his shotgun slung across his shoulder. There was one of Zoe walking through the woods.

One sketch she had drawn and torn to bits: Alan, his face twisted in hate and rage. In the middle of the night, several weeks after her hospitalization, the image had invaded her mind, and she had worked furiously. When it was done, she punched it full of holes and tore it to shreds. She had not seen him dead, but it would be a long while before the memory of him falling, reaching for the gun, and the sound of the crack when she lowered her cane that second time would fade from her memory.

On the positive side, she had had no problem with Ménière's disease since the shop opened. At times she forgot about it completely, when she was busy or looking forward to something, like Lewis Treadwell's arrival. Knowing that she would see him again caused her cheeks to flush with anticipation. He had been kind to her, her ally and friend in that huge, old house for so many years. And tomorrow he would arrive.

38

LEWIS TREADWELL

Winifred sat on a chair drawn close to the big window of the living room, watching the driveway and waiting for Lewis Treadwell to arrive. He would come by cab from the airport in Anderson.

Expecting a car to round the curve up to the house, she was surprised to see a lone figure walking toward the patio. He stopped to catch his breath and view the scene, then shifted his suitcase to the other hand.

As fast as she could, Winifred eased from her chair. Her legs wobbled from excitement. At the front door, she leaned against the doorframe and waved at him. He waved back and quickened his pace.

"Lewis Treadwell," she called. "Is that you?"

"Madam. Mrs. Parker," he replied as he set down his suitcase. "Indeed, it is I."

She wished she were young and could run to help him. "Where is your cab?"

"He dropped me at the road. He seemed in a huge hurry to depart."

"Oh, dear. How awful of him," she said.

He was almost to the patio now. He had not changed; he was still tall and trim. Theodore had developed a pot-belly in his later years, but Lewis Treadwell bore himself as erectly as when he had come to work for her mother-in-law at age forty-two. Only his gait had slowed, and his fine, aesthetic face bore the lines of age, as hers did.

She had always thought him handsome, and he still cut a fine figure for a man in his seventies. Warmth spread through her, and she was glad for this chance to appraise him without seeming rude.

And then he stood before her, extending his hand. Impulsively Winifred stepped forward, reached out, and hugged him. Surprised, he nearly fell backward over his suitcase. They both laughed, and she took his arm and guided him into the house.

"I am going to call you Lewis," she said, "and I expect you to call me Winifred."

It was unexpected and rather amazing, the way Lewis Treadwell took to the country. Winifred had known him only in a city environment, where he had been restrained and formal, as befitted a butler. Within days of his arrival, Lewis purchased a bicycle and set about exploring Wal-halla.

"Walhalla's a delightful town with many fine old homes," he told Winifred and Zoe, as he stored his bike in the rear of the shop. "I pedaled a ways toward Seneca. When I build up my leg muscles, I'll try for Clemson. I've always liked university campuses."

"Why not get a car?" Zoe asked.

"You see and feel the countryside so much more intimately from a bicycle," Lewis replied.

At Moore's on Main Street, Lewis bought overalls. "I've always wanted to wear these," he said when he appeared at dinner that evening. "Do I look like a farmer?" Despite the stiff, slightly baggy overalls, with that fine-boned face, he hardly looked like a farmer.

"More like a country gentleman about to inspect his estate," Zoe said.

Winifred could see that that pleased him.

Lewis fit right in. He listened attentively when Zoe spoke of her love for the forest. She, who was so private and so particular, chatted with Lewis as if she had known him all her life. Zoe even invited him to accompany her for a walk in the woods, which greatly pleased Winifred. She felt like a mother hen surrounded by chicks, and now there was a rooster in the barnyard.

Lewis helped Maudie press leaves and plant stems between wooden devices, reading the instructions as she worked. " 'Lay the leaves between absorbent papers, then slip the paper into the wood frame and tighten.' Press hard, now." He helped her press the wood. " 'In time,' " he said, picking up the instructions again, " 'the water will be gone, and the leaves will dry out and keep for a very long time.' "

He made coffee in the morning, helped Katie set the breakfast table, and at dinner time added a bowl with fruit or flowers as a centerpiece. He would have cooked the meals, but Maudie refused his help, insisting that she loved to cook.

Winifred worried that Maudie, who had come to be a nurse, was now engaged in chores of all types, helping Zoe redecorate her room and deal with her clutter, helping Kathryn with wedding details, and cooking. But Maudie looked happy, and Winifred's sketches captured the smile on her face, the light in her eyes.

In those tender days of spring, as leaves unfurled and flowers opened their lovely faces to the sunshine, Lewis and Winifred sparred with one another over gin rummy, as they had done many an evening in the house in Philadelphia while dinner grew cold waiting for Theodore. In all those years, Winifred and her butler had never exchanged a personal word, yet she felt a silent understanding existed between them. They continued now as they had been, sharing nothing of a personal nature.

But as the time grew closer to the wedding, Winifred grew more and more curious about Lewis—about his life, his thoughts and opinions. Did he live alone or did he have a wife stashed away somewhere? Or children? She knew that Theodore had invested money for him, and that when they parted, Lewis had a sizable portfolio, but what did he plan or want for his future? The more she thought about these things, the more melancholy she felt at the thought of his leaving after the wedding.

The wedding menu was catered by the Steak House Cafeteria. Chairs and tables had been rented, along with an enormous rose-and-pink-striped tent, and would be set up in the pasture near the summerhouse. Forty people sent in their RSVPs.

In April Cousin Emily and George arrived for an informal extended-family dinner that included Ruben and Olive, Abed and Gloria, Doc Franklin and his widowed friend Amy Tally. Maudie and Zoe prepared roast leg of lamb, baked potatoes, a green bean casserole, and a creamed corn casserole. Lewis and Winifred created centerpieces of dogwood and azalea blossoms for the buffet table, which had been set up on the patio. There were deserts: cherry pie, key lime tarts, and chocolate meringue pie.

When Winifred took a seat beside Lewis at one of the tables, Emily, across the table, winked at her, then stunned her by asking, "Winnie, do you still do your drawings? You had such talent." She turned to Lewis. "You lived in that house with her all those years, surely you saw them."

"No, madam," he replied. "If Mrs. Parker was an artist, I had no knowledge of it."

Emily looked Winifred squarely in the eye. "You still tear 'em up, Winnie?"

Winifred's face reddened. She could have strangled Emily.

"You draw, Granny? How absolutely marvelous. I always wished I could draw or paint," Katie said.

Winifred replied, "It's nothing, really."

The basket of rolls Emily was passing stopped in midair. "It is *too* something. Now, you just stop hiding your light under a bushel, like the good Lord says." The rolls moved on. Emily glanced at Lewis. "You really don't know about this?"

"I do not, madam," he replied.

"Oh, stop with the *madam*." Emily giggled and blushed.

"What do you draw, Winifred, landscapes?" Zoe asked.

"People," she replied. "Only people."

"What people?" Katie asked.

Winifred's eyes and voice softened. "I draw you, my dear, many sketches of you." Her eyes moved slowly across the eager group. "You, Doc, and you, Ruben, and"—she waved her hand around the table—"all of you."

"Show us, Winnie," Emily said. "Please show us."

To Winifred's dismay everyone echoed the request, everyone but Lewis.

"Perhaps we might wait until a little later," Lewis said.

He knew how she felt and was trying to protect her. Winifred seconded his words. "Later. This isn't the time. I'll show them to you all when I'm ready, and not a moment sooner." No amount of urging or pleading moved her from her resolve. But a plan began to form in her mind. She would select her very best drawing of each of them, take them to a frame shop in Clemson, and have them mounted and framed. They would be gifts for their kindness to her these many months.

39

THE FACE OF A SCHOLAR

Maudie remarked one day, when she and Winifred were alone, "Your friend Lewis has the face of a scholar."

"Why, yes, you're correct," Winifred replied. "And he reads copiously. He always has."

"Behind those wire-rimmed glasses, his eyes are wise and compassionate. I would have liked a man like that for a father. Does he have children?"

"I don't know," Winifred said. "I'm embarrassed to admit that I know very little about his private life."

"Well, you ought to find out."

Winifred agreed, but asked, "Why?"

"Because he's nice, and he likes you very much," Maudie retorted.

"Oh, Maudie, don't be silly." But it set Winifred thinking, and later that day, when she came upon Lewis standing on the porch watching a squirrel scramble up a tree, she said, "Hello, Lewis."

He turned and bowed slightly. "Madam, you look well."

"Oh, please don't be so formal, Lewis."

"Habit of long years' standing," he replied.

"Come, old friend," Winifred said, and his eyes registered surprise, then pleasure as she slipped her arm through his and led him down into the pasture. "Come, let's sit in the summerhouse. The pond is a wonder of activity these days: dragonflies hovering, bees buzzing, fish jumping."

At the summerhouse, they settled into wicker rocking chairs.

"I am content here in Salem with my family," Winifred said softly. "It was very hard at first, but much has changed, and I am a part of my family at last." They sat in silence then, and watched the long-winged insects that hovered just above the surface of the water.

"It's a lovely afternoon," Lewis said.

"Yes, it is. When the days are warmer, Zoe, Maudie, Kathryn, and I come down here in the evening. It's so peaceful and lovely. Sometimes there's an especially brilliant sunset, or we watch the way the light moves across the pond. In the city, with all those buildings crowding me, I never looked at the sky. And as you know, my husband didn't care for picnics or the country."

"Quite right," he replied.

"We always vacationed in cities: New York, Paris, London, San Francisco." She crossed her ankles. "Since I came here, I find myself remembering the sunrises in Goose Cove, where I was born, and the sound of the ocean. Odd, don't you think, to imagine one hears the ocean in a place like this?"

"Memories bring sounds as well as pictures to your mind," he said.

Their rockers moved in unison for a time.

"Where do you call home, Lewis?"

"When I left you, I bought a travel trailer, small but adequate for one person, and traveled for a few months around this great country."

"You did?" She learned forward. "And what part did you like best?"

"The green hilly parts, like New England, the Appalachians, the foothills of the Poconos."

"Where did my invitation to Kathryn's wedding find you?"

"I retain a small apartment in Philadelphia."

"That's where it went. That was the only address I had."

"I was pleased to receive it."

"Do you like this area?" Winifred asked.

"Very much so," Lewis said. "It is not as spectacularly beautiful as the higher mountains, but I have been told it is not as cold in winter. The high mountains are quite close at hand and can easily be visited, and you have marvelous lakes here in Oconee County."

"We do," Winifred said. "We must go for a boat ride on Lake Jocassee soon. It has waterfalls that spill from high mountains. We'll rent a pontoon boat. Can you operate a pontoon boat, Lewis?"

"I believe I have some small skill in that matter."

The silence that fell between them was comfortable. Then Winifred said, "I used to love poetry." She quoted, " 'All I could see from where I stood was three long mountains and a wood.'"

"By Edna St. Vincent Millay. Written at a young, impressionable age in Maine," he said.

"I was born on the Maine coast, in a poor fishing village. My father was a fisherman." Their eyes met with new understanding. "I made choices, Lewis. I gave up large parts of me—poetry, my sketching. I let the Parker family own me, control my thinking and behavior. When I look back on it, the bargain I made was almost Faustian. You were there much of the time. Could you tell?" she asked.

"I suspected that there were two Winifred Parkers."

"Winifred and Winnie, as my cousin calls me."

"May I call you Winnie, rather than Winifred? It seems more appropriate, since you are asking me to be informal."

"Winnie it is, then."

The long silences between them were as pleasant as the weather. After a time, she said, "I recall a time when you were quite depressed. I was so anguished over Steven's death then that I didn't care about anyone else's grief. Later I recalled my mother-in-law saying that you had lost . . . a wife?"

"Not my wife; she passed away giving birth to our daughter. My daughter, Angeline, was killed by a drunk driver when she was twenty-two."

"Oh, Lewis, how terrible. I am so very sorry." She rested her hand on his arm. "What a lovely name, Angeline. What was she like? Can you speak of her?"

"She was a beautiful young woman, quiet, serious, and loving. She was at the university in premed."

"What a terrible shame. You must have suffered greatly."

"Indeed I did. For some period of time, I struggled against suicide."

"We were right in the same house, and I didn't even know. I am so sorry, Lewis. So very sorry."

"It was not your business to know," he said. "You were my employer. Mr. Steven's death occurred one month before my daughter's passing, and it took every ounce of fortitude and courage I had to carry on day to day. Without the routine of my work, I think I would have ended my life."

"Does one ever completely recover from losing a child?"

Gently, he placed his palm over her hand. They sat thus, quietly soaking in the sight of tiny insects skimming the surface of the pond and the glitter of sunlight dancing across the water.

And then came Zoe's and Maudie's voices. The two women approached them, laughing. Swiftly, Winifred disengaged her hand from Lewis's and they exchanged intimacy for family fun.

The following day Maudie stood in the living room staring out of the window, wondering if she ought to consider leaving. She didn't think anyone would ask her to go. Should she raise the subject? Her primary charge was Winifred, who was very much better since the arrival of Lewis Treadwell. Maudie believed that he would stay in the area; he appeared to love the country. Her thoughts were interrupted when Zoe entered the room.

"I was looking for you. Are you excited about the wedding?" Zoe asked.

Maudie turned to face her. "Weddings bring mixed emotions."

"Do you wish you were married?"

"I'm forty-four years old, and I've never wanted to marry. But I'd like a wedding for the fun of it, if I could cancel the marriage afterward." She laughed.

"I cry at weddings, even if I don't know the bride and groom, when I see them coming out of a church or even on television," Zoe said.

Maudie steeled herself to broach the subject of her leaving. "I've been thinking. Mrs. Parker won't be needing me much longer, with Lewis here."

"Why do you say that? What does his being here have to do with it?"

"You don't see their budding romance?"

"Winifred Parker and her butler?" Zoe shook her head. *But if it were so, how would that change things? Nothing should change—not now, when for the first time in years, everything seems so right.* "I don't think that's going to happen."

"Keep your eyes on them. See for yourself," Maudie said.

"But if you left, where would you go?"

"Back to Greenville, I imagine. Hospitals always need nurses."

"This is silly—you can't be thinking about leaving! Winifred will want you to stay, whether there's anything between her and Lewis Treadwell or not. She's fine now, but you never know."

"We'll wait a bit and see."

"If you prefer to go back to hospital nursing, the hospital in Seneca is closer," Zoe said.

"I just thought—"

"Well, don't! I'd miss you. We all would." Maudie was such a good friend; Zoe couldn't bear to lose her. "Come on, let's go see how Katie and Jon's house looks, now that it's done."

They scrambled up the hillside and skirted the woods. The pond and the house fell away behind them as they rounded bend after bend, and it was soon clear to Maudie why she had not heard hammering, sawing, or other construction sounds all these months.

The land Katie had chosen rolled gently to the river below. Jon had situated the house facing south and west to take advantage of the sunsets. A wide covered porch wrapped the southern and western walls. Zoe and Maudie found the back door open and went inside. Two large bedrooms and bathrooms occupied one side of the house. An open floor plan included the kitchen with a high-ceilinged breakfast bay, and a bright and airy den. The living room sat just beyond, and a small office behind that. The high-pitched roof offered an attic, with room for expansion.

They sat on the porch on folding chairs left by the workmen. They could see the ridge of mountains on two sides, and a branch of Little River bounded the property on the west. Here the river ran wide, and Zoe remembered Katie saying that on still nights, when she and Jon sat on the porch and talked, the rush of water could be clearly heard.

Cleanup of the grounds still needed to be done. Pieces of building material lay here and there: a roof shingle, a square of tar paper, a can tipped sideways, spilling nails.

It was very still. "It's a lovely place," Maudie said.

"Yes, it is. I've been thinking about Winifred and Lewis. You really think there's more than friendship between them?"

"It's something in the way they look at one another. They've been friends for a long time," Maudie said.

"Perhaps they've loved each other and never recognized it," Zoe replied. "It would hardly have been appropriate for Mrs. Theodore Parker to be interested in her butler."

"Would you be thinking that she's changed a great deal, then?"

"She certainly has. But then, haven't we all?" Zoe left the porch and walked to the center of the cleared space that would become the front yard.

"You could end up with a family compound here," Maudie said. "If Winifred and Lewis married, they could build on your land too." She laughed.

Zoe kicked a small stone with the toe of her shoe. "They could do that, couldn't they? It would be very nice, a community of loved ones."

Maudie rubbed the back of her neck. "A fine idea. I'll be wishing it for you."

"I hope you'll stay with us and be part of any such community." The wind picked up and a piece of a cement bag drifted past them and wedged in a small shrub off to the side. "And I hope the weather stays sunny for the wedding," Zoe said, changing the subject.

"Are you excited? It's a mere two days away."

"I'm a little nervous about everything going smoothly, and having to walk down the aisle before the bride. All those people looking at me. I wonder what they'll think, now that they know about Alan."

"People around here like you, Zoe. They've known you for many years, and they know only kindness from you. If anything, they'll be saying how lucky you are to have such a lovely daughter getting married, and how well you look, things like that."

Zoe smiled. "You're such an optimist, Maudie."

"Better that than a pessimist. No one wants to be around a perennial pessimist."

They started back along the trail, and after a time Zoe said, "Can you find your way back to the house, Maudie? I'd like to go to the glade and be alone for a while."

"I can do that. See you in a little while."

Zoe could hear Maudie humming as she continued on.

Fallen leaves and pine needles padded the earth below the trees. Squirrels scattered as Zoe approached. This year the squirrel population seemed to have doubled, and a report on the evening news warned of an outbreak of rabies among squirrels and other wildlife populations.

It was a joy to be in the glade. Zoe settled her back against the tree she called Paris. "I've come to say how happy I am.

Katie is being married. Alan is dead. I like my mother-in-law. I even like shopping for antiques. And I've got a sincere and honest friend in Maudie." She looked at each tree. "You've grown up listening to me weep and complain about my life; now I want to share the good news. This glade has been a haven for me, and I'm grateful to you. I'm grateful for so very much: my life is rich with family and friends."

Zoe closed her eyes and sent her hopes for the future down into the earth to be absorbed by the roots and passed by the sap of the trees up, up, up to their very pinnacles. She pictured her dreams and hopes borne by freshets of summer wind to the wide universe.

And as she pushed up from the ground, she knew that she would visit the glade less often now, that her needs had changed.

40

THE WEDDING

On Katie's wedding day, they all awakened to a sky armored in dark clouds.

"It can't rain! Please, God, please don't let it rain." Katie dashed to the front door and yanked it open. She stamped her feet. "Go away, clouds. Go rain on Seneca. They need rain."

The ceremony was scheduled for four in the afternoon.

"Don't panic. I predict that the sky will clear. Wait a bit." Winifred stood beside her. "It will be just fine. I feel it in my bones when it's going to rain."

And then the rain began to fall slowly and steadily. There was no wind, no sense of a storm, just gentle rain, the kind that farmers love.

Katie began to cry.

Winifred put her arms about her. "It's early. You know how it can be here, rain one minute, sunshine the next."

"Even if it does clear up, everything's going to be wet. Everyone will be walking through wet grass."

"It will clear up and dry out," Winifred said with authority.

As if by her decree, at eleven o'clock the rain ceased. The clouds separated to reveal bands of blue sky, and from the house on Amorey Lane came excited shouts and happy laughter.

The sun dried the earth, and the grass gave up its shiny wetness. By three o'clock, people began to arrive. They clustered on the patio or strolled to the summerhouse, while others ambled inside and filled the house with light-hearted chatter.

Earlier the food had arrived in a large van and been taken to tables set up under the tent in the pasture. The florist had arrived at noon with sprays of white lilies and pink and red roses. Lewis directed the florist and shepherded people with the aplomb he had exhibited for years in the Parker household.

"Lewis is remarkable. He handles things with such ease," Winifred said to her granddaughter.

"But he's your guest. I don't want him to feel he has to work," Katie said.

"Lewis would be miserable standing around. He isn't doing this because he feels he must, my dear. He thoroughly enjoys taking charge, being in the center of things."

At three thirty the ushers led the guests across the pasture, which Ruben had close-cropped for the occasion, and which was indeed dry, as Winifred had predicted. Nary a cloud peeped over a hill or skittered across the sky.

There were exclamations of appreciation from the guests when they stepped into the glen where Katie and Jon would be married, for it was as magical, as mysterious, as a scene from *Brigadoon*. Willows dipped into Little River where two branches joined and formed a wider, deeper stream. Green light, reflected from the carpet of moss on rocky outcroppings, hinted at magic. A wind chime tinkled. Singing a cappella, a soprano filled the air with the Quaker song, "'Tis a Gift to Be Simple."

The Unitarian minister from Greenville stepped to the small peninsula. From behind the drape of a willow, the groom and his best man, Ruben, stepped forward. Moments later Zoe, in a pale yellow cocktail dress, moved gracefully down the pathway. Winifred followed with Katie, who had finally colored her hair as close to its original copper color as she remembered, on her arm. Winifred's lavender silk dress flowed about her ankles as she moved with regal grace. She handed Katie to Jon, then she and Zoe stepped away from the couple.

"I join my life to yours," Katie said, "freely and with love. I respect you and cherish you. I will listen with an open heart when you share your joys or your worries. I commit myself to understanding and accepting our differences."

Jon repeated Katie's vows, and added, "You are a gift to my heart. I pledge you loyalty and truth. I promise to hold you dear and respond to your needs, and to cherish you always."

With the rings exchanged, the minister proclaimed them husband and wife. They kissed and everyone clapped and cheered. All smiles, the couple strolled slowly back up the wood-chip-strewn aisle. The guests followed, and the glen grew silent except for birds twittering. Only Zoe remained, wiping her teary eyes, and Maudie, who came to stand beside her.

"Shall we go?" Maudie asked.

"Yes, I guess we should. They'll be cutting the cake soon."

"Winifred and Lewis are waiting for us in the lower pasture." Maudie slipped her arm through Zoe's. "She told me that Lewis is staying on in the area. He's taking Jon's old apartment in Walhalla."

"Amazing," Zoe said. "Just amazing. It's all going to be all right, isn't it, Maudie? You're not still thinking of leaving, are you?"

"When the time comes and Winifred no longer needs or wants me around, I will find work in this area and stay close by, my friend," Maudie replied.

"The house will be so empty. Perhaps you'd share it with me?"

"Aye. That I might."

They stepped from the glen and joined the older couple, who stood smiling in the sunshine, Winifred's arm tucked comfortably in Lewis's.

STUDY GUIDE QUESTIONS

The Winifred who first arrives in Westminster is not the same Winifred who walks her granddaughter down the aisle. We often hear that people don't change, that as people grow older they get more set in their ways—and of course there's the old adage that you can't teach an old dog new tricks.

1. Does Winifred's changing happen naturally throughout the story?

2. Is her changing believable?

3. How do you feel about people changing? What do you think could cause a major personality change?

Forgiveness is a major theme in this novel. We read and hear much about forgiveness, yet it is not an easy thing to do.

1. Do you feel, in reading this novel, that Winifred and Zoe are capable of forgiving one another?

2. Are you convinced that they are ready to forgive one another?

3. It has been said that being able to forgive is the ability to admit that we are like other people. Do you agree?

4. In your opinion, does understanding lead to forgiveness?

5. What does forgiveness say about these characters? Does it show strength, weakness, largeness of heart, insincerity?